ISBN-13: 978-0-578-52176-3

ISBN-10: 0-578-52176-8

This book has been years in the making and it would not have been possible without the support of those around me.

To my parents who always taught me to follow my dreams. My mom always promised me she would always buy me one thing no matter how old I got, and it was books. Thank you for fostering the love of reading in me.

To my husband who encouraged me to follow my passion and to finally finish this project. He supported me through late nights, angry writers block and baby sat our little boy with no complaint. I love you so much.

To my son, may you always follow your dreams wherever they may take you.

To my amazing editors Molly and Rachel from Content Chop Shop, without whom I couldn't have finished.

To my friends who never questioned my dreams and were the first in line to support.

Finally, to my friend Caitlin, who was the biggest dreamer I have ever met. She encouraged me to write and follow my dreams every day. Nothing was impossible. I miss you Caitlin, I know you are living in the worlds that you loved so much in your books.

The battle between good and evil began
before most humans even walked the Earth.
The good are born of the light, peace and
life. The evil are born in the absence of
light, hatred and blood. Eventually, the two
sides needed stewards to continue the fight.
These chosen few have fought for centuries,
to maintain the balance, but the balance is
shifting. Darkness looms to put out the
light.

Prologue

Myriad walked around the wooded area that she had known so well only a decade ago. She was a Fae, a magical being that was born of another realm.

"It means a lot that you came to visit, Myriad." She turned around to see her friend Padua.

"Of course, you only transition once. It feels like only yesterday that I was chosen for this task."

Padua nodded, "100 years goes by so quickly, it is such an honor to care for the birthing tree. I have seen so many lives come from these roots, lives that will come to protect us all."

Myriad smiled, "The Locrian are truly special. Thank you for inviting me for your final birthing cycle."

"Of course." said Padua. "You trained me when you served the tree, it seemed only right that you should be here when I leave."

Myriad looked up at the enormous tree with great reverence, her slight frame dwarfed by its size; her cropped red hair moving ever so slightly with the soft breeze. The temperatures were always pleasant and the weather always what is desired by the tree itself, whatever nourishment it required would be fulfilled.

"It never does get old, does it?" said Myriad.

Padua, nearly a foot taller, with long black hair, shook her head "It does not. This place, this tree, is far more than what it seems. It's as if peace itself resides here."

The pair closed their eyes and rested in the serenity. The breeze picked up, slightly blowing their robes in the wind. Padua's eyes opened.
She smiled at Myriad "It's time."

The Fae approached the tree as the roots began to glow and move. Standing back Myriad watched her friend at work. Slowly the first root rose out of the ground to present itself to Padua. She grasped the end gently and as she said a prayer and the end of the root opened to reveal the first Locrian.

"It's a girl," stated Padua, almost to herself. "Let's see what you shall be named." Pressing her forehead to the infant she whispered "Cassandra."

Myriad stepped forward. "May I?"

"Of course." replied Padua.

Myriad took Cassandra and clothed her in a white garment. She smiled at the infant and gently placed her in the arms of the apprentice. This Fae would take over the duties of tending to the tree. The apprentice disappeared through a tunnel; the tunnel led to a transport that would take all the newborns to the abbey where they would be trained and protected.

The next root climbed up to Padua. This was a boy. Again, she pressed her forehead to the child. "Donny, you will be strong young one." The baby laughed at her touch.

One by one the Locrian came to be; Bria, then Lyra, Liam and so on. 78 in total were born by the time the roots stopped moving. The number wasn't as high as desired but still a sizeable group to send. Padua began to pack up her equipment to ride with the infants to their new home, thus completing her transition back into Fae society.

Padua turned to take one last look at her home of the last 100 years. "It's hard to leave something so amazing."

Myriad nodded, "Your life will continue to be amazing my friend."

Padua nodded "Are you coming?"

"Yes, I wanted just a moment more."

"I understand I will see you in the transport."

Myriad closed her eyes and said a Fae prayer of blessing and thankfulness. Once she felt at peace she opened her eyes. To her astonishment, a root was glowing in front of her. It had risen out of the ground and was waiting for her.

Looking around she saw no one to assist but her, decades of training came back to her in an instant. Doing as Padua had, she held the root and accepted the Locrian into her hands. But this time there were two, and they were glowing. It happened so quickly that Myriad thought she had imagined it. There were never two Locrian born of one root. One was a boy and one a girl. The shock faded quickly as the girl smiled up at her and warmed her heart. Touching her forehead to the child's, she smiled as a tear fell from her eyes, "Margaret." The baby grabbed her face and smiled. At that moment Myriad's heart filled and she knew this baby girl was special.

The moment was lost as the boy let loose a blood curdling scream unlike Myriad had heard before.

Padua was returning from the transport. "Myriad, they need to leave before the…." She paused seeing what was in her friend's arms. "Two more? This is wonderful!"

Myriad stared at the boy. Something didn't sit quite right. She looked into his eyes, they flashed black. It put fear into her soul.

Padua approached her friend, "We need to take them to the transport."

"Yes of course," said Myriad, finally pulling her gaze away from the boy. "I named the girl but would you mind naming the boy?" She passed the child to her friend.

Smiling, Padua touched his forehead with her own, "Michael." Padua turned to her friend, "Come, we can't be late."

Myriad wrapped up Margaret and carried her to the transport. The baby nestled into her and quickly fell asleep. This child would forever hold a piece of her heart and she would watch over her for all eternity.

10 years later

Myriad sprung out of her bed with a feeling of dread. She walked quickly through the hallways of the abbey. All of the students were asleep; it was quiet except for a rustling coming from the courtyard.

She slowed down her speed in an effort to go unnoticed as she tried to get a better look at what was creating the noise. She was taken aback at what she saw. Michael was trying to get the gates open on his own while Margaret stood next to him staring off into the distance.

"Michael, what are you doing?" She approached with caution.

Michael paused and turned with a devilish grin on his face. "We are leaving, professor."

"It's a new moon. With all the Droch out it isn't safe."

His smile deepened, "We can take our chances."

"This is lunacy! Come back now, the both of you."

"You see, dear professor, that is the problem. You all think I am crazy. But maybe I am the only one who sees the Locrian for who they truly are...evil." He glared at the Fae, "I know you planned to get rid of me but I will save you the trouble, Margaret and I will be free of your contamination."

Myriad focused on the girl, "Margaret, sweetheart, come away from there and back to your home."

"She can't hear you. I have made sure of that. In time she will come to see you as I have."

Myriad took a closer look at Margaret. He had done something to her, bewitched her into some sort of trance.

All of her anger pooled inside of her and a ball of fire produced itself in her hand.

Michael saw and brandished a knife as he stood behind Margaret. He placed the blade to her throat. Margaret continued to stare blankly, unaware of what was going on around her. "Tisk Tisk professor, you should know better being a Fae."

Myriad took a small step back. "You won't hurt her Michael."

He sneered with a look in his eyes that burned Myriad to the core. " No, my dear Fae, you would never hurt her, but you don't know me at all."

Myriad became frightened.

Michael's eyes became dark, "I will kill her to get what I want, what I deserve."

Pressing the knife into Margaret's neck, a trickle of blood appeared. Margaret remained a mindless drone, captive to whatever Michael's plans were.

Suddenly, from a door behind Michael, Headmaster Asher Murphy and professor Bryan Doyle emerged, curiosity lining their faces. Their sudden appearance had the fortunate effect of startling Michael, causing him to turn out of reflex. Myriad let the fireball fly - stunning him into unconsciousness before he could turn back around.

"What the hell is going on?!" Said Asher. "I wake up to a noise and now you are shooting fireballs at our students?"

"He was trying to escape with Margaret." Myriad approached her with caution, "He

14

bewitched her and somehow she is completely unaware of anything around her."

"He wanted to take her tonight? On a new moon? That is suicide. What did he plan to do?" asked Bryan.

"I am not sure." Myriad knelt in front of her student, tears forming in her eyes.

Asher stood staring at Margaret and ruminated on the amount of power it would take to create and maintain this kind of hold on someone, especially while unconscious.

"We have to get rid of him, now, no more waiting, no more chances."

"What? That is crazy. We have never gotten rid of one of our own." said Bryan.

"There is something inherently evil about him Bryan, I have watched him for awhile. He needs to go. Tonight."

"Have you lost your…"

"I agree, Bryan," Myriad said. "There is something not right with him. I would never usually permit something like this but Asher and I have discussed it. He needs to go, look at what he's done to her. He is dangerous."

Bryan looked long into Margaret's eyes; the lifelessness therein chilled him to the core. He turned and nodded in agreement.

Asher picked up the unconscious boy, "Open the gate, I will place him outside, it is my responsibility."

The two obeyed. Asher walked cautiously outside, keeping an eye on the horizon for any sign of the Droch. It was rare to find them near the abbey, but still, one should be cautious. "Myriad, curse him from this place so that he cannot remember the location and will not be able to find it should he choose."

The shield was strong and the Droch had yet to find their sanctuary after hundreds of years. Locrian could always find the abbey when they left, it was like a homing beacon in the back of their brain. This instinct was removed from Michael, so he would not be able to find his way back.

She walked over to the boy and placed her hand on his forehead. Speaking in a long-lost Fae language, she cursed him from ever finding the abbey again.

"Close the doors." She commanded.

The sound was deafening. They had never had to turn on one of their own, and each knew it would haunt them for the remainder of their days.

Myriad turned her attention to Margaret. How was she going to break the link between them?

"I think if I bind her powers it will sever the connection between them." She said, as if to herself.

"Wait, she has powers too?" asked Asher.

"I haven't witnessed it but it would be logical to assume she does even if she isn't aware of them since her 'twin,' as we have called him, does. If I perform the binding it should sever the link and wake her up."

"Try it and see," said Bryan.

"Wait, she won't be hurt will she?" Asked Asher.

This was very out of character for the headmaster; the events that transpired had obviously shaken him as well.

"I would never harm her."

Asher nodded, "Proceed."

Myriad stood in front of her and pressed her forehead to Margaret's just as she had done when she was born. Speaking in Fae, she searched the child's mind and heart to locate her powers. She found them, not really active as of yet, but they were present and strong. Myriad bound the girls powers. The binding ensured the power would release on her 21st birthday when she received her Locrian powers and immortality with her class; when they all returned to where they were born, to join in the fight against the Droch. The Droch were also born from the earth, from the dark underbelly. Unlike the Locrian, the Droch were born immortal and ready to fight. Their numbers increased in the world whenever a great evil was being committed; their only purpose was to fight and feed. They live on the blood of humans, Fae, Elves - anything that would quench their thirst.

Myriad said another spell when she felt Margaret waking up. As she put her back to sleep she caught her and laid her in the grass.

"It is done. She is asleep. I didn't want her to wake up here not knowing what was going on." The others nodded in agreement.

"What should I tell her when she wakes up and Michael is gone?"

Asher paused, "We tell her nothing."

"Really Asher? Because I'm pretty sure she is going to notice that he is gone," said Bryan.

"No, she won't. Myriad, I want you to erase her memory of him- from every member in her class."

"What?!" She was aghast. A moment ago he was worried for her safety and now… "Asher, that is not so easy, there can be damage done and it's not exactly legal."

"I accept all ramifications of this. Do it. The memory of him is far too dangerous. Given time it may be necessary to share the information, but not now, not when they are so impressionable."

Myriad threw her arms up in resignation.

"Why not? I am throwing all my morals out the window tonight," said Myriad. She again touched the child's forehead with hers, searching through all the memories of her "brother." It took some time, as Michael was ingrained into her entire being. She had other friends but he seemed to isolate himself with her, separating her from her peers. The images that she saw disturbed her. What he did when they were alone was horrifying. He experimented on animals and other creatures. She could feel Margaret's sorrow and confusion. She also picked up on a few mutterings about "true immortality". Locrian were immortal, like the Droch, but both could be killed in battle. What was he planning to do? Although the choice to banish Michael was justified, her heart ached for the pain Margaret had been put through suffering alone for so many years.

"It is done."

"Good, please continue with her class. Bryan, take her to her room, tomorrow will begin as normal." Asher walked away.

Myriad followed Bryan. "Have you ever seen him like this before?"

"No, but lately he has become more withdrawn, the balance is shifting Myriad."

"I know, I can feel it." She paused at the entrance and looked back to where Asher disappeared. She could make out his shadow, hunched over.

"We are so desperate to survive; I just hope we make the right choices along the way."

She continued into the abbey with Bryan, erasing the past in hopes of making a brighter future.

Chapter 1

Margaret awoke with a start. She looked at her clock, it was 4:00 in the morning and now she was wide awake. This was not a good way to start the day. Resting her head back on her pillow she tried to remember what woke her; something about fire, earthquakes, maybe...the harder she tried the more it slipped away as dreams do. Whatever it was had her heart racing and she knew she wouldn't get any more sleep.

Climbing out of bed she put on the same outfit she had been wearing for the past 20 years: athletic shorts, sweatpants, t-shirt, and a hoodie. Layers were always important; in Ireland the weather can change drastically from morning to night, but more importantly, her classes were physically demanding so athletic attire was required. Her hoodie and pants bore the emblem of the Locrian tree, and she wore it proudly. It matched the brand that she was born with on her wrist, something all Locrian carried. Their motto was also printed below on her clothing so they would always remember their purpose in life.

She peered into the mirror before exiting her room. Margaret was muscular, could hold her own in a fight, but would never be seen as masculine. She had shoulder-length dirty blonde hair that was seldom tamed and she had piercing hazel eyes. Scrunching her nose in disapproval, she pulled her hair up off her neck into a ponytail. Not the best look but it would do for 4:00am.

Margaret was approaching her 21st birthday when her last name would be bestowed upon her and she would take her place in Locrian Society. Her name and place in the Locrian hierarchy would be given to her by the same tree that gave her life. All other Locrian born on the same day as her would attend the ceremony, marking their uncommon births with celebration. After they are granted

immortality, they never age and always
appear to be 21.

She looked around her room for shoes.
Despite how small her room was, she had a
tendency to lose track of things. There was
a twin bed, desk and closet, all made out of
the most beautiful oak. Her walls held
pictures of Ireland; the cliffs of Moher,
the town of Kilkenny and Blarney castle were
a few of the locations that adorned her
walls. Having never left the abbey she was
always curious about the country she resided
and was destined to protect. Her favorite
part of her room was a giant picture window
that overlooked the courtyard. On a clear
day she could see the moors in the distance
and the rolling hills of Ireland.

Finding her shoes underneath her bed she
headed out the door to walk around the
grounds. She loved walking around when no
one else was awake; it was peaceful.

She opened her door onto a long corridor lit
by gas lanterns. Not a requirement, as the
abbey had electricity, but an aesthetic
choice which she loved. Truthfully, the
abbey lacked many modern conveniences.
Everything that they knew about the outside
world was brought in by the professors.
Music was still played on record players,
books were dated and few. Margaret had read

The Great Gatsby so many times it was
falling apart. The professors gifted it to
her after the 15th time she had read it. The
way that Gatsby lived so lavishly and the
sadness that surrounded his life was very
intriguing to her. While it was an annoyance
to have so few things to indulge in at the
abbey, reading the book taught her that
material possessions did not make you happy
but rather true relationships with people in
your life was what mattered most.

As she exited to the outside corridor, she
paused to take a deep breath of crisp
morning air. Looking out past the courtyard
to the Irish moors she could see a slight
mist hung in the air under the remaining
streams of moonlight. She leaned on the
archway soaking it all in. From the top of
the abbey you could see for miles on a clear
day, but no one could see in. Only those
with Locrian blood or those sworn to protect
them could find this place. For their own
protection, the magic deters any human from
wandering too close. As a result, it was a
Haven. Margaret took another deep breath.
The sun would be rising soon, and then
coffee would definitely be in order.

Lost in thought, she failed to notice that
someone else was also wandering the grounds
at this ungodly hour. As a hand touched her

shoulder she jumped, startled at the presence.

"I am so sorry; I didn't mean to startle you," said the all-too-familiar voice of one of Margaret's favorite instructors.

Turning, she came face to face with Myriad. Myriad had once watched over the Locrian tree and because of her devotion to the Locrian she was granted the opportunity to train them. Her specialty was battle tactics. Standing at five-foot-two the Fae was still quite intimidating with her fiery red hair and a gaze that made you feel as though she saw into your soul. She had emerald green eyes that were so pure it was like staring into the gem itself. Today she wore her typically flowing cloak that was light green; this complimented her hair quite nicely. She always wore robes that were pastel in color, she claimed that it was to bring her love of nature into her clothing. Due to the rigor and intensity of her class, Locrian are not permitted to study under her until they are 18-years-of-age. Even though Margaret was not her pupil until a few years ago, she couldn't remember a time when the Fae was not a presence in her life.

Margaret adjusted, looking at her professor "It is completely alright."

"What has you up so early?"

Shrugging her shoulders "Just a nightmare.
One I can't even remember."

Myriad took a deep breath in, "Dreams can
tell us a great deal about our lives - past,
present, and future. And sometimes they
simply awake us to enjoy a gorgeous sunrise.
Would you care to join me?"

She smiled, "As long as that sunrise comes
with caffeine I'm there."

The pair continued their walk around the
ancient corridors flanked by stone walls
built roughly 700 years ago. As they made
their way into the dining hall the sun was
just beginning to peak above the trees. The
room itself was open to the outside through
grand archways that could be sealed with
double windows in the event of inclement
weather. Just outside the dining hall was a
raised glade that allowed the inhabitants to
see far across the land to the horizon. It
was the perfect spot to watch the sunrise.

Coffee in hand, the pair sat down to enjoy
one of nature's most beautiful shows.

Margaret paused for a moment as the sun sent its first ray of light towards their faces. "Does it ever get old?"

Myriad turned toward her pupil, "Sunrise? Never. I have seen thousands over the centuries and in many different places. The scenery may change, and the years pass, but the beauty never grows old."

As a member of the Fae, Myriad was hundreds of years old. No one truly knew her age, and no one dared to ask, but like the Locrian she was immortal unless killed in battle. However, the Fae, unlike Locrian, did appear to age. It was a status symbol to their people.

Margaret seemed to relax. "Good, I never want to take things for granted no matter how long I live."

Myriad looked at her pupil, "Never let anything be taken for granted young one. Every day is a gift even when you have lived as long as I have."

The quiet peace of the morning was interrupted by the steady hum of voices.

She stood up, peering over her shoulder at the dining hall that was steadily filling up. "Well, break time is over I am afraid, I must get ready for class. I will see you later."

Margaret stood and inclined her head to her professor in a gesture of respect.

Myriad turned and smiled. She always enjoyed her conversations with her student. She found the young Locrian to be wise beyond her years and she understood the ways of the Fae like no other Locrian she had instructed. It was refreshing to be with someone who didn't constantly fill the void of silence with chatter. Margaret knew how to appreciate the moments given to her through an appreciation of nature and time.

Bria, barely awake and disheveled, found her way to the coffee maker. Breathing in the first few notes of the Columbian nectar she didn't notice her best friend sneaking up behind her.

Margaret saw the opportunity and sprung, "Hi Bri!"

Bria nearly fell over backwards, taking her coffee with her. Splashing some on her hand, it burned like a son of a bitch. "Shit! You scared me to death! If you had made me spill any more of my coffee you would have been dead, I swear!" Bria, standing at five-foot-four, had short red hair in a pixie style cut, and bright green eyes.

Smirking Margaret saddled up beside her friend to give an apologetic hug. "Oh no, I would never. Besides I need my second cup."

Taken aback Bria replied. "Second? How long have you been up, woman?"

"Long enough to see the sunrise - and a good one too." The pair settled into a nearby table.

"Why in the hell would you do that? Was it on purpose?"

She couldn't help but chuckle. "No, it wasn't a choice. I had a nightmare. By the time I settled down I was so awake it didn't matter. I figured I would jump on the first pot of coffee before the other vultures arrived."

Bria nodded and hugged her cup like it was the source of all life on the planet, "Good plan." She sighed and breathed in the heavenly scent.

Bria had been Margaret's best friend since before she could remember.

Looking at the clock on the wall there was only a half-hour before the start of the day. "Well you better fuel up Bri, you know what today is."

Her eyes grew wide. "Oh shit No! No! No! No! It's evaluation day again? Already? Didn't we just do this?"

"We do it every month, Bri, it's not a surprise." She shook her head.

"I know, I just hate it. It's exhausting and I honestly do not like fighting with all the weapons."

"Bri, we have to use weapons."

"You know what I mean. I hate using knives and axes."

Margaret agreed that it was exhausting. Using all the different types of weapons was frustrating when you excelled at one over another but it was good to test your skills to see where you would be successful. Thinking about the thrill of it always put Margaret in a good mood, and seeing her friend's frustration honestly made her smirk.

Bri looked at her friend "What?"

"Did you know when you are pissed your cheeks match your hair."

"Shut up, Mags. Of course you are excited; it's a pissing contest between you and Donny."

"Oh come on, you hold your own pretty well."

"Yeah, with a longbow, not everything else."

"Come on Bri, at least it changes the pace for the day and we don't have to undergo instruction."

Bria shrugged, "I guess this is fitting, I woke up wanting to hit something today."

Her friend laughed. "What's up Bri?"

"Just not sleeping well either I guess. Maybe my insides were telling me what was coming."

Margaret loved her friend. Bria was not introverted in terms of her social surroundings, but for some reason she was always a bit self-conscious in a fight. They were being judged after all, but when she had a long-bow in her hand it was beautiful.

"There is not enough coffee in the world for this," said Bria.

Margaret gave her friend a nudge "Come on girl, let's kick some ass."

Bria chugged the end of her coffee, "Oh, once I get my bow, the ass will be thoroughly kicked."

Chapter 2

Instead of going to the classrooms the students all headed to the gymnasium, but it wasn't a typical gym. There was no work out equipment or basketball hoops. Instead, what existed was anything the Locrian needed to simulate battle scenarios. Combined with Elf and Fae Magic the room was supplied with anything they needed. The environment could morph from a dense forest to a dry desert or even a monsoon climate if they chose. On the day of evaluation the professors made it an ever-changing landscape to see which of the Locrian would perform the best and last the longest against the simulated Droch.

As everyone entered the gymnasium, the bleachers that surrounded the arena began to fill with younger students and other professors. In the middle of the floor stood professor Bryan Doyle who taught the usage of knife and battle axes, and next to him Donny, Margaret's competitor and friend. Standing beside one another, Donny and Bryan could be brothers. Donny stood at six-foot-two and Bryan six-foot-four. Donny wore the standard uniform and Bryan bore his traditional all-black attire. Bryan also had his long black hair pulled up off his neck in a ponytail that only he could make look intimidating. The biggest difference between the two was the scars and tattoos that covered Bryan's body. The tattoos represented the decades of his life on earth. Students often tried to analyze them in an effort to place the time period from which they could have originated. One in particular on his upper bicep indicated that he could have been part of ancient Rome, but others were too difficult to tell. Bryan was secretive about his past.

Like many of the professors here, their age was a mystery as was their past. The students could tell that the scars that adorned his body were not all the result of battle and probably indicated living conditions that were undesirable at some point in his life. But there was no asking about their history. This was something that the older Locrian kept to themselves and it was respected. Maybe one day, when they were considered equals, they would be privy to that information, but for now they would remain in blissful yet curious ignorance.

Donny saw the two girls enter and walked over. Margaret grinned as he approached.

"Hey girls, you ready?"

"Sure am. Be ready to have your ass kicked,"
said Margaret.

Donny grinned. "What about you, Bri?"

"Shut up Donny."

Donny took a step back. "What's with her?"
he asked Margaret.

"Guess," She said raising her eyebrows a
bit.

"Bri, really? It's not even that big of a
deal. You get to 'play soldier' for a few
hours without actually dying. In my book
it's a win."

"Of course you think it is, you leap at the
chance to 'perform' in front of everyone. I,
on the other hand, am tired of 'playing
soldier.' I would rather do it for real."

"I get that, I do. But for now let's have
fun, ok?"

"Again, shut up Donny."

Margaret shrugged as the room became silent;
all the Locrian in their year proceeded to

stand in front of Bryan Doyle to receive instructions.

He stood with his arms crossed, "Today your endurance will be tested. Each phase will last one hour during which time you will only be able to use specific weapons to survive. At the end of each hour the landscape will change as will your weapons. There will be no break until there is a last man or woman standing. If you are killed by a Droch you will be removed from the simulated landscape and dropped outside the boundary where you can observe the remaining competitors. Any questions?"

No one spoke, but Margaret regretted not eating breakfast this morning. Typically, the trials were an hour long with a break at the end of each. This was a whole new ballgame. The limitation on weapons was not surprising, as there was always some type of stipulation, however, the uninterrupted sparring hadn't been implemented previously.

Bria just looked at the two of them. "Excited now?"

"Alright, I admit it this could suck, like really suck," Donny said.

"This is so motivating," said Bria.

Margaret raised her brow. "Let's just stick to our normal plan. We stay together and we win."

Bria and Donny nodded.

Margaret walked over to get her weapons. She surveyed her options and selected a dirk, a traditional fighting knife, with an emerald green inlaid hilt, and a sheath to hold it to her waist. She grabbed some throwing knives for distance kills simple in nature but deadly when wielded correctly and a battle axe for decapitations. Even though the Droch were simulated it would still not be "killed" unless done in the appropriate way. She hoisted the axe on her shoulder and headed onto the floor.

Donny joined the pair, stacking up his own choice of weapons. The way that he held his weapons and the confidence with which he handled them made many of the students regard him with respect. Not just in the way he fought but also in the way that he carried himself. While he wore the same sweats as every other student, he stood out with his shaggy blonde hair, brown eyes and muscles that showed through his baggy outfit.

He walked toward them with a boyish grin and an axe comfortably resting on his shoulder.

This weapon was his bread and butter. He snickered, "Ready to get dirty?"

Bria made a face, "Just keep me alive until I get my bow."

"You got it."

Margaret whispered to Donny, "You always know what to say. Let's kick some ass."

He couldn't help but smile at her enthusiasm, she loved everything about this, and he greatly admired her for it.

Once equipped, the Locrian stood in a circle. The arena began to shift to the first battlefield. The lights dimmed to simulate fighting beneath the moon. Droch only appear at night because the sun is too toxic for their bodies.

Margaret stood ready as the environment changed. Looking over at Donny and Bria she smiled, "I never get tired of this." Donny returned the smile and Bria rolled her eyes.

The arena finally formed and it appeared as if they were in the streets of Dublin. The others in her class disappeared behind walls and buildings, immersing them completely in the landscape. Margaret cursed under her breath, "This means there are innocents."

Margaret took point, with Bria on her heels and Donny pulling up the rear. Heading down the first alley near Temple Bar she scanned the area. Noise came out of the bars with the chatter of human voices, and the sounds of guitars being played. Moving quietly through the streets she heard a subtle growl ahead of her. As she focused in on the noise she came upon a Droch preying on an innocent and drinking her blood. Droch required fresh blood and flesh to survive. The most grotesque thing that Margaret had learned about this species was that they would kill and eat their own in order to sustain themselves. If humans and other creatures are not available, such as Elves and Fae, the Droch will kill and eat their weakest member.

The Droch had glowing yellow eyes and a horn coming out of the right side of its skull. The left side appeared to have been sliced off. Its skin was a deep red with black swirls under the surface. To the woman it was feasting on it would appear to be human, but the Locrian could see through the cloak. Once bitten, the victim became numb, almost paralyzed, and unable to scream or fight. Even in the simulator it made her skin crawl. If they showed themselves, the Droch would kill its victim and flee. They needed to give the woman a chance.

Margaret turned behind her and motioned to Donny to take the shot. She pointed to the roof as a possible vantage point for the attack.

Donny signaled back and began looking for a way to get to higher ground. There was a balcony on a fire escape that protruded far enough out into the alley without showing his position. Once at the top he realized he would have to hang one-handed to get the angle he needed and not expose his location. The Droch was only 25-feet ahead of him so he felt the risk was negligible. He hated targets with innocents involved; it put his nerves on edge.

Hanging over the side he took a deep breath, "You got this." He knew he had to hit it just right in order to deliver a killing blow. The only way to truly kill the Droch was to decapitate it, or hit its brain, where the ore of the Locrians' weapons would seep in and destroy. All the weapons for both the Droch and Locrian were ancient in fashion, forged from the ore beneath the soil of Ireland. It was discovered long ago that the ore used for the weapons was the only thing capable of killing both races. The first true war against the Droch was fought over the ore pockets that surrounded the countryside. In the end, the Locrian and

Droch both retained a few pockets and the fighting has continued ever since. The battle of good versus evil never ended. The Locrian ore depositories are located under every outpost. Each is responsible for forging and maintaining its own weapons. Modern day weapons were not used by the Locrian or Droch, they had never been trained to use them. In this way, the Locrian and the Droch are forced to fight in a more traditional way, making this exercise strangely civilized by relying on hand to hand combat. Decapitation was the preferred method to kill a Droch because there was no chance of survival. Hitting it in the heart worked as well, but took longer. The ore would have to spread throughout its system in order to kill it and by that time the innocent could be dead.

Donny took aim and let it fly, hitting the Droch in the temple just below the severed horn. The Droch went limp, the light leaving its eyes as it slumped to the street.

He slid down the fire escape.

"Nice shot!" Whispered the pair. Hesitant to reveal their location in case something else was watching, they slowly emerged from the shadows to check on the victim. She was lost in a daze but breathing, and pale. Still unable to move on her own, they carried her to the nearest pub with music playing. They placed her just outside the doorway ensuring that she would be found. The light from the bar should keep the Droch at bay. Artificial light could not kill the Droch but it was still an irritant.

Ducking back into the shadows they began to move again, in and out of alleyways. After a few minutes they heard another growl, this time from above them. Looking up, a Droch was perched staring hungrily at the trio. This one had two horns spiraling around its head in a ram-like fashion, and claws dripping with blood. Clutched in its talons was a sword, which they all understood if this was not a simulation, could kill a Locrian.

The Droch shifted, ready to spring down on top of them.

"Spread out!" Yelled Margaret.

The beast leapt from its perch, slashing with its sword as it landed in the middle of the three. It was hacking erratically with no pattern at all, making it difficult to calculate its next move, and space was becoming an issue in the tight alleyway.

Towering over them, the Droch's momentum was powerful. Margaret hesitated to make a move until more space was available.

"We need to draw it out into the street!" she shouted. Bria nodded and took off at a sprint.

Sliding under the swinging of the blade Bria narrowly avoided the Droch's sword. Hopping up, she headed for the open courtyard. As she took off running the Droch was caught off guard and began to make chase. Droch were not incredibly stable on their feet when moving quickly, making fighting in groups beneficial to the Locrian.

Out of the alley, Margaret and Donny pursued from behind as the Droch chased Bria. Bria spun, raising her battle axe to fight, while Donny and Margaret took up positions on its left and right. Margaret swung and caught the Droch in its right side. This only pissed it off and it turned toward her with its sword raised. Just then, Donny caught it on its left side and Bria rose up and cleaved it's head in two.

Margaret smiled "Good hit."

Bria walked over to pull out the axe and for good measure sliced off its head. Wiping the green blood off her weapon she grimaced. "Even when it's fake it's gross."

The three of them chuckled.

Their revelry was interrupted by a scream. Taking off in the direction of the noise they arrived in time to witness a Locrian get taken out by a Droch. The student was lying in a pool of his own blood and looked to be dead, not just simulated, but actually dead. This caused a queasy feeling to hit Margaret's stomach. After a few seconds the 'dead' Locrian vanished from the simulation.

"Wow, that was way more realistic than in the past," said Donny.

The Droch who had 'killed' the student, heard Donny and began stalking toward the trio, wielding two swords.

Bria looked toward Donny "Well, shit."

"Fan out! Give it more than one target," yelled Margaret.

Watching the swords carefully spinning, it was obvious this Droch was way more adept than the one they had just killed. Margaret tried throwing a knife but it was quickly deflected. Donny made an attempt, and then Bria, all with the same result. As they regrouped, the Droch swung its sword toward Bria nicking her arm as she averted the full force of the blow. Margaret hit the beast on its side but it ignored her.

The Droch focused in on Donny, blades spinning wildly. Looking at his friends he had an idea. "It can't stop all of us at once," said Donny looking at Margaret and Bria. "On my count; three, two, one GO!"

The trio launched throwing knives at the Droch's head from three different directions. He managed to block two but one found its way home.

The knife stuck it dead between the eyes. "Mags you threaded the needle on that one!" said Donny.

She smiled; as much as they were always in competition with each other she did value his compliments. Donny was the best knife-thrower in class, so she was a little surprised that hers had been the one to break through.

They fanned out to gather their knives, still staying alert, and then moved back into the shadows to wait and see if there were more Droch in the area.

The group continued ducking in and out of alleyways in anticipation of the next attack, but none came.

A buzzer suddenly sounded, announcing the end of the first hour. Professor Caleb Murphy appeared, as if from a hidden doorway. He dressed in a less sinister fashion than Professor Bryan. Caleb typically sported dark wash jeans and a band t-shirt of some kind; today it was Led Zeppelin. He had shaggy blonde locks, giving him a bit of a hair band vibe, which explained most of his t-shirts. His past, like the others, was shrouded in mystery but it was one of less violence than Professor Bryan based on the state of his skin. He too bore tattoos from all over the world, but again their origin was difficult to place. The most popular ink amongst the students was a Metallica tattoo that he said he got in the 1980's. During class he often warmed up the room by playing Enter Sandman on his record player. His specialty and instruction was in swordsmanship, specifically broadswords.

As he stood before the trio, the remaining Locrian suddenly appeared around them as the walls dissipated. "The first hour is up. For the next hour you will be restricted to swords only. Place your other weapons in front of me and choose from the swords in front of you."

As if out of nowhere, several types of broadswords appeared in front of them. Margaret reached for the four-foot-blade, with a black hilt featuring the logo of the Locrian on the end. Standing at 5'8", the longer blade felt more natural in her hand than the slightly shorter option. Bria, being a few inches shorter, selected a three-foot-blade with a red hilt. She felt more comfortable wielding a sword than an axe or knives so she was more than happy to return them to the pile. Donny opted for the largest of the swords with a three-and-a-half foot blade which suited his height.

"Hey Bri," said Margaret "Thanks for luring the Droch out of the alley."

Bria shrugged "I hate enclosed spaces."

Margaret chuckled at her friend's response, it was almost impossible to give her a compliment.

While the trio practiced with the new arsenal, the landscape began to change and dropped all the Locrian together in an open field. Margaret took quick stock of their numbers and assessed that most of the students were still in the competition.

Being in the open field made her feel
vulnerable. There was nowhere to go.

Above one of the rolling hills, under the
light of the artificial moon, she could see
movement in the distance. Shadows appeared,
dotted with the yellow eyes of a massive
horde of Droch.

"This will be fun," she said to herself.

Chapter 3

Headmaster Asher Murphy sat overlooking the arena filled with his staff and students. He liked to present an air of professionalism and was wearing a black button down shirt, black slacks and a brand of Italian shoe whose name no one could pronounce. His hair, black like Bryan Doyle's, was pulled into a topknot. Many of the professors enjoyed long hair because, centuries before, when most of them were born, it was a sign of strength. Asher also bore many scars from battle but Bryan's would always put his to shame. Bryan and Asher were born of the same class but that was not widely known or discussed. They enjoyed their anonymity.

Bryan Doyle, Asher's longest and best friend, sat to his right and Myriad to his left. Myriad designed the new arena the students were currently exploring, and had made it much more realistic and difficult to complete.

Myriad leaned forward "Is this holding up to your expectations, Asher?"

"Surpassing the expectations. This is truly remarkable. And they cannot see us at all?"

She shook her head, "No it's as if the room does not exist until they are killed."

"The killing looks realistic as well," said Bryan. "What is behind that?"

She paused, hesitant to answer, "Basically, they do die for about 30 seconds until the arena registers that they are no longer 'in play'. They will also retain the injuries that they incur in the arena, other than the killing blows, of course."

Bryan gave Myriad a questioning look, about to protest.

She put up her hands in defense. "Not my idea." And tilted her head toward Asher.

"Asher, don't you think this is a bit much for them?"

"Bryan, don't you remember what we went through when we were their age? There was no school, no safe haven. Seeing monsters among humans and not knowing what they were. Being hunted by these monsters and not knowing why. Living among humans and wondering why we weren't the same. Getting our abilities and not understanding what we truly were up against until we were finally joined with other Locrian and trained. We were not in a cushy environment like these students are. Furthermore, I believe that we have been doing our students a disservice by not giving them scenarios such as these in the environment that we have. This is still safe but will prepare them for the harsh realities to come. We need them to be the most prepared they can be. We are losing too many when we send them to the battlefield. We cannot afford for our numbers to dwindle as they have. The time for action has come my friend, and believe it or not, I feel that this is the best way to do it - while they are still here for another year."

Bryan glanced at Myriad, feeling out her opinion on the subject. She was always one to protect the students.

"I have to agree, Bryan. As much as I hate to hurt them, or see them upset, I would hate for them to die even more. Here they can learn from their mistakes and hopefully save their lives for the future. Not just for their sakes but for all our sakes."

Bryan nodded. It was true. They went through hell while learning to take care of themselves, but that was what this abbey was supposed to protect the new generation from. Obviously something had changed outside of these walls if Asher was resorting to these types of methods for instruction. That would be a discussion for another day. Today he needed to focus on the students and what they needed to learn.

Bryan watched as his students battled through their second hour of simulation, unprotected in a wide-open field, engaging in hand-to-hand combat with nothing but swords. He had to admit to himself that it brought back cherished memories of fighting alongside friends, but also the difficult ones of burying many that he loved.

He watched in awe as the battle unfolded before him, amazed at the talent of his students, proving to him, and his fellow professors, that they were doing something right.

The Droch kept coming, one after the other. Margaret, Donny and Bria, were all holding their own. Fighting side-by-side and helping one another, they were beginning to make a sizeable dent in the Droch population. With decapitation being the preferred method to kill the enemy, Margaret and her friends left nothing to chance. Her adrenaline fueled her. Succumbing to exhaustion or outright failure were not options.

In the middle of a kill strike the bodies and Droch suddenly disappeared. Margaret looked down to see that she was covered in green goo; and red. Looking closer she saw a gash down her arm, nothing severe but it hurt like a bitch.

Another door appeared and Professor Murphy O'Sullivan stood in the middle of the field. Murphy was probably the most relaxed member of the faculty. He often appeared as if he was ready to go to the beach with his shaggy dirty blonde locks and boot-cut jeans and Ron Jon Surf Shop tank top. Why he always insisted on dressing like he was in 90 degree weather instead of a steady 60 degrees was a mystery. Unlike many of the other professors, his skin was devoid of scars and tattoos. His hands were dried, cracked and calloused from teaching archery over the years and from the many years before when he used his talents to kill.

"The next hour is about to begin. Place your swords in front of me and pick up your longbow and arrow quivers. Your quivers will automatically refill through the program so there is no need to grab extra arrows."

"Alright, this is more like it. Let's kick some ass, people!" screamed Bria.

In an instant the swords and professor Murphy disappeared. The students were now on what appeared to be a wall at the top of a hill. Margaret looked to her right and left, realizing that less than half of the Locrian remained after the previous challenge.

The trio stood together once again. Bria prepped her bow, "I may be taking that ass kicking back - do these bows feel heavier?"

"I think it's our arms, not so much the bow," said Margaret, feeling fatigued for the first time.

"Yea I was hoping that wasn't it."

The Droch began to advance across the horizon. Galloping on all fours, they were fast moving targets. Bria took aim and fired first, her love of the longbow evident in her skill. Her first target scored a direct hit to the skull and the Droch fell and skidded across the grass as it died. With their energy draining, each Locrian understood that if they didn't get a headshot, the battle would become longer and more tiring. At first this wasn't so difficult, but the beasts kept coming. Not having any kind of ground support made relying on the archery very difficult. Margaret was growing weaker with every pull of her bow string. She wasn't sure how much more she could handle. Taking a chance to look around as she reloaded, she realized there were even fewer of them left. If this kept up they would be over-run. The Droch were adept at climbing and using their claws for grip. Almost every arrow she shot now went straight down to try to knock them off the wall. For the first time since the simulation started Margaret began to truly worry. She didn't want to die, not even a simulated death looked appealing.

"Guys, I can't take much more of this," she shouted over the growling of the Droch.

"I can't either," replied Bria.

Just as Donny glanced to the side toward his friends, a Locrian standing to his right was hit by a Droch coming over the wall. The boy cried out in pain and collapsed. It was so real and disturbing that Donny briefly hesitated before firing off a shot at the Droch, hitting him in the eye and sending the beast over the wall.

Donny looked around, his eyes went wide, "Where is everyone else?"

It appeared that Donny, Bria and Margaret were the final three in the simulation. As they were taking stock of the situation, a Droch silently climbed over the wall and caught Donny unaware. Unable to defend himself, the Droch, using his talons, grabbed Donny by the throat and pulled, leaving him gasping for air with a chunk of his throat missing. As he dropped his weapon and reached for his throat, the Droch finished the job - slicing off his head and sending his body flying off the wall.

"Donny!!" Yelled Bria and Margaret.

While they were distracted, another Droch rose up above the wall and brought its sword down on Bria's head, lodging it in her skull. With the sword still stuck in her head, she reached out for Margaret and fell forward. The beast pulled the sword out of Bria and turned toward Margaret. Still in shock, she didn't even try to defend herself as the sword sliced across her throat.

Darkness surrounded her for a matter of minutes. Margaret awoke gasping for air, Bria and Donny beside her. All three received the touch of the healers Lyas and Lorien, twin Elves who aided with injuries and illness of the Locrian. The Elves looked down at the trio as they lay splayed on the ground. Margaret quickly grabbed her neck.

"Relax, young one," said Lyas, "The injury is not permanent; however, you will be a bit sore for a few days. The injury on your arm is deep and will need tending to."

Margaret was stunned. This was far more than what she or the others were used to. The crowd was silent. There was no talking, cheering, anything, just silence. Once bandaged, the three were escorted to the bleachers to sit with the others from their class. A cursory inventory of everyone's faces confirmed that the rest of the Locrian seemed as stunned and jarred as she did. After all, it's not every day that you die.

Chapter 4

The silence was deafening. Asher heard Myriad choke back a gasp when the final three Locrian were "killed." It took him a moment to recover as well; the deaths were so realistic he was brought back to a time when he saw his own friends die, but there were no second chances for them. He knew he had to say something to the mass of stunned students so he made his way down the bleachers, each step echoing in the silence.

He took a moment to gather his thoughts as his eyes scanned the crowd of exhausted faces. "This is a day I do not want you to forget. This is a lesson to you all, even those of you 10 years their junior." His arm swept over the Locrian who had just gone through hell. "This is the world you will live in when you leave. It is harsh and unforgiving, but with training and practice you can survive and make a difference in this war." He paused, looking out over the lives he had to protect, "All those who instruct the younger class, please remove them from the gymnasium at this time."

No one spoke as they all exited the room one by one. The young Locrian averted their gazes from their professors; their heads hung low.

Asher looked at his pupils; they were battered and worn down. This was a lot harder than he thought it would be.

"I owe you an apology. The intensity of the simulation was my idea, to prove a point and to better prepare you for the fight that is to come." He crossed to Margaret. "Even though you were the victor Margaret, the simulation did not stop because I wanted you all to experience reality. I am not sorry for wanting to prepare you, but I do apologize for deceiving you. I know that I owe you an explanation of what occurred here today. It is time that you learned a little more about where you come from."

He began to pace the room.

"There was a time, centuries ago, when Locrian were born and didn't know who they were or what they were destined to do. In my time we were lucky to find human homes that were welcoming where we could be raised as one of them. Others were not so lucky." Asher's gaze shifted briefly to Bryan.

"When the time came to be named, we were
pulled by the tree, by an unseen force, back
to where we were born. It was then that we
truly discovered who we were. Over time we
created the abbey to ensure the safety of
future generations, which allowed our
numbers to grow and greatly aided us in the
war against the Droch. The tree, that now
creates Locrian every ten years, had been
producing a class every year. The drastic
increase between years of creation,
resulting in fewer classes of Locrian, has
made it much more difficult to hold the
outposts and cities. As a result, the
process of your emergence into Locrian
society has recently changed."

A look of confusion came over the students.
They had not been told how they would
integrate into Locrian society after leaving
the abbey.

"After your naming you would have gone into
the cities around Ireland where your talents
were most needed. You would have been
assigned a mentor to help you grow in your
abilities and you would have protected the
streets of the cities in which you lived.
When the time came, you would have joined
the rotation at the outpost, serving for a
few months and then returning home to
recuperate in an effort to mitigate

exhaustion from the endless attacks. This process has worked for us for hundreds of years, until recently. We have come to realize that there are not enough Locrian holding back the Droch forces at the outpost. All who are available have been called back from the cities in order to hold the outposts and to protect the humans and our future. What this means is, for the foreseeable future, there will be no rest for the weary. You will, upon your naming, be sent to the outpost that needs you the most. You will be fighting continuously. That is why we tested you as we did today."

Myriad and Bryan listened to Asher with the same shocked rapture as their students. They had always believed that this reality would come to pass, but learning that it was happening now was painful nonetheless. To show their support, they walked down to stand with Asher.

Visibly bolstered by the presence of his colleagues, he continued, "Your lives will be difficult. You will be tested. You need to have the ability to fight in any situation for hours on end, or you will not survive. The class behind you will provide some relief, but without the proper training those 10 years will feel impossible. If we do not succeed, we let our people down, but more importantly, we let the world down."

Margaret didn't know what to do or say. None of them ever really knew what came after life in the abbey. No-one mentioned it, not until it was time to leave. While fighting was always something that she loved to do, now it seemed all too real. The idea that this pain and exhaustion she now felt would be her life every day was daunting.

Myriad stepped forward. "I know this is a lot to process. I am not sure what, if anything, you were expecting your lives to be outside of these walls. I know hearing this may be intimidating, scary and confusing. The reason we are doing this now is to give you a fighting chance at survival so that eventually you can have the life that Professor Asher spoke of. You will complete these trainings once a week so that you will get used to the rigor. The rest of the time you will train as you always have, with one exception, my class will be conducted via the simulator every day. This will provide you with multiple chances to engage in different battle tactics and situations before going through the entire attack sequence on Fridays. Our hope is that with time and training this will not be a difficult task to complete. We want you to take the remainder of the day to nurse your wounds, eat, recharge and process this

information. Tomorrow the real test will
begin."

———————————————

Margaret felt helpless. Her world was
crumbling. How could they be expected to
survive this? Bria and Donny left to find
food. How they were able to eat, she didn't
understand.

She found herself wandering the courtyard,
eventually coming back to the spot where she
had sat that morning. A lot has changed
since then. She hadn't been sitting long
when Myriad appeared beside her. She wasn't
really sure how she felt about the Fae in
that moment or if she even wanted company.

"You don't have to talk to me if you don't
want to but I am here to listen as I always
have. I can imagine you are a bit upset
about the situation, and maybe even with me
for my involvement in it."

Margaret took a deep breath, feeling her
emotions rise to the surface. She leaned
forward with her head in her hands and tried
to focus on breathing. It was all so
difficult to process.

Myriad watched her pupil "I know you are upset, I can see it."

"Please don't tell me how I feel right now because I'm not sure I even know how I feel right now." Margaret said, her hands covering her face. She leaned back and looked at her professor with a hint of a tear in her eye. "I don't know why this is affecting me more than the others. They seem fine and I can't even think straight."

Myriad touched her shoulder "You don't know how they feel just as I don't know how you feel; everyone deals with information in a different way."

Margaret sat quietly for a while, her eyes focused on the horizon.

"I always knew our purpose; I just hoped we would have more of an opportunity to live a life like the one professor Asher talked about. A life not consumed by fighting. Now we must face battle every day for a decade, in hopes of surviving until our relief arrives. It seems impossible."

Myriad wrapped her arm around Margaret's shoulders, "Nothing is impossible. We will prepare you the best way we know how." She looked into the young Locrian's eyes. "You will survive. We will prepare you for your destiny. And in terms of time, you will have eternity to live the life you want." She knew exactly how Margaret felt. Her youth had been filled with war and violence, just like Margaret's would be.

Taking a deep breath, Margaret looked at Myriad, "Is it really that bad out there?"

Myriad looked to the horizon and nodded. "Yes, young one, it is. The numbers are dwindling but numbers are not everything. The Locrian that are fighting right now are some of the best I have ever seen. You will not be alone. They are holding the ever-growing number of Droch at bay, waiting for you to come to their aid. All we can do is help prepare you, protect what we have, and hope it is enough to keep the balance and peace."

"The Droch are drawn to the power of pure evil. If the Droch numbers are increasing there must be some type of great evil that has emerged," thought Myriad.

"How is this going to work? I mean we have been training our whole lives and couldn't last three hours? That was horrifying."

Myriad nodded knowingly, "The exercise was created to be difficult on purpose. You do not have your Locrian abilities yet, nor

68

were you using your preferred weapons. Asher took it to an extreme to prove a point. It will get better, easier. We are doing this so you have the best chance of survival after you leave us. You WILL survive, young one. Now go, enjoy your friends, help them grow and understand. We will get you where you need to be if you want it badly enough, which I know you do."

She took a deep breath and looked out across the country she was born to protect. She nodded and took off toward the dining hall to be with her friends.

As her eyes scanned the crowd for Donny and Bria, Margaret swore to herself that she would survive and if she had any power or choice in it, her friends would survive as well.

Chapter 5

Dragas sat upon the rudimentary throne
constructed for him from the subterranean
rock of his home, his gaze taking in the
number of his followers. The Droch dwelled
deep beneath the surface of Ireland where
tunnels and caverns intertwined in an
underground maze.

He did not appear as the others did. His
skin was red and black, and his eyes yellow
but no horns adorned his head, no blood
dripped from his lips and unlike the others,
he still felt a sense of modesty wearing a
cloth to hide his privates.

Everyday more Droch came to fight under
Dragas' rule. Birthed from mud and filth,
Droch are born ready to fight. There was no
training required. With each passing day the
Droch grew in number. His plan was finally
coming together.

Dragas was very proud of his minions. They
served him well and each night grew
stronger. Every moment brought them closer

to what would ultimately end the world as they knew it and spawn a new world where chaos reigned and the Droch had dominion over the earth.

The new training schedule was brutal. The Locrian practiced fighting techniques for eight hours every day. They bounced between knives and battle axes, to swordsmanship, archery and hand-to-hand combat. In the morning the class was divided in order to have their technique reviewed in a smaller setting. There were 4 groups of students taking turns with each instructor. Three groups of 20 and one of 19 giving their class 79 in total. At the end of the first four hours the students were allowed to rest, eat, and rehydrate. The remaining four hours were spent in the company of all the instructors while Myriad coordinated the battle simulations. The students worked in teams and Myriad paused the simulation after each mistake was made in order to allow the Locrian time to recover and rectify their mistakes. If they failed, they died, and the next group rotated in to try to complete the simulation, learning from the previous group's errors.

Margaret was so exhausted she lost track of time and days. Every night she fought to remain upright in the shower and was barely able to drag herself to bed after nursing bruises and cuts from the training exercises. She tried to stay positive but exhaustion overwhelmed her and wore her down. This was her life now for the foreseeable future. The only positive was that she was so tired every night she never had a hard time falling asleep but the morning always came too soon. It had only been a week; and tomorrow was the next full battle exercise. They would be put back into the arena and fight until only one stood or everyone died. It was a terrifying experience that left death at the forefront of everyone's mind.

She limped back to her dorm room, ice pack on her neck where Bria had landed a blow earlier that day. She didn't remember climbing into bed as she fell asleep. She awoke with a start, yet again, from a horrific dream. This time she remembered a bit more. Lava spewed up from the earth and Droch had overrun the land. She rolled over and looked at the clock, "Shit." It was 4:00am again and she had a long day ahead. Try as she might, she could not get back to sleep. As she got dressed she thought about caffeine - a necessity. Food - a possibility.

She walked towards the dining hall hoping some coffee would already be brewing. She was in luck. Someone else had gotten up to face the day as well. Picking up a coffee mug, she gestured to the Elven cook with a sign of gratitude.

"I know this is a big day for you all so every Friday from now on I will be open a bit early just in case you need something."

Margaret had only ever seen the cook in the confines of the dining hall, had never conversed with him around the abbey, but she felt a momentary rush of affection for this little man, "Thank you very much."

The cook moved closer to her, and as he approached, Margaret realized he had a sunnier complexion than his Elven counterparts in the infirmary and he possessed long jet black hair.

"Thank YOU young Locrian for fighting this fight and continuing to do so. You not only protect the world for humans but for creatures such as my kind as well. I know that you do not have a choice in the matter, but I know you take pride in what you do and it is appreciated."

She was floored and didn't know what to say.
She had never been thanked for doing what
was expected. She nodded to the Elf as he
went back to his station. She poured her cup
of coffee, grabbed some toast and peanut
butter, and headed out of the dining hall.
She knew it would be crowded shortly and she
wasn't in the mood to be surrounded by
people just yet.

She wandered around the empty grounds until
she found herself in the arena. She walked
in, took her coffee, and plunked down in the
middle of the floor. There were no Droch
after her, no screaming or yelling, just her
and the quiet. She closed her eyes and
visualized a more peaceful place. She
thought of a place where Droch didn't plague
her, where she could just be Margaret with
her friends, her family. She pictured a
beach with waterfalls and crystal blue water
and felt a warmth on her face that did not
exist in Ireland. No fear existed there, no
problems, no worries, just peace.

She was so focused on this imaginary
paradise she almost didn't hear her
professor approaching.

Myriad sat beside her pupil. "Margaret, what
are you doing here so early? Shouldn't you
be resting?"

She let out a breath "I was attempting to do that just now," she said, slightly upset about being disturbed. Although Myriad had always been one of her favorite professors, the ongoing drills designed and enforced by her had caused her to fall out of Margaret's favor. It felt like they had already stopped living and began their life-long journey and pursuit of survival for the sake of mankind. One week had already begun to destroy her; what would a lifetime of lifetimes do if she was lucky to survive that long?

Myriad looked taken aback "I didn't mean to disturb you. I was merely concerned because of the hour." She began to stand.

Regaining her composure, she stopped her professor, "I know. I apologize for my short response, I was just meditating to try to channel my emotions."

"I can see that. I know that there is anger in there, and some of that is directed at me."

Margaret slumped her shoulders, not wanting the professor to be correct but knowing that she was. Myriad had always been a person that she felt at peace around, but lately she was full of anxiety. "It's not so much directed at you professor, just the situation in general. I am not pleased with any of the instructors lately. I'm doing my best to keep fighting and take these opportunities to learn so that we can survive, but I just feel pissed off! We went from being in a school to a military institution overnight. This is our life now, professor, and we don't even get a final year to enjoy it before the fighting consumes us because it already has."

Myriad understood what the young Locrian was going through. Regardless of the fact that they were born to do this task, they were still living and breathing beings that had emotions, formed friendships, and wanted to live.

Myriad looked at her pupil, one that she cared a great deal about, "I do not know what to say to ease your pain."

"I don't want anything to ease it; I just need a reason to fight, to live. And if there is no future for us it's hard to fight and get up every day. Maybe that is why we are weak in number; we feel too much and grow too weary. The Droch have no emotions, they only know how to fight. I don't want to turn into a mindless drone like them. I need to believe that this will end and we will live."

"It will, you will. This is why we are preparing you, and what we are all working so hard to achieve. Your life can be long and fruitful you just have to put the fight in first."

She nodded, wanting to believe the ancient Fae who had lived through periods like this before.

Myriad stood and walked away leaving Margaret alone again to think. If she could be good enough to survive the simulations, maybe she could survive the real thing and that gave her hope.

Eventually the room filled with her classmates. The younger Locrian would not observe them again until just before they were to enter their new roles. The trials began as they had before, starting with axes and knives, then swords, then archery. This time around more of them advanced to the archery level. Margaret, Donny and Bria all completed the scenario along with a few others. The next hour was knives again. It was a rotation geared at inciting exhaustion. That was how they would fail.

Myriad sat with the others and observed her pupils; her children that she had watched grow. The individual elements of the trials were real situations, but in reality, the

Locrian would never be forced to use only one method of attack, in small numbers, in multiple locations in one night. The purpose was to train them for the worst case borderline impossible, scenario so that when they were able to succeed, reality wouldn't seem nearly as difficult or so she hoped. She saw how battered and tired the students were and she felt like she had betrayed them. Her job was to train and prepare them, but this seemed more like abuse. She had to believe they were doing the right thing, but at what cost? Margaret was the last to be killed again and Myriad flinched every time she fell. All she could see was the newborn child she held in her arms that night long ago and it was a pain that was tough to bear.

Margaret hated failing at anything, especially something that made her suffer the pain of her own death and that of her friends. Donny and Margaret made it to the second round of swordsmanship but Donny was cornered by two Droch twice his size when he was cut down; and she was left without support which resulted in her decapitation. Bria almost made it to the swords but an axe caught her in the temple when she let down her guard to check on the others.

Margaret walked with the rest of the class
to the infirmary to get patched up from the
wounds that they incurred. She really wished
she could avoid receiving killing blows to
the head because it was giving her massive
migraines. As she passed the younger Locrian
in the hallway she couldn't help but notice
the stares. Her face was bruised and
bloodied. She couldn't help but wonder how
this must look to them and how scary the
prospect of going through these trainings in
a few years must be for them. Through her
exhaustion she mustered up a smile to give
them and to her surprise they smiled back.
She had almost made it to the infirmary when
she saw Bria sitting just outside on one of
the abbey's ornately carved wooden benches.

She crossed over to her friend, "Bri aren't
you going to go in?"

"Yea, I just hate dying, ya know it just
isn't good for my self-esteem."

Margaret chuckled a bit. "I don't think that
dying is good for anyone's self-esteem. But
at least it isn't permanent."

"True story. These head injuries suck
though. I can barely see straight my head
hurts so badly."

She nodded. "I agree. Just means we need to work harder, or invest in aspirin."

Bria smiled. "You always know what to say."

"Sarcasm?" asked Margaret.

"No I mean it."

"Thanks Bri. I'm not feeling so optimistic lately, so I'm not sure what good my words are doing."

"It's not really so much what you say, it's what you do to back it up. We all know this new schedule sucks, but you take it in stride. You haven't seemed discouraged at all, and that in itself is encouraging."

Margaret smiled, "You are really serious. Alright, well I will make you a promise; I will have your back, as long as you have mine."

"That is what I am here for," smiled Bria. "But I do need some help with swords and knives. I'm just not as quick as you and Donny are."

"I need it with archery, I can't hold that bow as steady as you do, and I need to work on my grip strength."

The pair began to walk into the infirmary.

"It's not too hard to build it up; just do what I do."

"What's that?" Asked Margaret.

"I do grip exercises at the gym and when I feel like I can't hold on any longer I picture the most annoying person I know and imagine that holding my hand there is keeping their mouth shut for as long as possible."

Margaret looked at her friend, "Donny?"

"Yep!"

The two began to laugh and couldn't stop. It was a sound that the professors hadn't heard from any of the students in the last week and apparently it was contagious. Suddenly the entire infirmary was full of laughter, from jokes and silly banter and the result of pure unadulterated exhaustion. And where there was laughter there was hope.

Chapter 6

As the days progressed, classes became less taxing and returned to the friendly competition the students were accustomed to. Donny and Margaret were back to their normal bantering, much to Bria's chagrin; and the focus of the trials shifted to team building and away from the morbid news from weeks prior.

Margaret felt better about her future, apart from one small annoyance that she couldn't seem to get over. Her dreams about the Droch were becoming more and more frequent. She was beginning to think her subconscious fears were manifesting as she slept and it made it extremely difficult to get a restful night's sleep. Though, she had to admit that things were beginning to look up.

She walked toward the classroom that was scheduled for knife and battle axe instruction. The weather was beautiful and she was enjoying the warmth of the sun on her face - a rarity in Ireland.

"You ass hole! I'm going to kill you!"

Margaret heard Bria's screams all the way down the corridor as she made her way to the training room. The outburst didn't worry Margaret - she had a pretty good idea of who Bria might be yelling at.

"You could have killed me, you idiot!"

Margaret entered the room and saw Donny pinned to a wall; Bria held him with a knife at his throat. She looked so pissed off that Margaret actually had some concern for Donny, but not much.

Donny, with his hands in the air yelled "Calm the hell down Bri, there is no way I was even going to scratch you! You know how good I am."

Putting the knife a bit closer to his throat, "That cocky attitude is what I'm talking about Donny, you're not that good. If you do it again I WILL cut your balls off."

Despite his precarious position, Donny began to chuckle, but quickly stifled it as he saw the fire in Bria's eyes refuse to dim.

Slowly Bria lowered the knife and moved away as Margaret approached the pair.

"What the hell did Donny do now?" She said with a smile.

"The idiot decided to practice his motion accuracy."

Margaret looked around the room noticing the lack of targets.

"I'm confused."

Bria whirled around "He practiced on ME! He decided to see how close he could throw the knives without actually hitting me."

Glancing around the room again she spotted the knives. She couldn't help but laugh. "Come on Bri, you have to admit that he's pretty good."

She shook her head "No, not this time. Do not side with him on this just because it's 'cool'. I was terrified. I had no idea it was happening - I took off running!"

This time Margaret had to hold back a snicker at the picture that appeared in her head.

"The little shit didn't even stop when he realized how pissed off I was." Bria turned toward Donny one more time "I mean it Donny.

You better watch your balls, because I will come for them."

Margaret tried to calm her friend down.

"Bri he wouldn't have thrown it if he thought he would hit you, loosen up."

Bria's face flushed. While it was true that Margaret was always in competition with Donny, whenever it was something like this, the two of them teamed up on her. They loved pushing Bria's buttons and it pissed her off to no end.

Turning on her heel Bria headed off toward the dining room. "Screw you both, Ugh!"

"Let her get a drink and she will cool off," said Margaret.

Donny nodded. "Thanks for that, I know how close you are."

"I know when she is being unreasonable. Plus, when her feathers are ruffled it can be entertaining. And yes, we're close, but when it comes to stuff like this" she gestured around the room "You and I are on more of the same page than she and I are."

Donny nodded with a smile. "Well I kind of don't blame her, I got a bit closer than I anticipated on the last one you can see it there." Donny pointed to the far corner, they walked over to the knife, and Margaret could see a few of Bria's hairs stuck to the blade.

She leaned in to take a closer look "Ok, that is a bit close," she stood back glancing at Donny, "maybe I should have let her cut your balls off."

"Truthfully I was lucky; if her hair had been shorter I might have gotten skin."

"I have no issue with you pushing yourself and testing your limits, and this was pretty cool, but if you ever actually hurt my friend I may have to beat you up just a little bit. And probably let Bria have your balls," she shrugged. "It's only fair."

Donny smiled.

Turning from him, Margaret reached for the knife just as Donny did and their hands touched. She dropped her hand immediately, shocked by the sensation that pulsed through her fingers. Just then, Bria returned to the room with the rest of the class and professor Bryan.

"Donny, if I ever hear about you using living beings, that are not Droch, for target practice again, I will hang you from the rafters - Am I understood?"

Donny's face went white "Yes professor Bryan."

Donny grabbed the knife and began to clean up his mess, looking over at Margaret with a sheepish grin.

Professor Bryan removed his hoodie and revealed a black tank top and his sculpted muscles. "Thank you, Donny, for unintentionally leading me into our exercise for today. We're practicing on moving targets. Don't worry Bria, they're wooden."

Bria took it in stride. "As long as they resemble Donny we'll be alright." Their classmates laughed, lightening the mood for the moment.

He continued, "I want you to pair up. You must stop the object charging at you, aka the Droch, with a kill shot, before it gets within striking distance. Find your partner." He took a moment to look at his students, their faces suddenly focused, and he felt a sense of pride. He went back for a moment and thought of Asher and himself as young men competing in the woods with axes, knives and swords. It was a different time, but the threat remained the same.

Donny leaned over to Margaret, who hadn't realized he had walked up behind her, "Want to give it a go?"

Peeking over at Bria, Margaret shook her head. "No doubt it would be fun, but I think I'll hang with Bri today. Siding with you earlier means I need to earn back some lady loyalty points."

Donny, looking utterly gut punched, shook his head, "Maybe next time."

Margaret was confused. They were never partners. It was always a competition between the two of them. Why was he taking it so hard? She walked over to Bria, "Partners?"

"You sure you don't want to be with your buddy over there?" Bria snarked.

"Are you kidding? You're super pissed off, if you can channel that into the exercise, we're sure to win. Besides, I want to be on the friendly side of your fire.

Bria smiled, "Oh I'm going to kick his ass."

The pair started toward the table to grab some knives. "What was Donny talking to you about before?"

"He wanted to be partners today, but I told him I had to be with my girl."

Bria looked over her shoulder at Donny who was glancing in Margaret's direction, "That's weird, he's never asked you that before has he?"

She shrugged "No, but I figure maybe he's getting nervous that I'm gonna beat him. Or maybe he's worried about getting stuck with you!"

"Alright, now that you're all paired off the competition will begin," Said Bryan "Those who stop the Droch the fastest will be the winners. Donny and Margaret, you and your partners will go last."

Margaret grinned - this was a testament to the professor's faith in them.

The new training schedule made the competition much more intense, which she loved. Not only was it more difficult overall, but it also helped to increase her friend's capabilities which meant a higher chance for survival for everyone.

Professor Bryan stood with his arms crossed. "Alright, the Droch target is placed 50-feet away. Whoever stops the Droch furthest from them wins. The catch? Both of the team members must make a killing head shot."

"Well shit, speed is not normally on my side," said Bria.

"Bri you've gotten so much better and you don't have to be fast, just be accurate. Picture Donny's head that should do it."

Bria smiled with a determined look in her eye.

One by one, Margaret and Bria took advantage of watching their classmates make the mistakes they would try to avoid. The furthest stop out so far was 20-feet. Donny was partnered with Cassie, a tall, gorgeous blonde whose hair was always infuriatingly perfect. At nearly six feet tall, she spoke eye to eye with Donny about strategy, and as Margaret glanced over at them she felt a brief pang of jealousy. What was wrong with her? She needed to refocus and distract herself from whatever weird feelings were going on inside of her if she was going to win today. She paused, reminding herself that Cassie was probably the worst knife handler in the class which would be helpful in beating her and Donny.

Donny and Cassie went second-to-last. He threw his knife after just a few seconds making his killing blow immediately. Cassie took longer, making several throws and missing the target entirely. Donny slid behind her to help her with her aim and Margaret began to fume. What was going on in her head?! This is Donny, the boy that has driven her nuts since she could remember. Finally, Cassie hit her mark. It wasn't enough for a win, they ended at 18 feet, but Cassie walked away with a smile; she had never done a killing blow with a knife before. Margaret knew she should have been happy for her, but the image of Donny standing behind her, guiding her knife-throwing hand was embedded in her head.

Finally it was Margaret and Bria's turn. Margaret took a deep breath to focus, her friend needed a win today. Aiming, she focused on only one thing as she took her stance and narrowed her eyes on the Droch target. The Droch began to move and she let her knife fly, hitting it at 45-feet. That was the farthest hit so far, giving Bria more of a chance. "Take your time Bri, don't worry about anything else, just focus on the target." Bria let her knife fly and connected right between the eyes.

Margaret's eyes went wide "Holy shit you did it Bri! That was amazing. You hit it 30 feet out. I told you - you can do this!"

Bria stood stunned for a moment, then shaking it off, turned to Margaret, a huge smile on her face.

Their classmates swarmed around Bria to congratulate her on the win. Margaret let her friend revel in her victory.

Professor Bryan came forward. "Congratulations Bria, how did you hone that focus in?"

"Well I can't take all the credit because Margaret helped me focus, but the real credit goes to Donny," Bria said, basking in the moment.

Professor Bryan seemed confused. "Donny?"

"Yes. If he hadn't pissed me off so much this morning I wouldn't have pictured his face when I threw the knife." Donny scrunched his face in her direction; tongue out, like a brother annoying his sister.

Everyone roared with laughter. "I appreciate the solid use of motivation." Retorted professor Bryan. "I am just glad that she didn't confuse the Droch target with you Donny." Professor Bryan jabbed Donny in the ribs.

"I am not going to live this down for awhile am I?" Asked Donny.

"That would be up to her," Bryan pointed in Bria's direction.

Margaret smiled as she backed away, gathering her stuff quietly to leave the room and head to the next exercise a bit early. She wanted Bria to savor her own success without her in the way.

Margaret was already warming up when the rest of the class came into swordsmanship. "Hey where did you go?" Bri asked.

She continued to go through her stretches, "I've won a lot of things but you truly conquered that event and I wanted you to have that moment on your own. You deserved it."

Bria gave Margaret a hug, "Thank you, but anything else we win together, we celebrate together."

Margaret smiled, "Deal."

Professor Caleb Murphy entered in his usual laid back fashion wearing jeans and a Rob Zombie t-shirt. No one really knew if Caleb Murphy was an old roadie or if he just appreciate good music, but regardless, he stood out in a crowd.

"Alright people, apparently I have not been as 'intense' in my training as I need to be, so we're going to amp it up today." Caleb said, groggily.

Bria nudged Margaret, "Do you ever wonder if he's just high on life, or something stronger?" Margaret attempted to cover her fit of laughter with a cough as everyone turned to look at the pair.

Unphased, Caleb continued, "I want you to experience some training that we went through when I was a young Locrian. We partnered up and the match did not end until blood was drawn."
The students exchanged worried looks. Was he really asking them to hurt each other?

"Ok, I'm betting on the stronger stuff. Has he lost his mind?" Whispered Margaret to Bria.

Professor Caleb looked at the room full of stunned faces "Listen, I'm not asking you to kill each other, it'll be just a nick with the training swords. The tips will be blunted and you'll have to avoid the face; helmets must be worn for this exercise. I don't need someone losing an eye. I want to condition you to fight with your wits and not always go for the kill shot. You may be forced into battle to fight with a less lethal weapon and be required to wound or slow down your opponent until something better can be found or you can get to help. It's just an exercise."

It was clear that Margaret and the rest of her classmates still felt a little uncomfortable at the idea of intentionally injuring each other.

"I will pair you up with your equal in swordplay." He began to walk around the room. "Margaret and Donny, you two will be together, that is a given. Bria, I'll pair you with Lance, I think you'll complement each other well."

As he continued to pair off the rest of the group Margaret leaned into Bria. "You got this girl."

"Hell yeah I do! Do me a favor?"

"Sure, what?"

"Take Donny down, would you? I'm still a bit pissed from this morning."

"You got it."

Bria was still seriously amped up from her victory. Lance stepped over to Bria and handed her a helmet. Bri had known Lance for quite some time, but she couldn't tell you much about him other than the fact that he was extremely quiet and introverted, but a very skilled fighter. Bria took it as a compliment that Caleb paired the two of them together.

Donny approached Margaret, helmet in hand.

"You ready to do this, slugger?" Asked Margaret.

"Take it easy on me Margaret, my ego was already dealt a painful blow today."

"Huh? Oh come on Donny, it's not like I haven't beaten you before. And you should be proud of Bri, she definitely deserved a win today after your 'target practice'.

"Yeah, that's what I meant." He shook his head and put his helmet on.

Before Margaret could question what Donny was going on about the match began.

The sparring went on for a while until only three pairs remained. Donny and Margaret, Bria and Lance, and Cassie and her partner Lyra. Professor Caleb allowed the six

Locrian to take a break and get water before returning to the mat.

"Since all of you have held up so well I'll allow each pair, one at a time, to engage each other, so the others can learn from your technique," Caleb said as he lounged in the corner. "Cassie and Lyra you can go first."

Lyra and Cassie faced off, going back and forth parrying each other without a direct attack for several minutes. Either they were exhausted or measuring their opponent. Finally, Lyra lunged but Cassie quickly blocked her. Cassie spun and kicked Lyra back. giving herself some space. Lyra lunged again, very off balance, allowing Cassie to pin her sword to the floor and kick again causing Lyra to fall back. Cassie's sword caught Lyra on the thigh and a tiny drop of blood seeped out. Lyra looked relieved that it was finally over. Cassie helped Lyra up and the pair shook hands.

Bria and Lance went next. Bria was concentrating harder than Margaret had ever seen and her form was better than just a few weeks prior. Lance was also laser focused. Suddenly, as if she had lost her mind, she sprinted directly at her opponent, throwing him off entirely. She jumped at the wall behind him, using the momentum to send her towards Lance who was already off balance, and took him down in one fell swoop. Once he hit the mat she stood over him and put a small mark on his shoulder.

Bria had the biggest smile plastered across her face as she helped Lance up. He removed his helmet and bowed in respect to her. The class began to cheer and her cheeks flushed as she walked off the mat to join the rest of the group.

Donny and Margaret went next. Donny was unnaturally quiet during the match, his usual joking and bantering traded in for stoicism. They went back and forth for quite some time and Margaret began to get tired. Fatigue caused her toe to catch on the edge of the mat, and as she fell, Donny rushed to get the advantage. She rolled out of the way just in time and was able to catch Donny in the gut with the hilt of her sword. He hit the mat where she had just been, the wind knocked out of him. Margaret staggered to her feet and marked her victory on the back of his arm.

"Good match buddy," she said, helping him up. "I love sparring with you."

"Thanks, just not my day today I guess," he said with a slight smirk.

"Hey" said Margaret, following him to put the equipment away. "Are you ok? You aren't acting like yourself."

"I'm fine," Margaret was unconvinced. "How would you feel if you lost two of your best events in one day? Don't worry about me." He said, nudging her shoulder.

He was right. If she had lost two events she would probably be handling it worse than he was. Still something seemed off.

Caleb watched as his students left the room and smiled. He thought back on his training as a young boy, his memories of bonding with the other Locrian more through training than anything else. The battles wore them down, but the bond they had training lasted a lifetime. It gave them the trust in each other to survive. He stood to prepare for the next group, this time with a smile and his eyes a little brighter.

Bria caught up with Margaret in the hallway. "It's getting a bit cold out don't you think?"

"Yea," said Margaret, distracted as she pulled on her hoodie. What started as a nice sunny day had turned cloudy with a drizzle and a chill set in the air.

Margaret was zoned out, her gaze a million miles away.

"Anything wrong?" Bria asked, as they passed other classmates heading toward the swordsmanship room.

"Ya'll look rough today!" Yelled a boy named Liam on his way to Caleb Murphy's class.

"Wait until you get there," yelled Bria "I hope you brought bandages.

Liam's face sunk.

"Haha - that was fun." Bria turned toward her friend, anticipating a retort as well, but she was still lost in thought. "Mags, where are you girl?"

"Huh, sorry. I don't know. Donny just seems off today and I hope it isn't something I did."

"What did he say?"

"He said he was just having a bad day. Losing two events in his best areas has him down."

"Well duh! He never loses at knife throwing and honestly you would be flipping your shit right now if you had lost in swordsmanship.

Plus, I also semi kicked his ass earlier today. A boy can only be handed his ass by two beautiful women so many times in one day before he starts having issues."

She had a point. Both of them hated to lose, and in comparison, Donny was probably handling today 100 times better than she ever would.

"You're right," Margaret said, perking up a bit. "On to the next?"

"Yep. I'm having a great day and this is my domain! I only wish they allowed us some shower time. I reek."

Caught off guard by her friend's statement, Margaret laughed.

"Yeah, but we all do so it's a collective stink."

The girls walked all the way to the back of the abbey, which was deceptively large with its outside corridors and just a few interior hallways. They climbed the spiral staircase with the wrought iron handrail toward the tower nearly eight stories up.

"Every day this seems further and further, especially now that we do two hours of work-outs before we even get here," Bria said.

Once they reached the top they were greeted by one of Margaret's favorite rooms in the abbey; second only to Myriad's classroom which was decorated in Fae artifacts and protective symbols that seemed to glisten on the walls. She covered the windows in tapestries which provided a relaxing environment for students to review battle strategies before entering the training ring. The tapestries allowed soft light from the sun to penetrate the room; this provided optimum relaxation and calm. It's something that Margaret took for granted until recently, only now realizing the importance of being centered before fighting. Lately it felt like the only thing in her life she could truly control.

The tower was covered floor to ceiling with rich rustic, wood paneling and expansive picture windows. A huge medieval door was on the far side of the room. It led to an overlook with a view that spanned miles and miles into the distance over the expanse of Ireland. It was the best view in the entire abbey. The door hung open providing a clear view of the balcony and allowing the cool air to fill the space.

Murphy O'Sullivan came in through the opening with a smile on his face. "Alright people, it's target practice day." In his

light colored jeans, flip flops and muscle
tank top, he looked like he'd be more at
home at a beach shack than in an archery
tower. Everything about him screamed beach
bum or hemp enthusiast. He grabbed a poncho-
style hoodie to put on over the sleeveless
tank and lead the students outside.

"I have placed targets along the treeline,
some are closer than others, as you can see.
Some will require more focus and attention
to detail to hit. The more you hit, the more
points you get, and of course the more kill
shots the better. Each of you will have
different colored arrows so that I can tell
who has hit each target. Any questions?
Good. Take your positions."

Margaret grabbed the purple arrows and Bria
grabbed the blue. Donny slid down the row
towards Lance and grabbed the black arrows.
Margaret peered out at the tree line, some
of the targets were barely visible. How
could she even see it to hit it, let alone
land a kill shot.

Margaret squinted, "Bri, can you even see
all these?"

"Yes, barely, but yes."

She was a natural archer with vision
Margaret couldn't explain. It would not

surprise her if Bria's last name turned out to be O'Sullivan on naming day, lord knows it was her talent for sure. Not to mention her passion. Her face lit up when she had a bow in her hands and the bow became an extension of her body. The names that are bestowed on the Locrian reflect their talents and the talents of the founders. O'Sullivan is the name given to archers, Doyle to those who are strong in knives and axes and Murphy to those who excel with a broadsword. This was why all the professors went by their first names instead of their last to omit confusion. The last names bestowed on them signified their place in the Locrian hierarchy.

"You will shoot until your arrows are gone. In Three, Two, One, Go!"

All the students took aim but few looked as confident as Bria did. Arrows seemed to disappear too quickly and it was very difficult to see if they even hit a target, and if they missed, how to adjust. Professor Caleb walked the line once everyone finished and tallied the points. Gifted with the sight of a hawk at his naming ceremony, which is what Bria would get if she too were named O'Sullivan, he never needed binoculars or anything to spot where the arrows had landed.

"Lance, very respectable you hit 15 targets out of 20 arrows; four were kill shots, 19 points. Donny, again, very respectable, you hit 16 targets, 7 kill shots, 23 points. Cassie, 13 targets, 1 kill shot, 14 points. You're getting better Cassie." Cassie grinned, beaming with pride. Murphy continued down the line, "Margaret, very nice, 17 targets, 9 kill shots, 26 points. I like your technique. It's clear you can't see the furthest targets so you concentrated on the closest ones. And Bria, 19 targets, 12 kill shots, 31 points. This is a new class record. I am pleased to announce that you increased your scores as a class from last time which you should all be very proud of."

"Bri you are an animal today! I do not know how you do it with those targets."

Margaret gave her friend a huge hug. She was genuinely proud of her.

"Way to go Bri, you too Margaret," said Donny "Archery is never my strong suit."

"You still did really well Donny," said Bria.

"Thanks. Would you mind if I walked with you guys?"

"You never have to ask," said Margaret.

"Well I've been a bit of an ass today so I wanted to make sure it was safe."

"You're forgiven. I just need to grab my stuff."

"I'll help," said Bria. Glancing over her shoulder at Donny she caught him looking toward Margaret. "See, I told you he was ok."

Donny waited for them at the door to begin the long walk back down the staircase. This next class was honestly the trio's least favorite. Hand-to-hand combat. In this class they learned how to bring down a Droch without using any kind of weapon, or at least how to survive until help arrived, or the sun came up, if necessary. It was the most physically taxing class but lunch was scheduled in between class and the simulations, so at least there was something to look forward to.

"I am really not feeling this class today," said Margaret. "I can never picture an instance where I will be fighting and not have a weapon. I mean, you are kind of screwed at that point."

The trio made their way down the hall to the most visually boring classroom. The floor and walls are covered with thick, plastic mats for protection. There are no windows to let in natural light, and there are no personal effects of any kind placed on the walls to give the room personality. The students donned face gear, mouth guards and boxing gloves in preparation for sparring. Professor Xavier Doyle was the most eccentric teacher that the students had. He was very much a comic book nerd and fancied himself a true master when it came to martial arts. He used to fight with swords but one day gave them all up and found inner peace through martial arts. Margaret couldn't fathom putting down a sword in a fight.

Professor Xavier walked in wearing a black karate gi marked with the Locrian tree emblem. He was the shortest of all the professors coming in at 5'7". He had dirty blonde hair and was the only professor with what be might consider an updated hairstyle. His hair was cut short in a shaggy uneven fashion; the ends of his hair laying over the tops of his ears. His muscles were visible through the uniform which only added to the intimidation.

Xavier crossed to the middle of the room "Today I would like to see how you all fight in a group and how you work together. Professor Myriad set some simulators up here to project Droch for you to fight. It's not to the caliber of the training gym but I think it will serve its purpose."

The groans around the room were audible. Four hours of simulations in one day were enough. But now they had to do it without weapons? They would be wiped out. The Droch, by nature, are taller and wider than the Locrian, giving them an advantage when the Locrian do not have weapons to depend on. Given the realistic nature of Myriad's simulations in the training room they knew they were in for it.

Professor Xavier visually assessed the class, "Work together, and do not try to do too much yourself. If you get injured remove yourself from the simulation. It will end if all the Droch are killed or all of you are."

Donny spoke up for the first time all day. "Alright guys, I don't know about you but I'm really tired of having my ass handed to me by these simulated sons of bitches. You guys with me?"

All the exhaustion seemed to collectively leave their bodies as Donny's pep talk kicked in.

"We got this." Margaret said to herself.

Professor Xavier turned on the simulator and 20 or so Droch appeared in front of them, carrying their misshapen swords and axes. The Droch outnumbered the students 20 to one. Margaret sighed, losing some of her recent confidence, this would not be easy at all.

Initially the students took the offensive approach, bobbing, weaving, and dodging Droch weapons. Droch were not particularly good at fighting, just enormous and dumb, so their weaknesses were quickly revealed. Margaret, Donny and Bria were in close quarters. Bria noticed that Margaret's opponent tended to lean toward the right leaving its left side exposed. "Mags, dodge to the left." Margaret noticed this too and executed a sweeping kick to the Droch's knees causing him to lose his balance and fall. She pounced on his hand and he released his sword. Margaret quickly grabbed the weapon and decapitated the Droch.

Bria was still entrenched in battle when Margaret ran to her aide. As she sliced through his back he turned, distracted by the blow, and Bria did a spinning kick toward the beast. She grabbed for his sword, but when she went to slice it through his neck, his head was already gone.

"Sorry, did you want to do it?" asked Margaret.

"No worries, there's plenty more."

Word spread quickly of each student's success and the class continued to coordinate attacks. The "death toll" of the Locrian was minimal and soon all the Droch were defeated.

"I feel so awesome but so exhausted," said Cassie.

"I know, and we have to do this again this afternoon," sighed Bria.

"But on the plus side guys, we actually won. The simulator shut off - not us. I'd say that's a good enough reason to reward ourselves with some food. That, and the fact I am starving," said Donny.

A collective nod and fatigued cheer came from the room. It was a valiant effort made by all and it deserved to be celebrated, even if that just meant dining hall pizza.

Xavier Doyle watched as his students quietly shuffled out of the classroom, clearly exhausted, but hopeful. He smiled to himself, pleased at their victory.

Chapter 7

Lunch today was different than it had been during the past few weeks. The students were weary and dirty but the mood was light. Tales of beating records and winning matches spread around the room. Bria recounted the tale of her expert swordsmanship to those who were not lucky enough to bear witness to her victory.

Since the class was divided for instructional purposes, there were many stories circulating the dining hall that afternoon. The only locations in the abbey large enough for the entire class were the dining hall, Myriad's classroom and the gymnasium. The energy was already so positive and when all the students met that day in the dining hall, the energy soared.

The younger Locrian were in a positive mood as well. Their training had also recently changed. It wasn't as intense as the older class but still more rigorous than they were used to. Their class was smaller, with only 60 students. Margaret was jealous of them. Had her class been subjected to this level of training in their youth they would undoubtedly be feeling more confident about what was to come. But things were beginning to change, and for the first time in what felt like forever there was true joy throughout the abbey. The sacred Locrian tree was due to birth another class of Locrian any day now, and with numbers decreasing dramatically in recent cycles, everyone held out hope that the upcoming birthing would be fruitful.

The professors stood in the back of the dining hall, unnoticed. "It's good to hear them laugh again, and celebrate." Said Myriad. Caleb, Bryan, Murphy and Xavier all smiled.

"Today was a turning point," said Bryan. "Let them celebrate."

"I have not been so excited to witness something so masterful since my first Led Zeppelin concert," said Caleb.

The others shook their heads at Caleb's former rocker lifestyle. Secretly jealous of the talent that he was able to witness.

"I know what you mean," said Murphy. "The talent in this class is astounding and they are beautiful to watch when they are in their element."

Myriad smiled, "I think a reward may be in order."

Following lunch, the students made their way to Myriad's classroom to discuss strategy. As they approached the room there was something noticeably different, a floral smell wafted out of the classroom and met them in the corridor. The room itself had changed, gone were the work tables and maps. Instead there were hundreds of flowers lining the walls and covering the floor.

Myriad stood in the middle of the room with her eyes closed, looking radiant. Fae are in their element when they are in nature and they somehow become even more beautiful in this environment. Fae that are as old and experienced as Myriad are able to manipulate nature, and as such, she had merely opened a window and summoned the growth of the flowers to her classroom.

She opened her eyes, "Come in young ones, please, and have a seat on the carpet."

Margaret looked at Bria with a shrug, put her things down, and began to walk towards the carpet.

"Oh, please remove your shoes first," requested Myriad.

The students stopped and immediately returned to the entrance, removed their shoes, and walked towards the carpet covered in flowers. It was by far the softest thing that Margaret had ever felt beneath her feet. All she could think about was she would love to sink into the floral fabric and sleep. From the looks on everyone else's faces they felt the same way. Margaret also knew Myriad's room hadn't always been this big and she was convinced Fae magic was at work.

Myriad sat facing the class; legs crossed on a chair "Today we're doing something a little different, as you may have already guessed. I've heard about all of your victories today and I'm so proud. You have worked tirelessly every day for the past month and I think you need a break."

The whole room sighed in audible relief.

"So I guess I'm correct in my statement then."

Chuckles of laughter escaped the students.

"Today I'd like you to take some time to deal with your emotions, the good and bad. Please rest your minds and your bodies, I know they are spent. I encourage you to stay

here for at least an hour to meditate. The
flowers in the room will heal the body, mind
and spirit, literally. Their fragrance is
famous for it. You may already feel your
aches and pains subsiding. If you fall
asleep, I will wake you. Do not worry. Just
relax."

The Locrian began to lay down on the soft
carpet and to breathe deeply. Margaret was
glad to see she wasn't the only one who was
truly exhausted.

It felt as if only a few minutes had passed
when Myriad touched Margaret on the shoulder
to wake her. Startled, she shot up, trying
to figure out where she was. "Take it easy,
you're disoriented. You were out cold."

Margaret looked around and realized she was
the last student left in the room.

"Please tell me I'm not the only one who
passed out like that."

Myriad shook her head "Oh absolutely not,
you were just the last one I woke. You
seemed to need it more. I only woke you
because it's almost dinner time and I
thought you may want the chance to freshen
up before then."

"Almost dinner? So I slept for nearly four hours?"

The Fae looked at her like a worried mother would. "You were not alone, there is a lot going on, and I know sleep hasn't been easy for anyone lately."

Margaret nodded, getting to her feet "Yeah, that's for sure. Alright, I better go shower, I know I'm not smelling good at all. See you tomorrow, professor."

Myriad chuckled as Margaret ran out of the room. The sight of the sea of Locrian passed out on her floor had been astonishing. She knew the recharge was necessary and the flowers would aid their aching muscles. As she had watched them all sleep, she couldn't help but remember them as children and pray over them for their safety.

———————————

Margaret could not remember the last time she was able to take her time in the shower, instead of rushing through so she could get to sleep. She hadn't gone to the dining hall in weeks for dinner either, too tired to care. But tonight, thanks to Myriad's nap session, she felt truly alert. She was also starving. She definitely wanted some fries and whatever other greasy goodness she could pile on her plate.

As she entered the dining hall she could see that her sentiments were shared. Each student had a mound of food and was eating in near silence. The looks on their faces said it all, pure bliss.

Margaret took her turn at creating a pile on her plate and before she knew it she had selected a slice of pizza, fries, a cheeseburger, chicken nuggets and a side of nachos. It looked disgusting and delicious all at the same time. She had no doubt she could finish everything in front of her.

She scanned the room and located Bria and Donny sitting near the back. Clearly just getting food themselves, she walked over to sit with them.

Bria seemed perky this evening, "Hey Margaret!"

"Hey yourself, you look refreshed."

"As do you. I was out for about three hours, you were still cutting Z's when I left."

She was a little embarrassed by the statement "Yeah I guess I was more exhausted than I knew. What about you, Donny?"

"About the same as Bri, she was gone by the time I woke but it couldn't have been too long."

Margaret nodded "I could get used to the nap. Between that, the rug, and the flowers - geez."

"Yea," said Donny "I want those flowers in my room, I'm barely sore from today and my previous aches and pains seem to have disappeared."

Margaret stretched her back, testing to see if her muscles had also gotten some relief. "Myriad is a miracle worker."

"That's for sure," said Bria.

After dinner Margaret was so stuffed she could hardly move, she headed back to her dorm room. Even with the nap she still felt that rest was in order. She changed for bed and did something else that she hadn't been able to do for a while, read. She picked up her tattered copy of The Great Gatsby and relaxed.

It didn't take long for her to become tired and she fell asleep mid-read with her book on her face.

Margaret shot up in bed, awakened by a loud bang. Groggy, she made her way to the door and stepped into the hallway where she was nearly bowled over by Lance. "What's going on?"

Lance paused. "It's the new class of Locrian."

Margaret's eyes widened. She grabbed a sweatshirt and flip flops and took off down the hall. Reaching the front entrance she met up with Bria and Donny. All of the Locrian were anxiously awaiting the arrival of the new batch of infants. Lyas and Lorian were at the front of the group to receive them. The infirmary had been transformed into a nursery to accommodate all of the new arrivals until they could be placed into dorms. It was a massive undertaking but the twin elves were the best.

The carriage carrying the infant Locrian arrived in its enchanted state, appearing as a regular vehicle. Once the back door was opened, though, it revealed rows and rows of babies safely nestled in carriers.

Lyas and Lorian began to remove the infants from the car in their carriers, each one attached magnetically and with wheels, similar to a large load of shopping carts. They pushed the first group of infants past, then the next. Lyas entered the car a second time, but exited quickly with a solemn expression. Turning to professor Asher, the elf whispered in his ear. Asher's face paled.

"Are you absolutely sure?" The elf nodded and walked back in the direction of the infirmary.

Margaret was confused, "I wonder what the issue is? Where are the other babies? That wasn't nearly enough."

"It is strange, I hope nothing bad happened to them," said Bria peering through the crowd.

Asher Murphy turned towards his fellow professors with a somber look. He paused, having momentarily forgotten that the students were watching.

"Please return to your dorms, the excitement is over for now. Rest, you have training to attend to in the morning."

Confused, the students walked back towards the dormitories. They were all curious about what was happening but nobody was brave enough to ask.

Margaret did not want to return to her dorm, not yet. Something was wrong, very wrong, and she needed to know what it was. She began to head back to her room but darted and hid behind a divot in the wall. Bria and Donny noticed and turned to walk back towards her.

"What are you doing?" Asked Donny.

Margaret's gaze stayed fixed on the group of professors. "I have to know what's going on, something isn't right. We're coming of-age soon and I'm tired of being in the dark. I feel like we deserve to know."

Donny looked at Margaret with a grin, "Why don't you tell that to professor Asher then?"

She smirked, "I would but I prefer to listen from a safer distance."

As much as they knew Asher cared for them, he was still intimidating and would punish them if he caught them disobeying or challenging orders. The last time they had been in trouble they had to clean the bathrooms for a week. It was horrible and not something Margaret wanted to repeat.

The three settled into the shadows.

"Asher are you sure?" Asked Myriad.

"Take a look for yourself!" He snapped.
Myriad was taken aback. "I'm sorry Myriad
but I'm not sure what to do."

Bryan took a step towards the transport.
Peering in he shook his head, "There were
only 30? What does this mean for our race?"

Asher's head slumped. "That I cannot
answer."

"What do we tell the students?" asked
Myriad.

"Nothing. We go on as usual," said Asher.
"They have too much on their plates as it
is. So as not to draw attention, there will
be no celebration of the infant's arrival."

Myriad looked surprised "But Asher, they are
still important, they should be celebrated."

"They will be, in time. For now, do your
traditional prayer of protection over them.
Once we figure out this mess we can
celebrate their birth."

It was clear Myriad wanted to argue but
thought better of it and followed the others
out.

Margaret, Bria and Donny stayed silent as the professors walked away.

Bria turned towards the others with a look of shock. "There are only 30 babies? This isn't good guys."

Margaret turned to her friend, "No shit Bri. What good is all this training if there is nobody coming to relieve us?"

"This changes everything," said Donny.

Chapter 8

Margaret did not sleep well that night, which was becoming more of a habit than she cared for. All the rest she had gotten in Myriad's room the day before was squashed by the deep sinking feeling that they were all screwed. She decided to go for a walk; she couldn't stand being cooped up in her room any longer. She found herself out in the courtyard once again. There was something about this spot that calmed her. She sat on the rock just outside the doors to the dining hall, waiting for the sunrise to wash away her worries. She sensed the Fae approaching her and peeked over her shoulder.

"I know you heard what was going on with the Locrian, Margaret." She looked at the Fae wide-eyed in surprise. Myriad pointed to her ears, "Fae hearing dear. The three of you sounded like a wind tunnel with your heavy breathing. But don't worry, no one else knows you heard."

Margaret nodded and turned away in relief. Myriad invited herself to sit. Margaret took a deep breath not wanting to hear the answer to her upcoming question, "What does this mean for us?"

Myriad looked at her pupil, pausing before she responded. "I am not sure. Every class of Locrian since I have been alive has varied in number. Caleb's class was abundant, but he was born centuries ago when the tilt of the war was even worse than this one. His group numbered in the hundreds. But the original group, the founders, was but 50. I think they were hoping for a larger class, one that would even the playing field, and return the balance. Having the numbers we do now is definitely scary for everyone."

Margaret felt defeated. "We made such great strides yesterday and had such hope to have this happen is such a blow."

Myriad nodded and turned towards the horizon. She was proud of all they had accomplished in such a short period of time. The harsh methods that seemed so cruel before had forced them to utilize everything within them.

"You should still have hope. The founders were small but mighty. They managed to

organize and fight off an entire army. You
can too. Right now there are 169 Locrian
under this roof, all preparing for the fight
that is to come. If 50 Locrian did it
centuries ago, you can certainly do it now.
There is no reason to think that this new
information changes anything. Your class is
impressive, young one. One of the best I
have ever seen. Keep that in mind."

Myriad stood to give her pupil some space.

Margaret nodded then asked "Professor?"

She turned "Yes, young one?"

"How were the founders created again?"

Myriad paused.

"You know this story, are you sure you want
to hear it again?"

Margaret nodded, "Yes absolutely."

Myriad sat once again, "The tree was just a
sapling on the edge of Kilkenny when the
founders were born. Without the care of the
Fae, the babies were found by humans and
taken into homes. They were spread out all
over Ireland until the call to return to the
tree united them. The tree not only called
to them but to the Fae as well. It was then

the Fae realized how important the tree was and we took it upon ourselves to protect it. Until the first naming, the founders were the only Locrian to exist. On the anniversary of the first naming ceremony the Locrian tree produced the next class. This time there were 100 Locrian born and the Fae were there to welcome and protect them. The tree then began to produce a class of Locrian every year, gradually increasing in number, until the balance had been restored."

"How many were in those classes, do you know?" Asked Margaret.

"The Fae record the numbers of every class, but I cannot recall them all."

"I was just thinking, it seems that all the classes are even in number," said Margaret.

"I never thought of it, but I guess you are right."

Margaret paused, "Except for ours."

Myriad paused thinking of something to say, "I never noticed."

"Really? You know everything there is to know about the Locrian, but you never noticed that our class was different."

"Young one, don't consume your thoughts with such matters, I am sure that it doesn't mean anything," said Myriad.

Margaret looked off at the horizon, "If you say so."

Myriad turned and walked away, saying nothing more.

Margaret knew that the Professor was hiding something, why was their class different?

Myriad walked up the spiral staircase that was, adorned with gas lanterns. At the top of the stairs stood an ornate wooden door, with the Locrian tree carved intricately on its surface. Without knocking, she threw open the door to find Asher and Bryan in a heated discussion. Pausing, they looked at the Fae whose face was stark white.

"What is it?" Asked Bryan, as he crossed the room to hold the Fae up from falling.

Shaking, Myriad could barely control herself. "She is so inquisitive, why does she have to be so inquisitive?"

"She isn't making any sense Asher."

Bryan walked her to a couch. He wasn't sure she could stand on her own.

Concern filled the headmaster's gaze.

Asher knelt in front of the ancient Fae. "Myriad, look at me and focus. What is going on?"

Her eyes slowly met his, with a look of regret she tried to explain.

"I was speaking with Margaret. She had overheard our conversation last night about the newest class and was feeling a bit defeated, as we all are."

Asher stood, getting furious. "I can't believe she eavesdropped. I'm going to - "

"Asher, not the point," interjected Bryan. "Please, continue Myriad."

Bryan motioned to Asher to sit.

"Well, I was trying to boost her confidence by discussing the founders and how they were able to survive and hold the Droch at bay being so few. I reminded her that we have 169 Locrian at our disposal here, granted they are not all ready to fight, but they will be."

Bryan leaned back. "I do not see the issue, that seems like a fair statement."

Myriad shook her head, "Yes, but Margaret is smart and asked another question. She wanted to know why all the other classes of Locrian were even in number, except for hers."

Asher's face turned white as understanding set in.

He began to pace "Shit! None of them are supposed to know that Myriad! They were never to find out that there was another."

Myriad stood to confront Asher, furious at the way he was speaking to her.

"Don't you think I know that! I had to erase their memories once, I cannot do it again." She stared him down, "I will NOT do it again."

Bryan jumped up to make sure the two of them didn't get into a fist fight.

"Please calm down. Did she seem to suspect that there was another Locrian born into her class?" Asked Bryan.

Myriad shook her head, "No I don't believe so."

Asher let out a sigh, "If she does, we will tell her only what she needs to know and nothing more."

Myriad disagreed, "By doing that we may cause more problems. I cannot lie to her if she asks. She has more of a right to know than any of us do."

Asher looked out the window. "In a way, you are already lying to her. Omission is betrayal just as much as an outright lie." He turned toward Myriad looking her square in the eye. "If you want her to be safe, you will do as I say."

Myriad did not take kindly to Asher's threatening tone. "You are forcing that omission Asher; you are the one betraying her."

She turned to leave and Bryan caught her arm.

"Do you think that HE is the cause of this?" Bryan asked looking into her eyes. "That the issues the Locrian are facing are because he survived and is now out for revenge?"

Myriad paused and shook her head. "I do not see the connection. Even if he had survived, he would not have control over the birthing cycle."

Appeased for now, Bryan nodded and let her go.

Myriad opened the door.

"Myriad?" said Asher, with a look of concern. "Keep an eye on her just in case?"

Without turning around she responded, "I will, as I always have."

Margaret sat in the dining hall huddled together with Bria and Donny speaking below the hum "I am telling you something was weird."

Donny sat, thinking. "Are you sure the classes have always been an even number? I mean it's not like we were there."

Margaret glared at him "Donny, the classes before us and after us have all been even. Why would we be different?"

"Maybe it doesn't really mean anything,"
said Bria. "What if one of us passed away
when we were little, or the Droch attacked
the transport. We know things like that have
happened."

It did happen, but rarely. And if a Locrian
died in infancy they were buried in the
garden in the back of the abbey. To her
knowledge no children had been buried there
since the elves had come on staff. Infant
death just didn't happen. Droch attacks
didn't happen anymore either, not in recent
history. Births and naming ceremonies all
occurred on the eve of a full moon and Droch
did not attack during full moons. The
moonlight was too bright for their eyes and
could scorch their skin if it was clear
enough. This allowed the Locrian babies to
be transported safely and without conflict.

Margaret couldn't shake the feeling. "It was
just odd, I feel like I caught her in a lie.
If there was a death or an attack, why
wouldn't she say that instead of walking
away?"

"Is it really that big of a deal?" Asked
Donny. "So we have one less than normal?
Like Bria said anything could have happened
and maybe Myriad doesn't like talking about
it, or maybe she isn't allowed to talk about

it. It could have been something upsetting and they don't want us to know."

Bria was getting tired of the back and forth, she really didn't see the importance of it. She finally had enough and interjected, "The point is it could be any number of things and we have no control over this. It isn't affecting us so we need to simply let it go."

"Alright, fine." Margaret said begrudgingly. "I'll let it go for now."

Bria breathed a sigh of relief. "Now let's move on to more important issues. I completely suck at swordsmanship. I can't seem to get the flow that you two have, and I know you both want to work with the bow. Maybe we can get some practice in after the simulator? It isn't kicking my ass nearly as badly now. Is it bad that I'm becoming immune to dying?"

Donny and Bria's conversation faded to the background. Margaret knew it was out of her control but something didn't sit right, she was missing something. Her gut was telling her not to let it go and she always trusted her gut.

Margaret was a little tense as she approached Myriad's classroom. She didn't want to talk to the Fae. She knew there had to be a reason Myriad lied, so she told herself she wouldn't press the issue. She simply avoided any conversation, which was easy because of the scheduled simulation exercises.

That night Margaret skipped dinner, not from exhaustion but from distraction. It was as if she was grasping at air trying to recall something that just wasn't there. All she knew was that something was definitely wrong and she couldn't pin it down. She didn't blame Donny and Bria for letting it go so easily, it seemed so unimportant, but something rooted in her memory somewhere told her otherwise. She hoped to get some solace while she slept, to stop her mind from fixating on the situation.

As she sank into her dreams she was met with blissful silence, her mind was blank and relaxed. Then, she was falling, as if she was thrust into a nightmare. Suddenly she hit the ground hard. As she sat up she expected to be on her dorm floor but instead she was in what appeared to be Dublin. She had never had a dream so real, it was as if she was in Myriads simulation, but it was wrong. The Dublin she knew was bright, vibrant, and full of life, this was scorched and broken. Massive holes marked the pavement and the sky was so black that not

138

even stars shone through. Steam rose from the earth. Margaret walked over to one of the holes and saw a lava like substance. "This cannot be real, this is a dream," she said to herself. It had to be a dream, if it wasn't she had fallen into Hell on earth.

"Why does this feel so real?" She reached out above the opening into the steam and pulled her hand back quickly. She looked at her fingertips and they were red. "What happened here?"

She wandered through the streets, deserted. She thought there would be a human, a Droch - something, something that would be in this hell, but nothing.

"This does not feel right, this is more than a dream," she thought.

A whisper floated through the air *"Margaret"*.

She turned in the direction of the noise but no one was there, nothing moved. It was eerily silent. The only visible light came from the vents in the earth causing a red hue to envelope her surroundings.

"Margaret" Again, she turned, but nothing was there. She had to wake up.

Panicked, she began to run, not sure what to do, but trying to wake herself up. She leapt over cracks and crevices, acting in fear now. Her name echoed around her and she was terrified.

All of a sudden a Droch unlike any she had ever seen before dropped down in front of her, throwing her off balance she fell into a gaping crevice. She could feel the heat of the lava rising up to greet her. Throwing her hands up in reflex, she waited for the collision.

She shot up in bed. Drenched in sweat and panting, she looked around her room and thankfully everything appeared to be in order.

"What the hell was that!"

She jumped out of bed and began to pace. "*How is it still dark out?*" It felt like she had fallen asleep ages ago.

She caught her reflection in the mirror; her t-shirt clung to her and her back was soaked. Her hair looked like she had just stepped out of the shower.

"This is crazy," she said.

She ran her hands through her hair and was shocked to feel intense pain.

Margaret glanced down at her hands and realized they were covered with blisters. She noticed her pajamas had singe marks speckled throughout, some so severe they had made holes straight through the fabric burning her skin beneath.

"What is going on?"

She opened her door carefully, her hands were in agony.

She walked as fast as she could, not even taking the time to put on shoes or a jacket. The cool air felt good on her burnt skin. She rounded the corner and saw the welcoming entrance to the infirmary.

As she entered the doorway she saw Lyas and Lorian tending to the new infants. They glanced in Margaret's direction and touched their lips, to remind her to be quiet. When they actually saw her they froze.

She stood with her hands in the air "Something is wrong with me."

Chapter 9

In a matter of minutes Margaret was surrounded by Asher Doyle, Bryan Doyle, Myriad, Caleb Murphy, Murphy O'Sullivan and Xavier Doyle.

"Did she say how this occurred?" Asher asked the elves, as if Margaret wasn't even in the room.

Lyas and Lorian faced the professors "In a way, but we found the wounds so bizarre we had to contact you all. There is an aura of magic around her wounds. It's faint but there. Her clothes also retain the aura and they have scorch marks on them as if she was near immense heat, but she said she was sleeping and awoke with her hands and clothes like this. She came straight here."

Myriad looked concerned "I just don't understand what kind of magic could do this. Fae Magic can leave a trace but I don't know of any that would do this, especially to a Locrian. It would violate the treaty that we established long ago."

"Are we sure she was sleeping? Maybe sleepwalking?" Chimed in Bryan Doyle.

"She said she woke in her bed," stated Lyas.

This back and forth continued for quite some time. Margaret became irritated at the group treating her as if she wasn't present.

Standing in the group of professors, Margaret tried to regain her voice, "Could I maybe tell you all what happened instead of you playing a guessing game?"

They all paused, turning toward her. All of a sudden Margaret felt like a child, not like a Locrian less than a year from being their "equal." Her face flushed. Seeing this, the professor's expressions softened a little. Myriad stepped forward. "Of course, it was inconsiderate of us not to ask you directly." She gingerly sat the young Locrian down, her vacant expression becoming more and more concerning to the group.

"What happened exactly?" Asked Asher, stepping forward.

"I went to bed early because I have had a lot on my mind lately." Her gaze went to Myriad. "I fell asleep quickly but was launched into a dream. I know I have had it

144

before because I remembered bits and pieces, but this was different. Before, I was on the outside looking in, this time I was in the dream. It felt real, I could feel the ground beneath my feet and the heat in the air."

"Did you feel awake?" asked Myriad

"Yes, in a way. I knew it wasn't reality but at the same time I felt like I do now; Very conscious and aware of things going on around me."

"What did the surroundings look like?" Asked Bryan.

Margaret took a moment to gather her thoughts. The memory made her shiver, "It looked like Dublin, but a messed up version. The streets looked like an earthquake had happened. There were cracks and giant crevices. Storefronts were broken and fires were burning like looters had ransacked the place. Some of the crevices were so deep that lava flowed beneath the surface. It was completely void of people and Droch. It was dark, there was no sun or moon, the only light came from the red glow emerging from the crevices, it was unreal. Then a voice, a whisper, came out of nowhere saying my name. It completely terrified me so I ran. All I could think about was waking myself up. Then a Droch, unlike any that I have seen in the simulations, appeared out of nowhere causing me to fall into one of the giant crevices, towards the lava. I could feel the heat and then I woke up with singed clothing sweating like I ran a marathon, and blisters on my hands."

As if jarred awake, Lyas suddenly realized that the entire time Margaret had been sitting there her wounds had been exposed.

"Oh my goodness your wounds! I am so sorry. I'll grab the salve and bandage them." He quickly disappeared to retrieve the items.

Margaret nodded but the look on the faces of the other professors sent a shiver down her spine.

"What did the Droch look like?" asked Asher.

"He was almost human like. He had red and black skin but no horns. His eyes were yellow, and he had sharp teeth and claws, but he wasn't as tall as a normal Droch or as muscled. He also wore a loincloth." This fact was particularly weird because Droch did not care about modesty and never wore any clothing.

Margaret paused looking for answers in the faces of the professors.

"You have no idea what could have done this, do you? None of you."

Myriad wanted badly to comfort her. "I have never heard of something like this but that doesn't mean that we cannot find out. I still have numerous contacts with Fae far older than I, they may have heard of something like this. There has to be an explanation."

Margaret tried to feel comforted by the fact that she was surrounded by the greatest leaders of her time, but it didn't look like she was going to get answers anytime soon.

Asher approached her with Bryan in tow.

"Margaret just rest for the week, go to class but do not fight. It will hinder your healing," said Asher.

Bryan looked at the other professors, "Let's come up with a plan later this morning that will allow her to participate and learn without causing further harm."

They all nodded in agreement.

One by one the professors went back to bed, eventually leaving Myriad alone with Margaret, who was still receiving medical attention from Lyas.

"Wow, I sure know how to clear a room," said Margaret.

"Well you know, men," said Myriad playfully. Sitting down she looked at her student's weary face. "What's on your mind?"

Margaret's shoulders slumped "Some of the most powerful individuals in the world, with centuries of collective knowledge, cannot figure out what is going on with me, and it terrifies me."

Myriad rested an arm on her shoulders.

"We will, just keep me informed of anything that happens."

Margaret agreed.

"There is something else that I was thinking about," said Margaret.

"Yes?" replied Myriad.

"Do you think it's possible for me to die in the dream? I mean, it did this." She held up her hands. "What if it's worse next time?"

Myriad thought for a moment.

"I don't know but I'll work on something that Fae use to ward off bad dreams to bring to you tonight. It should help."

She nodded. Lyas was finishing wrapping her hands.

"Here is the salve. You don't need to ration it. Use as much as you feel is needed, it will help with the pain as well. Come back in a few days so that I can check on the healing. Remember to shower without the bandage each night and then re-wrap it."

The stinging in her hands was already subsiding. She got up and headed down the hall in a daze. She got halfway to the dining hall before it dawned on her that she was not only still in her pajamas but that she looked like she had been through hell, literally. She wanted to shower but knew the burns would sting so she redirected back to her room and changed into her daily uniform. She walked back toward the dining hall which was now packed full of students. Robotically she walked to the coffee machine and got herself a cup and headed outside. The noise was not welcome today. Her brain felt as if a thousand bees were buzzing around and she couldn't focus. The dream had done one good thing, it took her mind off what she was previously obsessing over. Who cared if

149

there were only 79 of them? She no longer did.

Donny tapped Bria on the arm and pointed at Margaret. They watched her walk slowly outside with her coffee. He nodded in her direction and the two of them stood to follow their friend.

"Mags?" Bria carefully approached her friend who was completely distracted.

"Mags? What is going on?" At this point Bria was sitting next to her with a look of concern.

Donny hung back waiting to see if he was needed, knowing sometimes guy advice was not the best medicine.

Bria looked back at Donny and shook her head in confusion. Donny walked over and knelt in front of Margaret and touched her hands, only then noticing her bandages. Fury lit in his eyes.

"Who did this to you Margaret!" Donny couldn't contain the anger in his voice and it clearly shocked his friend out of her trance.

"Shit! You scared the crap out of me Donny. Why did you sneak up on me like that?"

Bria touched her arm. "Mags, we have been here for a while trying to get you to talk to us. What happened?"

Margaret looked at her hands and a tear rolled down her cheek. The anger inside Donny built up. Whoever hurt her would pay. Rage filled his eyes as he began to pace. Before his anger got out of hand, Margaret told her friends everything, every last detail.

"What do you think it means?" Asked Donny, the fire in his eyes replaced by concern.

"I don't know. It's not like I was in a real place, in real time. It was Dublin but not the Dublin we know."

The roar of the dining hall was beginning to die down. The three of them realized that they needed to get moving or they'd be late to class. They walked in silence, not knowing what to say, and once they were in class their tasks quickly distracted them.

Even though Margaret could not actively participate, each instructor allowed her to pick the challenge for the day and aid in judging the victors. It was a welcomed distraction. Come lunchtime Margaret felt a little more like herself.

Over lunch the trio discussed the dream in a more productive way, now that the shock of it had worn off.

"What if your dream didn't feel like a dream because it's a real place," Donny asked.

Margaret looked confused, as did Bria.

"I don't follow, Dublin is a real place, sure, but not as Margaret described," said Bria

"Yes that's true Bri, but what if it doesn't appear the same because it's not from this time. What if it's from the past when one of the great wars reigned? Or it's from the future, predicting what is to come?"

"Shit Donny, really?!" Margaret exclaimed.

He looked a bit stunned. "I just thought if you didn't recognize it…"

"I know, sorry, it's just not really something I wanted to think about the fact that actual hell on earth could be in the cards."

"Is there a way to find out one way or the other?" Asked Bria.

"I don't know much about these things but I can ask Myriad. I know Fae can manipulate time and space through dimensional travel, maybe she knows of a way," said Margaret.

She didn't really want to know. It would be perfectly fine with her if she never entered that dreamscape again.

Margaret sat with Myriad during the simulations to help catch mistakes and direct the students. It was beneficial because she was able to catch errors as they occurred. Not being directly engaged in the battle provided a new and welcome perspective.

"Cassie? You missed that throw because you snapped your wrist too much. Try to finish your throw with your finger pointing at your target. It should help your aim. Let's reset the fight at the last Droch, and Cassie try it again."

"You are good at this," said Myriad.

She shrugged, "It's what you train us to do, besides it's a lot easier to see where mistakes occur when you're watching it from the sidelines."

Myriad nodded "Yes, but you anticipate problems before they happen. Most students would struggle with this despite the advantage of sitting on the sidelines."

"Thank you, I appreciate the compliment," said Margaret, still staring into the arena.

She began to play with the wrapping on her hands, thankful for the salve that was providing relief.

"How do they feel?" Myriad asked.

Looking down Margaret replied "Better, thank you."

The Fae inclined her head in a gesture of respect.

Turning to look at the Fae, Margaret said "I did have a theory about what happened. I spoke with Donny and Bri - well to be fair it was Donny's idea."

She turned to face the arena again and watched as Donny decapitated another Droch, taking particular notice of his muscles moving under his sweat-soaked shirt. Margaret's heart rate began to speed up and her mouth went dry.

What was wrong with her? Shaking her head she realized Myriad was still waiting for her to continue.

"Anyway, he thought perhaps, the reason the dream felt so real was that it took place in Dublin's past or future, and was showing me a glimpse of what is to come. It would also explain the Droch I saw and why it didn't look like any we've ever seen. Maybe it evolved from or into another type of beast entirely."

Myriad took a moment to consider the theory, "It's possible, however, given that the other professors didn't recognize the description you gave I would not think this could be a Droch from the past, but rather from the future."

The thought sent chills through Margaret's body. Myriad was right, if it had been from the past surely one of the others would have better understood her description. If this was a scene of what was to come - she couldn't even finish the thought.

"Is there a way to test that theory?" asked Margaret.

"When we travel through dimensions it's not an exact science," Myriad said, still keeping an eye on the Locrian fighting.

"Typically it's helpful if we're able to find something with a date or time, like a newspaper or a sign that assures us we have landed in the correct era. If you could find something like that if you're pulled in again, that could give you the answer."

Margaret nodded. This could potentially answer some questions and give them an idea of how to stop it from happening again. She did not want to be pulled back in again, but if she was she would be sure to stay more alert.

Myriad looked at her pupil, seeing that contemplative look on her face worried her.

"Margaret do not go looking for trouble, I would hate for you to be hurt again."

"Don't worry professor, the last thing I want to do is relive that nightmare."

Myriad relaxed a bit. "I made you the Fae talisman to protect you from bad dreams as I said I would."

She reached into her bag and pulled out a beautifully woven gift that Margaret thought looked very familiar.

"Uh professor? This is a dream catcher, the Fae don't make these, the Native American

people do," she said with a smile. Locrian
are privy to human history so they can study
them and be more like them when they enter
into the world and live among them. This
helps them avoid drawing unwanted attention
to themselves.

Myriad feigned an offended look.

"Who do you think taught them? We serve,
nurture, and appreciate nature as they do.
We felt them worthy of such a gift. The
magic is real in that, hang it above your
bed and I am confident it will help."

Margaret smiled at the Fae, tucking the gift
into her sweatshirt pocket and watching her
friends again.

Dragas collapsed in a heap once the
connection was severed. It took a lot of
energy to pull the Locrian into the dream
with him but it would be worth it. Pulling
himself up he meandered drunkenly across the
room. He pointed towards a smaller Droch,
"You! Will you commit to serve me through
your life?" The small Droch walked over to
his master and stood tall anticipating what
was to come. He stared Dragas in the eye
prepared to bravely meet his fate. Dragas

took his claws and tore through the Droch's flesh pulling out his still beating heart, and consumed it to regain his strength. As he ate the Droch's heart, its memories and energy infused themselves into Dragas. A bloody smile spread across his lips as he absorbed another's life completely. He left the carcass to be feasted on by his minions.

His plan was falling into place. The Locrian were crumbling at the outposts and the intelligence he received of the birthing cycle was good news as well. Their race was dying and soon the dream that he had showed the unsuspecting student would become a reality. The Droch would emerge from the underground tunnels and live on the surface, forever shrouding the earth in darkness. It was only a matter of time.

The Droch around him cowered in fear but also in respect. They understood what he was capable of and this power earned their loyalty.

"The plan is nearly complete," he proclaimed. "Soon we will no longer hide in the shadows living on leftover droppings of the battlefield. Soon we will be victorious, and they will be the ones cowering in the darkness!"

Grunting echoed through the cavern, erupting into a beastly roar. Surely the nearby Locrian would have heard it, the echoes emerging from the caverns. *"Let them hear,"* thought Dragas, *"Let fear consume them."*

Chapter 10

The next few days were fairly boring for Margaret. Attending classes she wasn't able to participate in made the days long and monotonous. It did, however, afford her the opportunity to catch up on some much needed sleep. The dream catcher that Myriad had given her was working well. She had been dream-less for an entire week. She was grateful, but also a little frustrated. As much as she didn't want to experience the dreamscape again, she was also incredibly curious about the mystery surrounding the entire situation. And the only way to solve the mystery was likely through her return to the altered reality.

Her hands improved every day but the brand new skin was very sensitive. Most of her calluses were gone and it was now very difficult for her to grip things with the intensity that she used to. Even though she was told not to, she practiced sword and knife techniques on her own to ensure she remained on par with her classmates. The new skin on her hands allowed blisters to develop quickly due to the limited practice she was doing on her own. She was hopeful that they would soon return to calluses, but for now she lived with the discomfort.

Margaret made her way to the infirmary in hopes of being cleared to take part in class. Lyas shook his head, "I told you not to participate in class."

"But I wasn't participating in class," she smirked.

Lyas ignored her and kept working. "Seeing as you will do it anyway, I may as well clear you for instruction."

"Really? Thank you so much!" Margaret hurried out of the infirmary before Lyas could change his mind.

As she walked excitedly towards the dining hall she ran into Bria and Donny.

Donny smiled "Does that happy walk means that I can finally redeem myself in knife throwing?"

"It sure as shit does but you won't be redeeming anything."
Donny wrapped her into a supportive hug and then draped an arm over her shoulder.

She was grinning from ear to ear. "As long as Bria is my partner you're going down." Donny laughed, and she noticed that his arm lingered on her shoulders a little too long. Trying not to make things awkward, she squeezed his waist in a gesture of thanks and slid out of his embrace. As she turned around she noticed that Donny's cheeks were flushed.

This confirmed what she'd been thinking since the day their hands touched - he liked her. "Crap," she thought, "This will not end well. He's Donny, he's like a brother, an annoying brother at that. How could this happen?" Her gaze lingered on his face. "Although, he is pretty adorable when he's embarrassed. No! Stop thinking like that, he's your friend. Just a friend." Even if she did have feelings for Donny, he was one of her best friends and she knew it would not end well. She decided not to address it unless it became an issue, which she hoped it never would.

Margaret followed Donny and Bria into the dining hall and found her gaze lingering on Donny's behind. She flushed; she needed to wipe thoughts like that out of her mind.

After enjoying a leisurely breakfast the trio headed toward the first class of the day.

Walking a bit more upbeat than usual Donny said, "You guys can pair up however you like, but you're both going down today, I can feel it."

Margaret rolled her eyes. "Donny, seriously, was it really that big of a deal? You only lost because you had one of the worst knife handlers in the class as your partner. If you had been partnered with Bria you would have beat me."

The group side stepped several of the ten year olds running to class, obviously late. Margaret smiled at them.

"No, it's not that, it's just fun to be in competition with you. Doesn't mean the same to beat someone else," he winked.

This time it was Margaret's face that went red. She walked away, hoping nobody noticed. It's not that Locrian don't have relationships, they do, but she had personally never been in one and wasn't exactly sure what to do with the extra attention.

Professor Bryan was standing in his classroom already, looking like he just had a workout and was seriously pissed off.

"Alright my little knife wielders, today is the day we challenge you a bit more with targets that not only move toward you, but also come from different angles. No partners, you're going solo. You'll have ten targets. Once you take out the first moving target another will appear. Your job is to identify and take out each target with a kill shot as quickly as possible. You will be timed. If the target gets within ten feet of you, you are automatically eliminated. Any questions?"

Bryan Doyle was never much for greetings. His eyes scanned the room and landed on Margaret. His eyebrows arched in mild surprise.

"Margaret, did you get the all clear?"

"Yes sir," she grinned.

"Good, we've missed you. Would you like to go first?"

She looked at her hands nervously. She was a little concerned about her skill level given their condition. She met her professor's gaze, "Yes sir, I would be happy to."

Her classmates patted her on the back offering encouragement as she made her way to the center of the room where the table of throwing knives waited.

The knives were laid out so that the students didn't need to use a belt. She tested their weight in her hands and it felt surprisingly good and natural. She took a deep breath and nodded to professor Bryan to start the challenge.

The first target came from the very back of the room, roughly 50 feet away. She took her time, aiming carefully. She wanted to avoid throwing more than necessary in order to protect her hands, if possible. She let the first knife go when the target was about 30 feet out and nailed it in the forehead. The second target simulated a Droch charging on all fours, coming at a more rapid rate, and it took her two tries but she got the kill shot. This went on for what felt like forever and her nerves were starting to fray. The last target came down from above, taking her by surprise so much that the Droch got within the ten foot limit and she was eliminated.

She froze, and the buzzer sounded. It was the loudest sound she had ever heard, she had failed. The knife she held in her hand fell to the floor and her head hung heavy on her shoulders. The room went silent. She couldn't bring herself to look at her peers.

She couldn't remember the last time she had set that buzzer off. Still unable to move, her heart pounded fiercely inside her chest, she wanted to run, but her legs wouldn't move.

The silence was broken from the back of the room. "Well done."

All eyes were on the professor, usually silent during challenges, expecting the Locrian at this point to help each other with mistakes.

Margaret stared at him with a look of confusion. "I failed professor, or did you not notice?" She said, sounding a little snippier than intended.

He shook his head. "That's not the point, Margaret, your time was phenomenal until that last target appeared. If you'd hit it you would have eliminated 10 in just under 45 seconds. I noticed, though many of you may not have, that Margaret still has blisters on her hands, making holding a knife difficult; aiming and throwing accurately even more so. My guess is you were practicing when you shouldn't have been, but that's not much concern – my point is that if your hands had been healthy there's no doubt you would have succeeded. This task is not easy, as everyone else will soon see. The lesson today is do not give up, even if you are injured or out numbered, it may save your life."

Margaret made her way back towards the others and received smiles and pats on the back, feeling more pitied than accomplished. She slipped to the back of the class to watch the other students take their turns. With their faces full of determination, each student stepped up to the challenge. And one by one, they completed it. They won. Each and every single one of them, even Cassie, the worst in the class, beat the challenge.

Bryan kept a close eye on Margaret as she watched each student claim victory. He walked up beside her, "You did that."

She looked at him, confused.

"What?"

"Their victories are because of you Margaret."

She turned toward him "I'm not following?"

"I designed this course to be nearly impossible. When they watched you fight to the end, even with an injury, it showed them they had to fight just as hard, if not harder. Things do not always come easily to you, and it's good for them to see that, to see you struggle, because you don't give up. You just made the entire class stronger through failure. Sometimes we have to fail in order to truly win."

Margaret looked at Lyra who was currently competing, hitting target after target. She shook her head. "I think you did that with your speech, professor. They looked at me with disappointment. I felt it."

He turned to face her.

"They looked at you with fire in their eyes. Look there," he pointed to the center of the room, "Lyra just finished, watch carefully."

She stood watching as Lyra collected her knives after successfully defeating the challenge. Once she reset the course for the next Locrian she looked at Margaret and nodded in respect.

Margaret was stunned. Did she really inspire her class? She turned to Bryan.

"Professor? I want to go again."

He grinned. "I thought you might."

She walked back to the center of the room, feeling every eye in the room on her.

Grabbing the knives she stood at the ready. The pain from her hands was a distant memory. The knives became an extension of her body, she enjoyed the feeling of cold steel on her skin. She nodded and it began. She didn't think this time, only reacted. She heard nothing, and saw only the targets and before she knew it, it was over. No buzzer sounded and she had done it. A weight was lifted. She glanced over towards Bryan Doyle and he nodded in respect.

The class cheered and Donny and Bria came running towards her. "Holy Shit! Did you see what you did?" asked Bria.

She looked at her friend, "Yeah Bri, I just did it, I finished!"

Donny shook his head "No, look at your targets."

Donny pointed around the room, every target had one knife in it, directly in the forehead. None of the targets had come close to within the ten-foot boundary. She looked at the table and only 10 knives were missing. She had hit ten targets, ten kill shots, with ten knives.

She looked toward the professor, "What was my time?"

"37 seconds," said Bryan Doyle. "A new record." More cheers erupted around the room. Professor Bryan approached Margaret. "Who is the inspiration now?"

Margaret smiled "I am."

Bria hugged her friend who still seemed in shock. She stood back, holding her friend's hands.

"Mags you're bleeding."

All of her blisters had burst and a small trickle of blood was running down her hand.

"Absolutely worth it," said Margaret, wearing the largest grin either of her friends had seen in a while.

Her winning streak continued throughout the day. Sword fighting presented more of a challenge but she sealed her victory by conquering the task. Even though she was edged out by Donny who was not so subtle in his triumph. All she could do was laugh, her world was getting back to normal. Archery was by far the hardest, per usual. She placed last but still completed the challenge and Bria won overall so it counted as a win in her book. Hand-to-hand combat, while rough on her palms, didn't prove as difficult as she had imagined it would. Some fresh wounds opened up on her knuckles but they would eventually turn into new callouses. Every challenge in every class was a step toward feeling like herself again.

By lunch Margaret's confidence had returned. She re-bandaged her hands to keep the blisters from re-opening but she was feeling so good she hardly noticed the pain. News of the day's events began to spread to the other Locrian in her class. During the planning phase for the simulator the other Locrian huddled around her more closely than normal, looking to her for answers. During the exercise her class banded together to attack each group of Droch. They all moved as if they were on giant weapon. They had always worked together, but today it was unified, harmonious, and fluid.

The day had gotten off to a nerve-wracking start, but ended with the students feeling as if they had all made a huge leap forward in their training. That night laughter filled the dining hall. The mood was so positive that no one wanted to go to bed. Eventually exhaustion took over and slowly, one by one, all the other students went to bed until only Donny, Bria and Margaret remained in the hall.

"I guess we should hit the sack, we have to do all of this again tomorrow," said Bria.

Margaret didn't want this day to end, professor Bryan was right, out of failure can come great triumph.

She sighed, "You're probably right."

The three of them walked down the main corridor together until they reached the hallway that led to the north and south dorm rooms.

"You know after all this time you'd think that we could be in the same dorm hall," said Bria.

Margaret smiled, "But then what would you have to complain about at night?"

Bria stuck her tongue out in a playful gesture. "Alright dorks, see you in a few hours." Bria turned and headed to the south dorm rooms and Margaret and Donny walked toward the north dorms.

Donny paused at her door and seemed a bit uncomfortable. "You did really well today and it will only get easier."

"Thank you, so did you," she said with a sheepish grin. "I'm sorry you didn't get the redemption you wanted."

He shook his head "It was worth it to see you do so well and be so happy. You've had a rough time lately."

Margaret nodded in agreement.

"I did miss competing with you. I won't take that for granted again," said Donny with a smile.

"I appreciate that Donny, I do."

Margaret's heart sped up a bit as the pair continued to linger in front of her door.

Donny hugged her goodnight but didn't leave. He leaned back and looked her in her eyes. Margaret's heart continued to pound as they stared at each other in silence. Donny leaned in and gently kissed her lips. Margaret froze and closed her eyes. It lasted only a few seconds but her brain went numb. She lost all ability to think or move. He pulled away and her body quietly screamed *NO*. It took all she had not to reach for him and pull him back in for another kiss. His lips were so warm and soft, she could still feel them.

She stood completely still, shell-shocked. Did she really have feelings for Donny? She was so confused.

Donny smiled, "Glad to have you back."

With a little pick-up in his step, he turned and walked towards his room, leaving Margaret stunned. She eventually fell into her room after fumbling with her doorknob for what felt like hours.

"*What was that?*" She thought to herself. "*I mean I know what that was, but what is going on with me?*"

"Holy shit," she blurted "I like Donny." She flopped onto her bed with a smile. "What the hell am I gonna do?"

Chapter 11

Over the next few days Margaret didn't know what to do when she was around Donny. She began dreading classes because she didn't know what to say to him. Even when Bria was around she found herself staying silent or leaving early to avoid conversation.

How could one little kiss have made things so complicated? She loved the way that kiss had made her feel. She felt more alive in that moment than when she had a weapon in her hand. But she was not a typical girl, she always put fighting and honing her skills above guys; when she had been approached in the past about dating, she was never interested, her training always had come first. But this was Donny, and now she had no idea what to do. She hadn't even told her best friend what had happened and began to feel silly ducking into the bathroom or nearby classrooms whenever she saw Donny in the hallway alone.

Until recently, she had never even pictured a future with a guy in it. All she thought

about was surviving, but maybe there was
more to life than simply surviving.

Seeing Donny coming down the hallway she
sprinted for the ladies room, coffee in
hand, telling herself that she would
eventually have to get her shit together and
face this situation head on. She peeked her
head out and watched him walk into the
dining hall. "Hey." said a voice from behind
her.

She nearly jumped out of her skin and almost
spilled her coffee.

Margaret turned and was relieved to see that
it was Bria who had surprised her and not
someone else. "Bri really? You gave me a
heart attack."

Bria gave her a look.

"What?" said Margaret.

Bria crossed her arms. "Don't 'what' me.
What is going on with you and Donny? You're
bobbing and weaving all over the place like
shrapnel is flying around whenever you see
him coming."

"So you've noticed?" said Margaret.

"Do you notice this?" Bria mimicked her, sprinting across the foyer and ducking behind a column nearly taking out several 10 year olds in her wake.

"Sorry guys." The 10 year olds shook their heads and continued on towards the dining hall.

Margaret covered her face. She really couldn't be that bad, could she?

"So. Spill. Something clearly happened. You won't look at him and you duck into the bathroom to "pee" more times than humanly possible. And you've barely said two words to him in almost a week, or me - me! So I know that you're hiding something. What gives?"

Margaret walked toward the bathroom door. "It's nothing."

Bria chased her, "Oh no, you are not getting off that easy! Something happened, if I didn't know any better…" She paused and stopped walking. "Wait! No way! Did you guys kiss?"

Margaret stopped in her tracks. Her cheeks flushed immediately.

Bria ran to catch up to her.

"Oh I knew it! I knew something was going on," said Bria.

Margaret felt her heart pounding. "Keep it down ok Bri, I'm not even sure what to do yet. I know I should have told you but I didn't know what to say."

"Why? I'm happy for you guys! Wait, unless - was it bad? Is that why you won't talk to him?"

Margaret looked at her friend like she had grown three heads. "No, it was amazing I just don't know what to do. I mean, it's Donny. Who knew I could ever like Donny?"

Bria cocked her eyebrow. "Ummm everyone?! You guys have made goo-goo eyes at each other for the past few months. Everyone knew you liked each other. Well, except for you."

Margaret leaned on a nearby wall with her head tilted back. She felt like she might be sick. "It was that obvious! Ugh, I'm so embarrassed."

"Why? This is great! Finally!" said Bria, joining her against the wall.

Margaret looked at her friend. "I just don't know what to do now. I hate being this crazy ball of emotions. I've made such a mess of things by not talking to him. Do you think he's mad?"

"No, I just think he needs to know you're into him so he doesn't think he made a mistake in kissing you. But, he hasn't said anything to me."

Margaret took a deep breath.

"Ok, I'll talk to him. Ugh, I can gut a Droch without a second thought but I can't work up the courage to talk to a guy I've known my whole life. What is wrong with me?"

She began walking again with Bria. "Since when did you get so good at relationships?"

"Since Cassie moved across the hall from me. You learn a lot about what not to do by watching that one. I do have to hand it to her, she has quite the parade of suitors, but none ever last. I guess even with looks like hers it's not easy."

Margaret let Bria lead her back into the dining hall, feeling uneasy after what her friend had said. "Geez, I don't know if I feel comforted or terrified by that statement."

They chuckled and looked for Donny.

Margaret noticed him in the corner, lost in thought with his coffee. She realized more caffeine might do her some good, maybe boost her confidence, so she grabbed a second cup and headed in Donny's direction.

"Hi," She said, approaching cautiously.

Donny nearly spat out his coffee when he realized she was talking to him.

"Can I sit here?" she asked.

Still surprised, Donny scooted down to allow her some room. "Uh sure, sure. That would be great." He stared at her for a second. "Don't take this the wrong way, but you DO realize you're talking to me, right?"

She punched him in the shoulder and turned her gaze to her cup of coffee, wishing it would somehow calm her nerves.

"I'm sorry for avoiding you, I just didn't know what to say. I mean, you're one of my best friends, and suddenly there were lips involved."

He looked down. "It's ok. It was a mistake, clearly, so let's just pretend it didn't happen."

Margaret felt like she had been punched in the gut. "A mistake?"

He looked at her. "Yea, isn't that why you've been avoiding me?"

Franticness kicked in. "No, I… I just don't know what it's like to have a boy interested in me. That was my first kiss and it was wonderful. I just don't want to screw anything up with our friendship, and now I'm rambling so I'll shut up."

She wanted to slink out of the dining hall, run to her room, and never emerge from her covers, but she stood frozen.

Donny was grinning from ear to ear.

"What?" she asked.

"Mags I'm so happy you're so confused because it means you like me too. I honestly haven't known what to say to you either so you avoiding me wasn't entirely horrible."

She smiled. "I do like you."

Donny reached for her hand and the pair sat quietly, appreciating the moment.

After a while he spoke. "Just so you know, we don't have to do anything you're not

ready for, we don't have to tell anyone
until you want to, no one has to know."

She cleared her throat. "Well SOMEONE
already knows."

They both turned to see Bria staring at them
awkwardly. She quickly bolted behind a plant
as if they wouldn't notice.

"Is that what I looked like all week?" asked
Margaret.

"Worse."

Margaret punched Donny again.

"What was that?" he asked.

"For letting me look like an idiot for that
long."

He smiled and just held her hand, clearly
the happiest he has ever been.

The next few days were blissfully normal.
Everyone in class continued to work
together, becoming more and more fluid.
Donny and Margaret kept their relationship a
secret, which wasn't easy given that Bria

had a tendency to run her mouth when she shouldn't. Donny told her if she let it slip he would use her as target practice every day for a week. He was pretty confident she would keep her mouth shut. Every night Donny and Margaret waited until everyone else left the dining hall and he would walk her to her room holding her hand and hug her goodnight. Ever since that first night he hadn't kissed her, or even tried. It was something Margaret longed for but she knew Donny was respecting her wish to take things slowly. This might just be a little too slow.

Her sleep remained dream-less, which she didn't really mind. Everything seemed to be returning to normal, or at least whatever normal was for them now.

A few days later, Bria, Donny and Margaret were enjoying some Elven made pizza when they heard shouting from the courtyard. As they exited the dining hall the students heard the guards yelling "Riders approaching - open the gate!"

The towers at the abbey were more of a formality than anything else. There was never true use for them because of the cloaking protection, but there was always someone stationed in them just in case.

Margaret and the rest of the Locrian ran to the front gate to see who the mysterious riders were. Six of them came bursting through the gate at a full gallop. Locrian tended to favor ancient rituals and preferences, such as traveling by horseback. The elder Locrian had lived hundreds of years, and as such, things like riding on horseback were a comfort to them and a tradition that was passed down through the generations. The only exception to this rule was when large groups of Locrian needed to be transported. Traveling via horseback allowed them the freedom to avoid major roadways and if travel was required at night, the Droch were much more easily avoided.

At the head of the all-male group of riders was an Elf, followed by four Locrian and what appeared to be a Fae.

The Elf jumped down from his horse that had a beautiful tan coat and a black mane. He stood roughly at six feet from what Margaret could tell, and had long grey hair and a beard. The Fae matched him in height but had long black hair and a distinct absence of facial hair. He walked slightly behind the Elf leading them to believe that he was the one in charge. Approaching one of the guards he said, "I need to see Asher and Bryan now." The guards nodded and took the two guests into the abbey, leaving the four Locrian behind. It was interesting to see that leadership positions were not just held by Locrian but others that fight alongside them as well.

Asher and Bryan were in the office already when the visitors arrived. "Craine" Asher walked over with a hand extended for his friend. "It's good to see you well." "Likewise" replied Craine, gripping his friend's hand.

Asher turned to the Fae, "Dorien it's great to see you as well. Myriad will also be pleased."

The Fae grabbed Asher's hand, "As much as I would love to see her first, this is more important."

Asher nodded. He knew the unexpected visit wasn't routine. "What brings you here my friends?"

Craine gestured towards the table. "Let me better illustrate."
The four of them crossed the room to Asher's table where he kept a large map of all the outposts in Ireland. He updated it as often

as he could, keeping track of the number of Locrian lost, supplies needed, and other information important to the ongoing battles.

Craine leaned over the map.

"Something strange is happening and we aren't sure what to make of it. As you know, my outpost is the one right outside of Dublin. Historically it's always been the location we've kept most fortified because it is attacked more often due to the amount of people living in Dublin." said Craine. Asher nodded.

Dorien stepped forward "I'm here in Galway, another frequently attacked outpost. Not nearly as often as Dublin but we still get heavy fire."

"Yes, we understand this, what is the issue?" said Bryan impatiently.

Craine did not appreciate the tone of the Locrian. Returning his gaze to the map he began to explain.

"Recently there have been fewer and fewer Droch attacking our locations. We foolishly thought maybe we had started to wear them down, but no. Last night as we prepared for the new moon, which is always the worst night of the month, we received word that the Kilkenny outpost needed aid. We didn't know what to do because we were already depleted in number, and with the expected attack at Dublin we couldn't spare any men to aid them. However, the sun set and there were no Droch to be seen. I felt it in my gut, the Droch were moving on a less fortified outpost. We immediately went to Kilkenny to aid them, leaving behind a few Locrian in Dublin just in case. By the time we arrived they were nearly overrun. Dorien and his crew arrived shortly after and thankfully we were able to hold them off."

Craine paused to reflect on what could have been a massive slaughter if they hadn't reacted in time.

Bryan was confused. "Wait. We have been using the same strategies for years. How is it that all of a sudden these dumb beasts have found a way to rub two brain cells together to figure out the weaker outposts?"

"That's exactly why we're here Bryan, we do not know. Everything we know about the Droch is that they act on animal instinct. They fight to survive and prey on humans and magical creatures alike. But something has changed. What's even worse is that it's getting harder to kill them."

"What do you mean?" Asher said leaning forward.

"Arrows and knives to the heart always used to take them down within minutes. The poisonous ore acted quickly. But we've noticed that now it takes several shots to slow them down and eventually kill them. Unless hit multiple times in the heart, it does not slow. This uses more ammunition and time, which we all know is precious when under attack."

"What about swords?" Asked Asher.

Craine continued, "They seem to hold their potency for now as long as it's a head or heart shot. As do the axes. I believe it's due to the amount of ore in each weapon. If they're stabbed in the heart with a broadsword or battle axe they do not get up."

"That was good news at least," thought Asher.

Taking it all in he asked the question he didn't want to ask. "How bad was the damage last night?" asked Asher.

Craine bowed his head. "Not good. Half the Locrian fell at Kilkenny before we arrived. After we got there, minor injuries. I kick myself for not going sooner but I never thought they would attack there in full force."

Bryan and Asher absorbed this information with the painful quickness their leadership required. "I wonder what they're after?" Said Bryan.

Asher looked at Bryan. "What makes you think they're after something?"

Feeling the stares of all three individuals Bryan continued, "It was an organized attack. Something that took time to plan and has now showed their hand. Why would they risk that unless they're after something specific?"

"This could not be happening" thought Asher. *"It is one thing after another."*

Asher's face was white, he felt sick to his stomach.

Dorien, who hadn't spoken, came forward. "There's more, the dead and wounded on the battlefield..."

Asher and Bryan met Dorien's gaze.

"What about them?" Asked Bryan, almost afraid to hear the answer.

"When we went out to collect the bodies on the battlefield at dawn, they were gone. Same as with the Droch bodies, they're all gone. Severed heads remained, but the bodies themselves are being taken. The Droch heads disintegrate after sunrise but those of our own people are left, with no body to be buried with."

Asher looked at Dorien and Craine simultaneously, "What do you mean taken? By whom?"

Dorien paused. "At dawn, at the edge of the trees, I saw a Droch dragging one of our own into the caves. They're stealing our bodies, and not just those of the dead but also the injured."

Bryan crossed the room "Any idea why?"

Both Craine and Dorien shook their heads. "Nothing conclusive. We have speculated that it could be for nourishment if their supply is running low, but they've never done it before."

The thought disturbed them all and for a moment a silence hung in the air like a thick cloak.

What in the hell was going on? The world was
crumbling and the balance had clearly
shifted even more than they had initially
thought.

After awhile Dorien spoke up again. "There's
one more reason we came, can we bring Myriad
in here for this?"

Asher nodded and sent for Myriad to join
them. At this point he felt like nothing
else could shock him. He was wrong.

In a matter of minutes Myriad arrived,
confusion wrinkling her otherwise ageless
face. She spotted Dorien across the room and
the tall, black-haired Fae smiled for the
first time since arriving at the abbey,
softening his chiseled features. Myriad
walked briskly over to him and embraced him.
"It's good to see you well," she said. "As
it is you. I wish I was here for better
reasons," the Fae said solemnly.

Myriad had sensed that something was wrong,
and now she took a step back from Dorien to
absorb the mood of the room.

Dorien's gaze still hung on Myriad's face
for a few fleeting seconds, then he gave his
attention to the room. "I wanted Myriad in
here to ask a favor of all of you. We just
informed Asher and Bryan of the issues that

we are all facing, and I will allow them to share with you at their discretion, but we need help. The tables have turned and it is becoming more and more difficult to maintain balance. We need more Locrian. What we are asking is not easy, and we understand how this will sound but we have no choice. We need the new class to fight with us during the new moon cycle. Throughout the initial crescent, the new moon, and the following crescent, we need their help to maintain our numbers. They can return home afterward to continue training."

The professor's faces said 'no' without any of them saying a word. Dorien pressed on, "We wouldn't be here if we thought there was any other way to maintain the outpost. We wouldn't ask this of them if we had any other choice."

Myriad's heart caught in her chest. "They are not ready, they don't have their powers or their immortality."

Dorien approached Myriad and took her hands. "Myriad, I know what these children mean to you, but in a few months they will be joining us. If they wait until then there may not be much to join. This is a difficult time for us all. We need the bodies, as harsh as that sounds. The Droch almost took an entire outpost last night."

She looked deep into Dorien's eyes.

"Which outpost?" she asked.

"Kilkenny" replied Asher.

"But why would they attack an outpost that has never held much interest? It doesn't make any sense. What are they trying to get to?" She asked almost talking to herself.

"That was the same question that Bryan asked. What could they possibly want so much as to send the entire horde of Droch to one location?" Replied Asher.

"Wait, all of them charged Kilkenny? Were any other outposts attacked?" asked Myriad.

Dorien shook his head no, "They were nearly over-run when Craine and I arrived."

Myriad went white as a sheet, and Dorien quickly tucked his arm around her in support.

She looked him in the eye with a profound sense of fear.

Her mouth went dry as she whispered "I know what they're after."

Slowly she sat down onto the brown leather sofa, trying to gather her racing thoughts. "They're trying to find the tree," she said.

"The tree?" said Asher. "You don't mean THE Tree?"

She nodded "Yes, the Locrian Tree resides in the outpost in Kilkenny."

Craine looked at Myriad, confused. "Wait, IN the outpost? I've been there thousands of times and I have never seen it."

"It is well protected by Fae magic. Only those trained to protect the tree can open the entrance," she responded.

"How in the hell did you two not think of that?" Craine asked the two professors.

"Because they don't know where it is," said Myriad firmly.

The Elf looked confused. "All Locrian attend their naming ceremony there and they are allowed to keep the memory of their ceremony but as they leave the chamber there is a charm placed around it that wipes the memory from the Locrian so that they cannot recall the location. It is for the safety of the tree. The only beings in existence that hold the location of the tree are those that were placed in charge of the birthing process and protection of the tree. Beings like myself."

"So how would the Droch get a hold of that information?" Asked Craine.

After a moment, Bryan asked "Dorien, you mentioned that the Locrian were being taken off the battlefield, injured and dead; what about Fae? Are they also being taken?"

He thought for a moment. "We have had a few go missing, so it is highly likely."

Myriad was so confused. "Locrian are being taken? By the Droch?"

"Yes," replied Dorien, "We cannot reclaim the dead or even the injured."

More frantically Myriad asked, "Who are the Fae who have gone missing?"

He paused. "Moa' and Padua." Myriad, already sitting, managed to sink even lower upon hearing the names of her two closest friends. "I'm sorry you had to find out this way."

Myriad nodded. Her heart felt broken, but she would have to mourn another time.

Standing up, she turned to the others, "Padua knew of the location, but what doesn't make sense is how the Droch got the information out of her? No Fae would ever tell and to my knowledge the Droch have no way of communicating. From what I know they sound similar to a group of gorillas, grunting and growling at each other."

"Maybe they have evolved, or can communicate in other ways? We really don't know a lot about them other than their ability to maim and kill. But how do they know the location isn't important anymore, what's important is figuring out how we can protect the tree." Craine said.

"Myriad, is there a way to move the tree? To relocate it safely?" asked Asher.

She shook her head, "I am afraid not, Asher. The tree's roots are too fragile and go too deeply into the soil. The chamber that it resides in is specially made to nourish it and help it grow." She paused. "I do wonder if there is a connection to all this and the latest class of Locrian."

It was Craine and Dorien's turn to look confused.

"There were only 30 Locrian born from the tree in this last class," said Myriad.

Craine shook his head. "This proves that now more than ever we have to strike, the tide must turn or those Locrian will not live until their 21st birthdays."

Asher, impatient with the melancholy atmosphere, interjected a bit harshly. "Craine, we have heard your reasons and we will consider them justly. Please give us a night to decide and prepare. You and Dorien should stay the night and rest, after all, your journey cannot have been easy. We will have your answer in the morning. I know that you need men at the outpost so please feel free to send the four Locrian that came with you back to the outpost."

The two understood Asher had the last word, and gathered themselves up to leave. Myriad grabbed Dorien's hand. "After I'm done here I have a favor to ask of you if you do not mind."

Dorien inclined his head, "Anything for you. I will see you when you're finished."

When they had both left the room, Asher and Bryan looked at Myriad. "You're working with them the closest in terms of simulations, are they ready?"

She did not want to answer Bryan's question. This was not the position she wanted to be put in, but she took a deep breath and dove in. "Asher...Physically they have come a long way, and in the last few days they are moving beautifully together. They finally mesh as a unit but it is still so new. And I do not think anyone is ever emotionally ready to experience the loss of a friend or a fellow Locrian."

Asher began to pace, coming to terms with the inevitable. "Regardless, this is something that needs to happen. The two of you have spent the most time with them in training. Who stands out as the leaders of the group?"

Realizing that the debate of whether or not to send them was over, Myriad and Bryan's minds churned through the best way to help their students in the moment.

"Margaret for sure," said Bryan. "When she uses a broadsword it's as if it's an extension of her body. And her knife and battle axe abilities are phenomenal as well. The students really seem to look up to her and respect her."

Asher nodded and looked to Myriad.

"I agree with Bryan, Margaret is the leader in simulations. Everyone looks to her for advice. I would also recommend Donny and Bria. Both of them have leadership qualities."

Bryan nodded in agreement. "Donny is the best I've seen with a knife and battle-axe consistently, although Margaret does best him on occasion. Bria has the eye of a hawk when it comes to archery. She does not have the commanding presence that the other two do, although that is improving slowly. But the bottom line is the three of them have always fought together very cohesively, even before the entire class itself united."

Asher took a deep breath, knowing what the next few days would bring. "Ok, then it's settled. The three of them will be the leaders for this class; they will decide what happens to the Locrian on the battlefield because they will know them the best, not Craine. I will make that clear. Myriad, tell the three of them before you tell the group. When you tell the class have the trio stand with you in support. They have a full month to prepare, that should give them enough time to improve on a few things."

Myriad took that as dismissal and nodded to Asher and Bryan in turn before she left.

This will not be easy for them, she thought to herself as she hurried to find Dorien.

Chapter 12

Margaret was emerging from her room to head to dinner when she ran into Donny and Bria.

"Hey, are you ready to eat?" asked Bria.

Margaret nodded, "Yes, I'm starving."

Donny reached for her hand, which was becoming more and more comfortable each day. They made it halfway to the dining hall when they saw Myriad coming in their direction.

"Margaret, I was on my way to look for you. I think I know someone that can talk to you about the dream you experienced."

"Now?" She asked, looking at Bria and Donny, and thinking about dinner.

She nodded "He's only here for a short time, please come with me."

"Ok, well do you mind if Donny and Bria tag along?"

"Not at all dear, it's your dream. Come along." The trio followed as the Fae hurriedly rushed around the corridors.

Myriad led them through the abbey to the guest quarters. Margaret couldn't remember a time when she had been down these halls. For Locrian, their classmates were their family. There were no guests for them to host. Looking around the corridor, it reminded her of her dorm hallway with the gas lanterns. The difference was in the decor. On the student's hallway there were elaborate tapestries that lightened the corridors; the guest hallway was darker and decorated in a more medieval fashion with suits of armor. She paused in front of an ornately decorated red oak door. Knocking lightly she waited a few seconds for the door to open. On the other side Margaret recognized the Fae who had arrived earlier that day.

Dorien opened the door and smiled at Myriad, "Dorien, these are my students."

Dorien nodded his head in respect "Your favor?"

Myriad nodded, "Yes, Margaret has had some issues recently with dreams."

Dorien looked confused "Dreams?"

"It is similar to the issue that you have had in the past," she emphasized.

"Oh I see," Dorien sat down and gestured for the students to do the same. Margaret looked briefly around the room noticing the beautiful four post bed and tapestries that adorned the walls. Similar to the ones that hung in the students dorm corridors. "Margaret, explain to me exactly what is occurring when you dream."

She laid out in detail the dream and her experience, the burning sensation and the physical effects the dream had on her when she woke. When she had finished she realized she was sweating - just the memory of the dream had pushed her into mild panic as she relived the heat and searing pain.

Dorien thought for a moment, "Since receiving the dream catcher have you had any dreams at all?"

"No, none; it seems to have done the trick."

Dorien continued, "I believe that is true for now but what it sounds like to me, from my personal experience, is that someone or something is drawing you into this 'dream', this alternate reality, that while you are dreaming everything happening to you is real, which was why you burned your hands and clothes. I think the reason that you woke up is because the person creating the 'dream' did not want you to die, at least not at that moment."

Margaret looked shocked. She had thought of this fatal possibility but had shoved the thought from her mind since the dreamcatcher had worked its magic. "So you're saying these dreams could actually kill me?"

Dorien nodded, "It seems that way, but it isn't truly a dream, but rather a dream-scape. The dream-scape is shaped by the person pulling you in." Margaret looked confused and Dorien explained "I was trapped by an evil sorcerer, for a few years. My body was here but my soul was on another plane of existence. While there, everything that happened to me in that reality was real. I had to find food to eat and water to drink in order to survive. If I died in that alternate reality I would have died in real life."

Awestruck Margaret asked, "How did you escape?"

"Myriad freed me using the most powerful Fae magic in existence. Though it was forbidden she never gave up on me."

Dorien grabbed Myriad's hand and held it firmly, yet tenderly.

Myriad smiled slightly at the students confused faces, "Dorien is my husband."

All three jaws hit the floor.

"What!" the trio replied collectively.

She chuckled, "Yes, I know it is a shock, but Fae marriages are different, it isn't uncommon to go an extended period of time without seeing one another. Dorien actually taught here for some time alongside me but when the tide began to shift in favor of the Droch he realized he was needed in the fight. We see each other more than you know but our work is our priority at the moment because it is so important."

Margaret respected this as she felt the same way about her newly emerging relationship with Donny.
Still shocked, but anxious to hear more about this dream-scape possibility, Margaret asked "So in my dream, or dream-scape - do you think that this person or being will be able to pull me back in?"

"I think it will be very difficult if Myriad did what I think she did to that dream catcher. If you're pulled back, now that you're aware, there is a chance that you could have more control over getting out of the dream. We have no way of knowing until it actually happens so for now I wouldn't worry too much."

"If you do return to the dream you are to find me immediately once you wake up," said Myriad.

Margaret nodded, "Yes professor" she responded quickly, then more slowly, "Do you think this person is a sorcerer?"

Dorien shook his head, "That would be highly unlikely, from what I know they are extinct."

Myriad stood, "Now I know I interrupted your trip to the dining hall so please go and enjoy the rest of your night, I will see you in the morning. Would you mind meeting me in my room before your first class?"

The students nodded.

"It was very nice to meet you and thank you for taking the time to help me," Margaret said to Dorien.

Dorien inclined his head, "It was my pleasure young one, I know what Myriad's students mean to her."

Margaret, Donny and Bria all bowed their heads in respect and slipped out the door closing it on the couple so that they could be alone.

Margaret had another wonderful, dreamless night. It was amazing how much better she functioned on a decent night's sleep and she swore she would never go anywhere without that dream catcher again.

She walked down to grab a large coffee before heading towards Myriad's classroom. Bria had the same idea but she had yet to see Donny. Thinking he may have overslept, she grabbed him a coffee as well before walking with Bria to Myriad's class.

When they got there they realized that Donny had beat them and that he had gotten Margaret a coffee as well. "Great minds think alike," he said, handing her the extra coffee and kissing her on the cheek.

"You guys are disgusting, ugh," said Bria rolling her eyes.

"I think it's sweet, I always knew you two would get together," said Myriad.

"You did?" cried Margaret.

"I told you, everyone knew. Stop acting so surprised," Bria said with a smirk.

"Have a seat my children, we have a lot to discuss." Myriad's face became serious and the trio took their seats.

The light-hearted banter over, Myriad got down to business.

She took her time detailing all the information that she had received over the past 24 hours, even the parts that terrified her to think about. She wanted her students to be prepared and be able to cope with anything that came their way. The trio stood motionless and silent for what seemed like an eternity.

When she was done, Myriad paused, giving them a chance to process all the information. "Anyone want to say anything?" she coaxed after a few moments.

"We are so screwed," said Bria, putting her forehead on the table.
Donny looked at his friend, "Bri, I don't think it's that bad."

Bria lifted her head and gave a curt response, "Oh really Donny? Because to me it sounds like we're up shit creek without a paddle - without a boat even!"

Myriad looked at Margaret who sat in silence, her eyes looking off in the distance while the other two bickered back and forth. Myriad interrupted them. "Margaret, what are you thinking?"

Her eyes were fiery, but her voice was soft when she replied, "I think we can do it."

"Wait, what?" exclaimed Bria, "You think that this is a good idea?"

Margaret turned to her friend, "I didn't say that this was a good idea. I just said we can do it."

Bria looked aghast, "But we won't have our powers or our immortality before we face down the biggest problem in Locrian history!"

Margaret responded as calmly as she could. "Bri, I know it isn't ideal, but whether we go out there now or in a few more months, what difference does it make? I know we don't have our 'powers' but we aren't even sure what that will entail. Just because we get enhanced abilities doesn't mean we become invincible. And yes we are granted immortality but we can still be killed by Droch. We have trained for this and we still have another month to get even more prepared. Come on Bri, this is what we have been training for our whole lives, and now we finally get to do it."

Bri looked at her friend in silence. She was right; she knew she was right, she just didn't feel ready.

"I just feel like we're finally hitting our stride and now we have another obstacle in the way," said Bria.

Margaret nodded in agreement. She of all people could understand the emotional rollercoaster they had all been on the past few months. "I know, but we'll get through this. We've conquered all the other obstacles that have gotten in our way, I see no reason why we won't conquer this one."

"I agree" said Donny "We can handle this."

Bria nodded, "Ok I'm in. But if I die so help me Margaret I will come back and haunt you."

Margaret laughed "I wouldn't expect anything less."

Myriad breathed a sigh of relief when she saw how well they were taking the news.

Donny looked at Myriad, "Professor, may I ask a question?"

"Yes, Donny."

"Why are you just telling us? Where is everyone else?"

Myriad smiled, "I'm so glad you asked. You three have been chosen as the leaders of your class. It is an award that has been given to a select few in every class of Locrian."

"What does it mean?" Asked Bria, skeptically.

Looking at them in turn Myriad continued, "It means from here on out you will be in charge of the trainings, the battle plans, and the decisions that will put your people in harm's way. Once you are named and officially enter Locrian society, you will again receive leadership roles. It is a great responsibility but a great honor as well. For the next few weeks I will help you in any way I can to coordinate what you need. When you go to Kilkenny to fight you will be responsible for your group of

Locrian. If they fail, you fail, if they succeed, you succeed. It's a huge responsibility but one I know you can bear."

The three nodded their heads.

She looked at them with pride, "I'm telling the rest of the class this afternoon. There will be no simulations today. It will be your job to stand with me and help them to accept what must be done and do it with their heads held high."

Margaret realized that this would be one of the hardest things they had to do. Fighting simulations was one thing, fighting the real deal, without their powers, was something else. Similarly, convincing Donny and Bria had been an easy battle, but trying to convince 76 others was going to be an entirely different story.

Chapter 13

The day seemed to drag on. Margaret was not focused in her classes and her mind wandered constantly to how her classmates would take the news this afternoon. She decided not to eat lunch and sat outside enjoying the uncommonly warm weather. Donny went to sit with her.

"Anything on your mind? Other than the obvious."

She sighed, "I honestly do believe we can do this, that we can lend help to the Locrian who are fighting right now, but convincing the others isn't going to be easy."

The two of them sat outside for a while in silence.

"I think it will be ok," said Donny.

Margaret looked at him.

"It's like you said, we'll have to do this soon anyway, and it's a chance to make a real difference in the balance of things. It's a bit overwhelming since we don't have our powers yet or immortality, but we still have skills. We are Locrian and this is what we are destined to be."

She smiled, "You sort of stole my speech from earlier."

"I added to it a bit," he smirked, "But I do believe it. Myriad was right to choose you as a leader."

She reached out and grabbed his hand, "You as well."

Before they could stop themselves they leaned into each other and shared their first kiss since the night in the dorm hall. It was powerful and reassuring. Margaret knew that Donny was her partner on the battlefield as he always had been, but now he was also her partner in life. She felt that no harm could come to her as long as he was there. They parted and she leaned her head on his shoulder, it just fit.

Margaret sighed, "I don't mind if they know about us now, it just feels right to be with you."

Donny's heart sped up "I feel the same way, but I'm glad you don't mind because I'm pretty sure they all know now."

Turning around Margaret and Donny saw a sea of smiling faces looking in their direction through the dining hall doors. Bria was at the head of the group, grinning ear to ear.

Liam screamed from the back of the room "It's about time!"

Laughter erupted from the group and Margaret and Donny couldn't help but chuckle as their faces flushed from the slight embarrassment.

After a series of congratulatory high fives, hugs, and handshakes, the group made its way to Myriad's classroom. The room was different; she had used her magic again. Today it was filled with soft couches and chairs, and tapestries were draped over the windows to filter the sunlight, providing a very relaxing environment.

"Alright!" said Liam, "Is it nap time again?"

"Not quite Liam," replied Myriad. "Please take a seat."

They all sat, slightly confused. "There will be no simulator today."

The group exhaled in relief.

Myriad looked towards them, "Would the three of you join me up here?"

Margaret, Donny and Bria stood and went to Myriad's side.

Looking at her classmates Margaret knew what she needed to do to unite them.

She looked at Myriad, "Professor, do you mind?"

Myriad took a moment to comprehend what Margaret wanted to do and then nodded. Myriad took a seat at her desk and let the trio address the group.

Margaret leaned on an empty chair nearest her, "Look guys, there's something that we've been asked to do, something that is not easy, but I know we can handle it. Yesterday we had a few visitors to the abbey, I'm sure most of you noticed. They came to ask for help." She paused. "The Droch are winning, and the Locrian are dying. We have been asked to join them on the next crescent moon and fight alongside them for three nights - the crescent, the new moon, and the following crescent. Afterward we'll return to the abbey to continue our training." She took a moment to look at her peers. "I know you're in shock, I know what you're thinking that it's not our time and we don't have what was promised to us yet. But we will. In a few short months we'll be exiting this abbey never to return and earning our place in Locrian society. We have been asked to leave a little earlier in order to hopefully tip the scales between victory and defeat. I'm asking you to join Donny, Bria and myself in this quest. I know you may be scared and confused but we're here for you. We have one more month to train, but I believe we are ready. I don't know about you but I'm ready to make a true difference and stop killing simulated villains. What do you say? Will you join us?"

The silence was deafening. She had laid everything out on the table. She stared intently at the faces in front of her and did not waver. She remained confident and felt an air of confidence coming from Bria and Donny as well. The silence continued until a quiet voice chimed in, "Yes."

It was faint, from the right hand side of the room. Margaret's eyes darted there and she saw Cassie stand, slowly, her long blonde hair flowing past her shoulders. "Yes," she said again, louder this time. Her eyes holding Margaret's, full of trust and confidence.

One by one the entire group began to stand, mumbling "Yes," one after another, until the room got louder and was filled with cheers.

"Alright, alright sit down," said Margaret. "It's time to get down to business. Let's hunt some Droch."

Dragas was angry. Night after night he had tried to pull the Locrian back into the dream-scape he created but nothing worked. There was a magic blocking his connection that he could not bypass. He was getting closer, he could feel it, it was only a matter of time. But for now, the frustration continued. He paced back and forth around the dark cavern that he called home.

He detested living underground. Not because of the dark, because that was necessary, but because he was beneath these creatures he so despised. The Droch were powerful and strong and should be feared. Instead, they're forced to live underground beneath the feet of humans and Locrian. Creatures that should be beneath Droch feet. He could not wait for the day when the world would be his domain, when the dream-scape that he had painted for the Locrian would become a reality. He had a plan to break down the walls that surrounded her and pull her back into the dream-scape.

Dragas made his way down to the caverns that were used to punish Droch who got out of line. Punish was a kind word, it would ultimately kill them, and slowly. These caverns were similar to jail cells but they had cut outs in the sides of them where sunlight could stream through. Over the course of the day the Droch would slowly burn up and disintegrate, losing one body part at a time until the entire cavern filled with sunlight, obliterating them entirely.

This is also where they kept the enemies they retrieved from the battlefield. Sunlight couldn't harm them, but without food or water it wasn't a pleasant experience. The sun in the room made it quite warm and with no way to hydrate it was torture to the Locrian and other magical creatures kept inside.

Reaching the desired cell, he opened it, it was midnight and fully dark outside. The Fae was tied to the wall, she was weak. Restraints wouldn't be necessary except she had clawed at his face in protest, the wound still stinging. She gazed at him as he entered, still holding that fire in her eyes as she stared him down. "What do you want?" She asked with a bite to her voice. Dragas walked over to her, squatting before her. He grabbed her throat, making her look him in the eye. "You know, Padua begged me to spare her life, whimpering in weakness. Very un-Fae like."

Gasping for air Moa' choked out "I don't believe you."

Dragas squeezed a bit harder, "It makes no difference what you believe, eating her heart allowed me to know the location of the Locrian birthing tree. And I intend to burn it to the ground."

Her eyes went wide in horror.

"And now, my dear Moa', I heard you can manipulate dream-scapes and establish some sort of a psychic link between you and the being that you wish to meld with."

Gasping for air, "What do you need with dream walking?"

Dragas sneered, "Yes, that is what it's called. And thank you for confirming it."

Her eyes went wide as he raised his hand, claws extended, and reached into her chest, pulling out her heart. The Fae had life in her for a few moments afterward, making her last view of this life of Dragas eating her heart. Her empty body collapsed against the cavern wall, the light leaving her eyes. Licking his lips, Dragas felt the power course through his being.

"Let's see if you can hide now," he sneered, blood still running from his mouth.

Chapter 14

Margaret was on a high. The meeting had gone better than she hoped. She was so happy she was practically singing in the shower. She never sung in the shower, but what the hell. She belted out a few verses of "All You Need Is Love" by the Beatles, courtesy of professor Caleb's collection of vinyl. Exiting the shower she was grateful no one appeared to be in the bathroom with her. She was happy but not THAT happy.

She crawled into bed, too awake to sleep. She opened her book and attempted to read in an effort to turn down the buzzing in her brain. She felt like she could do anything right now. After a few hours of reading she finally felt relaxed enough to sleep and she drifted off with a smile on her face.

It didn't take long before she realized she was being pulled into a dream again, but this time she was conscious of it. She saw the landscape of the world ruled by Droch beneath her, as if she was viewing it from the air. She was falling toward it. Afraid

225

to be trapped there, instinct took over and she threw her arms and legs out in an attempt to stop herself from falling, and she did. She hung in the air roughly 50 feet off the ground looking at the world that had been destroyed.

"Ok I did not expect that to work," she thought to herself.

Realizing she had some control over the dream, she tried to move which resulted in a Peter Pan type movement where she zoomed across the sky. "Okay, this is new." She might almost enjoy this if the circumstances were different.

Looking down she saw a herd of Droch running in one direction. Curious, she used her newfound ability to follow them from the air. They all gathered in front of what looked like Temple Bar. Standing in front of the bar was the Droch from her dream weeks ago. He let out a blood curdling roar.

"Where is she?!" His voice boomed and all the Droch cringed, sinking away from him. The Droch closest to him made some grunting noises like he was communicating with the leader.

One of the larger Droch roared back, "What do you mean you do not know?! I felt her enter the dream. She is here find her!" The Droch dispersed frantically. Margaret's heartbeat quickened and she realized this was not a dream, this was a summoning. He was hunting her, she had to wake up.

She flew higher into the clouds and dust, hoping this kept the Droch on the surface from seeing her. "Wake up," she said. But nothing happened. Summoning all her strength she screamed "Wake up!!" and she sat bolt upright in bed.

She threw her covers off, "Alright that killed my good mood."

She ran to Donny's room and banged on the door. When he opened it, he was half asleep, but became alert as soon as he saw her face.

"What happened?"

She shook her head, "Not here, we need to get Bri and Myriad."

He nodded and they took off running down the hallway together.

When Margaret finished describing her dream, Myriad asked, "So you had control in the dream?"

Margaret nodded, "Yes, it took a lot of effort to take control, but yes."

Myriad paced around the room, "Who was the Droch leader? And he could talk?"

"Yes, just like you and me. And he could speak with the Droch and understand them. I never heard a name but they followed him, and they certainly feared him."

Myriad paused and sat down across from her pupil, "It would make sense that the Droch are attacking more strategically if they have a leader."

"But here is the biggest concern, he was looking for me. He knew I was in the dream with him. He said he felt me enter the dream."

Myriad had seen this before with Dorien. "He's using psychic abilities to create a very real dream world that he can manipulate and he somehow has the ability to link with you and pull you in. But I'm guessing he didn't anticipate you being able to manipulate it as well."

"How is that even possible? How does a Droch have that ability, if that's even what he is, and how was I able to control the dream?"

Myriad thought for a moment. "I'm not sure. That ability only exists within the Fae and Sorcerers to my knowledge, and I believe the Sorcerers are all extinct. I haven't seen one since Merlin's time."

The trio looked at each other, "As in King Arthur?"

"Yes," and that was the end of that.

"As for controlling the dream yourself, my only assumption would be that he didn't have full control because the dreamcatcher intervened. I made another dream catcher just in case the other ceased to work. Place this one under your pillow. The proximity of the dreamcatcher and using two of them of equal strength should stop him from pulling you in again."

Margaret nodded, "Thank you Professor."

"It takes a lot of energy to build a dream-scape, not to mention the power it takes to pull someone else in. Even if you didn't have the dream-catcher, there's no way he would be able to invade your dreams again tonight. I also have a feeling he's not adept at what he's doing. He is borrowing that ability somehow, which is why I believe the dream-catchers will stop him."

Her explanation put Margaret a bit more at ease.

Myriad was still concerned. There was no reason that a Droch should have this ability. If it was a Sorcerer or a Fae even the dream-catchers would be no match for them, but this was something she had never experienced. She had a sinking feeling in the pit of her stomach. The psychic link between Margaret and this Droch was eerily strong. There was only one being on the planet that Myriad knew could have that kind of connection with Margaret.

Donny broke her train of thought, "Professor? Why is it attacking Margaret? Why not anyone else? How does he even know about her at all?"

Myriad paused as if she wanted to tell them something, but she thought better of it. "I do not know, but I will do what I can to find out. For now, Margaret, ease your mind, you will not be burdened by your dreams any longer."

The three of them left the classroom and returned to their rooms in silence. Bria hugged her friends before making her way back to her dorm. Donny walked Margaret back to her room and without saying a word followed her in. He laid down on her bed and waited for her. She placed the dreamcatcher underneath her pillow and lay down beside him. He wrapped his arms around her and held her. This simple act touched her in a way that no one else had. Within minutes she heard him breathing deeply, signaling that he had fallen asleep, but he still clung to her.

Margaret couldn't fall asleep. The dream disturbed her but not nearly as much as the fact that her professor had lied to her again. She knew that the Fae knew more than she was letting on about the Droch from her dream. What was Myriad hiding? Why wasn't the Fae telling her the truth? There was a Droch after her, that knew of her, and she needed to figure out why.

Myriad stormed down the hall, pounding on Asher Doyle's door as soon as she reached it. "Asher, wake the hell up!"

Her heart was racing, "Asher!"

He swung open the door, hair unkempt and half-dressed. "What?!" he growled.

She pushed past him. "I'm done lying to her, Asher, she has to know."

He rubbed his face in an attempt to catch up. "Wait, what and who are you talking about?"

Myriad spun on her heel, "Margaret! She had another dream and was pulled into it by a Droch with psychic abilities. He knew her, Asher. She was able to control the dream in such a way that she was not caught, but he knew her. We need to tell her, what if it gets worse?"

Asher began to pace. "How do we know that this has anything to do with him?"

Myriad shot him a look that finally succeeded in waking him up. "Who else could it be? Why would anyone else be targeting her, or even know about her existence?"

As she watched Asher pace she looked around his room and saw clothes everywhere, stacked in piles and filth around the room. She scrunched her nose at the unkempt room.

He put his head into his hands as he sat down, frantically trying to think of anything else that could explain all of this. He finally conceded. "Alright we'll tell her, but not right now, not when she already has enough on her plate. Let's tell her after the first round at the outpost. She may be more equipped to handle it then."

Myriad sighed heavily. She didn't like the idea of keeping the secret any longer than she had to but she respected Asher enough to try. "Alright. But after that I'm not keeping the secret anymore because she deserves to know."

She stood to leave, "Clean up your room would you, you are a headmaster not a pig!" She slammed the door on the way out.

Dragas paced the room. How had she not been there? He felt her consciousness enter the dreamscape. He knew she was there, maybe she had hidden from him somehow? But the only way to do that in a dreamscape was to manipulate the dream herself. Did she have that ability?

He had tried to reconnect with her again but it was blocked with more magic than he could get around. He would have to put that plan on the back burner for now. His plan could still move forward, he just needed to capture Margaret in order to complete it.

All he had to do was wait for the right
moment.

Chapter 15

Margaret got up in the morning silently, not wanting to wake Donny as she climbed slowly out of bed. She slipped out to get coffee, accepting that she wouldn't be getting back to sleep and knowing she would need the caffeine boost. She saw Myriad sitting outside and decided to avoid her. It was too much effort this early in the morning to talk to someone she believed was lying to her. This realization hit her hard - they had always had such a good relationship, and she missed their intimate morning chats.

She sat down inside, taking stock of her day and making a mental checklist. The instructors had decided that Margaret, Bria, and Donny would now run the classes, with their guidance, to help solidify their positions as leaders and to give them practice calling out strategies on the battlefield. Margaret could admit that it was a good idea, but the mental strain of the added responsibility was hard to bear. For now, she welcomed this brief moment of silence so she could focus on the task at hand.

She took out a notebook and began writing down the skills she wanted to practice with different students. Going forward, all instruction was scheduled for the gymnasium so the trio could teach all the students at the same time and assess the weaknesses of the entire group. As she jotted down notes, she saw Myriad approaching her table from the corner of her eye, but she ignored her until the Fae tapped her on the shoulder.

Unable to hide the hurt in her face, she glanced over at her professor. "You could have joined me outside," Myriad said, noticing Margaret's pained expression.

"I know, but I felt like working." Margaret bent her head back down, clearly wanting her to leave.

Myriad's heart broke a little; she hated seeing her students so upset with her. *"Damn you, Asher,"* she thought to herself, although both of them truly carried the burden. "I know you're hurt Margaret, but I promise I will make this right."

Margaret looked up again, the pain on her face replaced with anger. "You could make it right by not lying to me."

236

Myriad paused as if she wanted to respond but thought better of it. She gave her pupil a nod and walked away.

Shortly after, Margaret saw Bria and Donny enter the dining hall. Donny still had the tousled look of just rolling out of bed, a look that was so adorable she couldn't help but smile. As he smiled back at her, she had a sudden realization that what was important in her life was standing directly in front of her. She would eventually figure out what Myriad had been keeping from her, but for now this was what truly mattered.

Donny wandered over to her, "Are you ok? You were gone when I woke up."

Bria spat out her coffee, "You were in her bed?"

Margaret laughed, "Overly dramatic much? Nothing happened, Bri, he was just keeping me company. I was still shaken up about the dream."

"Oh, right. Good boyfriend," she said, patting Donny on the head.

Donny shrugged her off, "I'm not a dog, but thanks."

"To answer your question, yes I'm fine, I just wanted to get an early start and honestly I could not go back to sleep. My brain was on high alert."

Donny understood. "I don't know if I could have slept either if I were you. What you went through was pretty intense."

She turned back to her notebook. "So I was working on a game plan for today. Everyone already knows to report to the gymnasium but we have to coordinate with all of them at the same time to assess for weaknesses, strengths etc."

Bria nodded, "We've all fought together before, we just need to hone our techniques and strategies."

Margaret knew that there was more to this than putting everyone in the same room to fight. "The difference is we need to learn how to multitask while fighting. We will be on high alert helping others and have to be able to adjust when needed. Also, we need to focus on each Locrian's individual skills so we know where they will best be utilized in battle." Margaret pulled out some diagrams and began relaying how she wanted to practice with each formation and weapon.

"Wow, you're really on top of this," said Donny.

Margaret smiled, "I've had a lot of time to think recently."

They made their way down to the gymnasium to set up.

Margaret wanted to make it a bit easier to evaluate the class. If they were in one giant group it would be difficult to differentiate each talent. "Maybe we should have different stations instead of everyone doing the same thing at the same time. Donny can supervise the knife and axe area; I can do the broadswords and Bri the longbows. That way we're each working in our best area. After an hour we can rotate them through until everyone has been to each station.

Donny nodded, "I like that idea. Everyday we can mix and match the students to see who fights better with one another until we're able to nail down everyone's strengths. Then we can hone in on each talent to make sure everyone is as comfortable as they can be with their identified weapon."

"Sounds like a plan to me, folks," chimed in Bria.

The class began to enter the gymnasium with the professors in tow. Margaret took a deep breath, "Here we go."

At lunch everyone's spirits were high. The instruction had gone far better than expected and the group seemed to have a little fun along the way too. Myriad approached the students cautiously. She knew that Margaret was mad at her and she didn't want to make the situation worse. "Pardon the interruption, I was just wondering how you wanted to run the simulator for today?"

Margaret acknowledged the professor, not wanting to hinder anything being done with training. "I was hoping to run some different attack plans that we've seen in recent weeks that had a lot of Locrian stumped. Also, is there a way to use the Kilkenny outpost as a backdrop for all the simulations so that we'll know what we're dealing with and can really familiarize ourselves with the layout?"

Myriad let out a breath she didn't realize she was holding. "Yes, absolutely. Do you need anything else?"

Margaret shook her head, "Not at the moment, thank you."

Margaret was not happy with Myriad but she would maintain a professional relationship with her. Regardless of her personal feelings she still held respect for the professor.

Myriad nodded and disappeared down the hall.

The simulator ran as planned with some of the more difficult situations thrown in. They all took turns learning how to defeat them in multiple ways until it became fluid and natural to anticipate the unexpected.

Over the next few weeks it was more of the same. Margaret was not bothered by dreams breaking up her sleep but her own restless brain was another story. The classes were going very well and everyone seemed to be clicking. Even students who truly struggled in the beginning, like Cassie, found her home with a longbow. Before anyone knew it a month had passed and the week of the new moon was upon them.
"This is really going to happen isn't it?" Asked Bria, as they sat together at breakfast the last morning before they were sent into battle.

Margaret nodded and couldn't help but smile, "Yes, it is, but I feel like we can do this, that we can help."

Bria smiled back, "I actually agree with you, I honestly didn't when we first started this venture, but I do now."

Margaret felt that something good was going to come out of this experience, she could feel it.

"What time is the transport coming?" Asked Donny.

"Tomorrow at dawn so we have time to acclimate ourselves once we get to the outpost," replied Margaret.

"You're really excited about this aren't you?" Said Donny.

Margaret's face lit up a bit more, "Is it that obvious? I mean, aren't you? This is the real deal, no more simulations. We can actually make a difference for our entire race over the next few days and that's really amazing."

Donny smiled. He loved her enthusiasm and drive, and he loved her. Though he hadn't said it yet, but he was one hundred percent over the moon in love with her.

"What?" Asked Margaret.

"Nothing, just thinking about how amazing you are."

She leaned in to give him a light kiss. She would never admit it first, but she loved him just as much.

There were no classes that day as they all needed to prepare and pack for the next few days. She knew they were ready but it was still quite a lot to wrap their heads around. Margaret was glad she wasn't leaving the abbey for good - this was her home and always had been. Leaving, even temporarily, was going to be hard.

She went to her room to pack and there was a knock on her door. Myriad was standing on the other side. She hadn't spoken to the Fae alone in weeks.

Myriad looked uncomfortable, "May I come in?"

Margaret stood back from the door allowing her to enter.

Myriad took a moment to look around Margaret's room focusing on the pictures of Ireland that hung on the walls and the pictures of her closest friends, "I don't think I've ever been to your room. It's lovely."

Margaret stood with her arms crossed, equally uncomfortable. "Thank you."

Myriad sighed, "Margaret I know it's been strained between us these last few weeks, and I know you believe that I'm lying to you."

Margaret, still standing with her arms crossed, glared at her professor, "Because you are."

Myriad shook her head, "I'm omitting information that isn't really mine to give."

Margaret approached Myriad from across the room. "Technicality." She paused, "You were always someone I could trust to be completely honest with me and you have failed me twice. Once when I questioned our class size, and now with the dream."

Myriad's head slumped on her shoulders; she clearly wasn't happy with the situation either. "I know and I'm not being fully truthful with you, but I've been given permission to give you all the information you want after you return from Kilkenny."

This admission only made Margaret more upset. "Why then? Why not now?"

Myriad looked her in the eye so that she would know she was telling her the truth. "We believe it will be a distraction for you given what you're about to face for the first time."

Crossing her arms again Margaret replied, "Who is 'we'?"

"Professor Asher, professor Bryan and myself."

"They know too? This is getting ridiculous! It's my life, I should be able to know about my life!" Margaret walked to the picture window and took a deep breath in an attempt to calm down.

Myriad crossed over to her, "I understand what you're dealing with. But please know, any information that has been withheld was done so because we feared for your safety. As you are now older and can handle the information it would be wise to give it to you. But not until after you return."

Margaret conceded for the moment. At least she would finally know the truth in a few days.

Myriad rested a hand on Margaret's shoulder, "Dear, don't forget your dreamcatchers, you don't want to get pulled into a dream while you're resting during the tough days ahead."

She nodded still peering out of the window, "Thank you for being honest with me. I hope this will be the trend going forward."

Myriad turned her around and grabbed her hands. "Please know that none of this was my choice. It was a majority decision and I lost. I care too much about you to have you mad at me. Be careful young one and come home to us."

Myriad kissed her forehead and placed her forehead to hers as she did the day she was born. "Be safe."

Myriad saw the determination in her eyes, the eyes she stared into all her life. The innocence was gone, and she was ready to face her future.

Myriad walked to the door, "See you in a few days," said Margaret. Myriad smiled, the future was bright indeed.

Chapter 16

The transport arrived shortly after breakfast. It was the same transport that delivered the infant Locrian to the abbey a few weeks prior. Outside it looked like a Suburban but inside it could easily hold an army. Margaret loved Fae magic.

The entire class piled in with Bria, Donny and Margaret pulling up the rear. All the professors stood nearby watching in silence. They looked on with pride as the transport departed. Margaret looked back and saw professor Asher, he inclined his head toward her and as he raised his head he smiled; she smiled in return at the rare sight.

Her gaze stayed locked on the abbey, as her home slowly disappeared behind her. As the last turret vanished beneath the line of the hillside, she turned her attention to her classmates. The atmosphere was tense and quiet, an air of anticipation lingered.

The trip did not take long; Ireland can be traversed in a matter of hours if you know where you're going, and if you're traveling by vehicle rather than horseback.

As they approached the outpost it was like deja vu thanks to Myriad's skillful recreation of the landscape during simulations. Waiting at the gate were Dorien and the elf that Margaret had seen. She was told his name was Craine.

The vehicle door opened and Margaret hopped out first followed by Donny and Bria. Craine and Dorien approached them.

"Welcome to Kilkenny, are you Margaret?" Margaret reached out and shook his hand. "Yes sir."

Craine had a look about him that told Margaret it hadn't been easy here recently. His tired eyes looked into hers, "Good, glad to meet you. Asher has told us great things about you and all your classmates."

Margaret smiled. "This is Donny and Bria my co-leaders."

Craine greeted them in turn, "It's a pleasure to meet all of you. I'm relieved to have you here, as you can imagine."

Margaret nodded.

Craine gestured toward the courtyard of the outpost. "Have your people unload, there is a bunk house that has been cleared for your stay. Once everyone is settled I would like to meet with the three of you in the hall, we have a strategy to discuss."

"Yes sir," replied Margaret. Craine and Dorien departed to tend to other duties leaving the young Locrian alone to explore.

"Not much for words is he?" Said Bria.

"No, but can you blame him? He looked destroyed," said Donny.

"Yes, but clearly grateful to have us," said Margaret. "Come on, let's get everyone unloaded, we have a lot to do in a short amount of time."

They unloaded their group and headed into the outpost. It was sparse but not nearly as depressing as she thought it would be. There were not many Locrian up and about, but it was morning and they were likely just getting to sleep. They found the bunk house that Craine mentioned. It was barracks-style with bunk beds lining the walls. The walls were sparse with no decorations. The windows held blackout curtains that were pulled back to let in the sunlight. She and Bria took the first set by the door and Donny the one next to it. The rest of the group dispersed through the room, quietly choosing their spots and unpacking. The ruck sacks they had all packed were the very same sacks they would use when they departed the abbey for good. It was strange to think that one's entire life could fit into a backpack but that was the way things worked. Locrian live simply, on purpose, knowing what their futures' hold.

Margaret did a quick scan of the room, "Donny can you do a brief walk around just to make sure everyone is doing alright?"

He started down the row when he noticed Liam struggling with his sheet. "You ok?"

"Yea, thanks."He stood and stared at Donny. "This doesn't feel real yet."

Donny nodded, "It will, and you'll be great." He patted him on the shoulder and continued down the rows to check on everyone else.

"Are you ok?" Bria whispered to Margaret.

Margaret nodded and looked around the room. "I'm actually doing really well, I think this is something that needed to happen to bring us all together."

Bria nodded, "I know what you mean."

Margaret took the dream catchers out of her bag and hung one above her pillow and placed the other underneath.

Bria looked relieved when she saw them. "I'm so glad you remembered."

"Me too" Margaret agreed.

"Everyone looks like they have the situation under control," said Donny returning.

Feeling confident that everyone was settling in okay, the three headed off to see Craine and Dorien.

Bria couldn't stop looking around, "This place is massive. The way everyone always talked about the smaller outposts I pictured a tiny shack."

"I know, I can't imagine what the one in Dublin must look like. How do humans not notice these things?" Margaret asked.

"Fae magic," said a voice from high above their heads. Looking up the trio saw a figure sitting in a tree. "Hold on, I'll come down to ya."

The man dropped in front of them, a Locrian with shoulder length blonde hair, and tan skin from being outside. His eyes were a blue-green and he was an unusually tall six-foot-five. He wore tattered jeans and a black long-sleeved t-shirt that showed off his muscles.

Bria couldn't take her eyes off of him.

The blonde-haired Locrian turned toward the group, "Sorry if I startled you, I'm Damien O'Sullivan, one of the archers here."

Bria was staring awkwardly. Margaret nudged her. Still nothing.

"Hi I'm Margaret and this is Donny and Bria," she said, attempting to divert attention away from her wide-eyed friend.

He crossed his arms and leaned up against the base of the tree. "Ah yes, the reinforcements from the abbey. I seem to remember you three when I was there. You were only ten-years-old last time I saw ya," said Damien.

Donny looked shocked, "You only left ten years ago?"

"Yep. I know it's hard to tell with all the anti-aging going on around here. Personally,

I love it. I'll be getting carded for beer when I'm hundreds of years old. Pretty sweet."

Margaret and Donny laughed but Bria just continued to stare. Margaret was beginning to wonder if she was having a stroke.

"What did you say about Fae magic earlier?" Asked Donny.

Damien glanced at Bria a little quizzically and then addressed Donny. "Oh that. Well, the outposts cannot be seen by humans, just like the abbey can't. Like the abbey, if there are humans in the area, they are pushed away from the outpost by magic in order to insure their safety. Unlike the abbey, the Droch can see the outposts because its necessary. With the outposts to distract them, the humans remain safe."

"Good to know," said Donny.

"Yea." Damien nodded, sticking his hands in his pockets. "Well, where are you guys off to?"

Margaret glanced again at Bria who still appeared to be in shock. "Craine asked us to meet him in the hall. Could you point us in that direction?"

"Oh sure, it's right over there behind the blacksmith's work station. Go past there, take a left and you can't miss it."

Donny began walking that direction, "Thanks Damien. Hopefully we'll see you around soon."

Damien looked at Bria and winked as she walked past. "You can count on it." Bria flushed and hurried to catch up with her friends.

Once at a safe distance Margaret elbowed Bria in the ribs. "Bri, what the hell was that?"

"What do you mean?" Bria asked, grabbing her side.

Margaret's eyes widened. "Are you kidding me? You stood there like you had been lobotomized."

Bria's face paled, "Was it really that bad? Do you think he noticed?"

"Yes," said Donny and Margaret in unison.

"I'm surprised you didn't drool all over yourself. You can never make fun of me again for freaking over Donny."

Bria glanced back towards the tree where Damien sat in the shade. "He's just so pretty."

Margaret rolled her eyes, "Oh god, come on Bri, now is not the time for crushes."

Bria could not stop smiling. "Margaret, he's an archer, do you have any idea how hot that is? And that hair! I just want to touch it."

Margaret paused and looked at her friend. "Listen Bri, if you can focus long enough to get us through the next few days, I will do my best to hook the two of you up, ok?"

Bria's eyes went wide, "Really? Ok now if that isn't motivation I don't know what is."

Donny made a fake gagging sound. "Ugh, women."

Bria whirled around to face Donny, "Ok Donny, you weren't much better fawning over Margaret for the last 10 years, always asking where she was, or what she was doing it really was ridiculous."

It was Donny's turn to be embarrassed, "Bri! That is the last time I ask you to help with anything."

Bria smirked, "Good, I put in a decade of work, that was enough."

A tight-lipped laugh escaped Margaret and the other two joined in as they approached the hall. They made the turn to the entrance and were immediately stunned into silence. "The hall" was an appropriate name for what lay before them.

The hall was a large rectangular room dimly lit by gas lanterns hung every six feet.

In the center of the room sat several men all watching the three Locrian approach. Margaret felt as though she was a child approaching a very adult conversation that she should not be a part of. They walked to the table slowly. Craine stood and gestured to three chairs that had been set aside for them. They each took a seat in silence.

Craine turned his attention to Margaret. "I trust that your people are comfortable."

Catching a lump in her throat, she replied, "Yes sir, as comfortable as they can be."

Craine nodded and dove into business, "Let's start with introductions. I believe that you all met Dorien when you were at the abbey."

The three of them nodded, "Yes sir," said Margaret.

"Next to him is Seamus O'Sullivan, he's in charge of the archers here. Next we have Magnus Doyle who coordinates the knife and axe wielders, and next to him we have Patrick Murphy who works with the swordsmen."

Margaret inclined her head to all of them. Silence hung heavy as they continued to stare at her. Craine leaned over and whispered "It's your turn."

"Oh!" She said, embarrassed that she didn't know the protocol.

"I'm Margaret and I do not have my name yet but I show promise with a sword, and I have been chosen as a leader of this team."

She looked at Donny. "I'm Donny and I too do not currently have my name but my preferred skills are knife and battle axe."

"I'm Bria, and like the others I do not yet have my name, and my talents lie in archery."

Craine and his men nodded in greeting.

Craine shifted in his seat in an effort to get comfortable, "Now we can get down to business. Dorien and I coordinate the men on the battlefield. We assess weaknesses and strengths and change tactics as needed. However, you'll be handling all of your people. As the attacks shift you will shift and your people will shift with you. You know your people better than I do so you need to make sure you place them where their strengths are. What I need from you is the list of names and talents of each of your classmates so that Seamus, Patrick and Magnus can coordinate as needed."

Margaret, Donny and Bria took turns running down the list of students and elaborating on their strengths and weaknesses, each having worked with them in various settings and with a variety of weapons.

Craine looked impressed, the three had comprehensive knowledge of their classmate's skills and abilities, proving to him that they certainly deserve to be here. You all really have done your work, I'll give you that. But the challenge will be the duration of the fighting. That has always been the struggle with newly integrated Locrian."

Margaret jumped in, "I think you'll find that we'll be more of an asset to you than previous new Locrian. We've been training extensively and I have every confidence that we will not hinder but rather enhance your fighting."

Craine nodded in respect for the young Locrian's gumption. Their confidence and level of preparedness gave him a sense of hope he hadn't had since the idea of bringing them onboard had been suggested. It was no secret that he didn't want a bunch of dead Locrian on his hands.

Craine shifted in his seat again, "I assume you're aware of what's happening to our people when left on the battlefield and not retrieved by sunrise?"

The three nodded.

Clasping his hands Craine looked directly at them, "Good. If you're injured get yourself back to the outpost as fast as you can. If you see someone injured and it's no threat to your life to help them get back to the outpost, please do so. We don't know why we are being taken or what is being done to those who are living, and I personally don't want to find out."

They nodded. "We will let our people know," said Margaret.

Craine leaned forward, "One last thing, go for the kill shots immediately. Our arrows and knives aren't working to slow them down like they used to. Headshots will take them down immediately but for some reason the heart is no longer as effective. When in doubt, decapitate. As you know, this means you'll have to get much closer to your enemy. It's more risky but also the most effective."

Myriad had prepared them for this. Every simulation encouraged head shots and decapitations.

Margaret acknowledged the concern, "We have been adequately prepared and have been training with an emphasis on decapitations."

Craine leaned back, becoming more relaxed, "If you don't have any questions I suggest you get some rest before tonight. I would like your group to meet with Magnus, Seamus and Patrick two hours before the sun goes down just to make sure everything is squared away."

Margaret inclined her head, "Thank you sir."

The trio stood and left the hall.

"That was a bit different than we're used to." Said Donny, as soon as they were outside.

"Yea, I felt like an infant sitting there. But Margaret, you were fantastic," stated Bria.

Margaret let her shoulders relax. She didn't realize how tense she had been.

Her mind was spinning and she hadn't heard the others speak, "Holy shit; that was the most terrified I have ever been in my life." She bent in half, trying to catch her breath. "I'm serious, I was petrified."

"But you handled it so well," said Bria.

"Mags" Donny said, holding her hands and looking her square in the eye. "Seriously, you're a natural at this, you may have been terrified, but you were amazing." He kissed her and gave her a reassuring hug.

They all decided to take Craine's advice and rest upon returning to the group, however, the rest did not include actual sleep for Margaret, and she was pretty sure it didn't for anyone else either.

Sundown was approaching quickly and emotions were on high alert. Margaret instructed her people to explore the outpost and familiarize themselves so they would know where they were going during the night. Before long it was time for everyone to meet with Magnus, Seamus and Patrick.

Basic instructions were given on the general locations in the outpost that they would be in charge of protecting. They were once again encouraged to return to the outpost as soon as possible if injured or the sun was rising. The group was dismissed shortly before sundown.

"Wow, they're really freaked out over the kidnappings." Said Bria.

"Aren't you? The Droch have behaved the same way for centuries and now, out of the blue, they change? If I had been fighting for as long as some of these Locrian have, it would do more than freak me out," said Margaret, leading the group towards the blacksmith to acquire their weapons.

The blacksmith had an amazing arsenal to choose from. One of the ore pits was directly below the blacksmiths station with stairs that led down into it.

"This is amazing," said Margaret. She selected a black broad sword with celtic knots carved into the hilt. It reminded her of her favorite sword at the abbey, and for a moment brought her back home. Donny saw a red-hilted battle axe and Bria found a four-foot bow made out of pine with a quiver to match. "Everything is so detailed and beautiful, like nothing I've seen," said Bria.

Admiring their weapons, they made their way back to the courtyard.

Looking at the last few lights of day Bria sighed, "I don't like the fact that I am fighting in the turret while you both are on the ground. It doesn't feel right that we are not all together."

"But we are," said Donny. "You will have our backs up there."

Margaret looked at the two people she loved most in the world, "How are you feeling right now? Really?"

Bria smiled at her friend and with some unnecessary concern in her voice she admitted, "Honestly? I'm excited, nervous and hopeful. It's a feeling that I haven't had in a while and I can't wait to start. I feel more confident than I ever have and I know once the fight starts I can focus on what we came here to do."

Margaret was overwhelmed with pride. She, along with everyone else, had come such a long way in such a short period of time.

Donny took Margaret's hand, "I feel the same way. I'm confident we will do what needs to be done to even out this war. We don't have much of a choice do we?"

"Mags, what about you?" Asked Bria.

She glanced at each of them and then down at her hands, "I'm nervous and excited, but also feel a great weight on my shoulders. What if I tell the group to do the wrong thing? What if someone gets hurt? It's a lot for one person."

"It IS a lot but it's a burden we share. You are not alone." Bria hugged her friend and Donny wrapped his arms around them both.

"We better get to our posts," said Donny. "See you in the morning Bri."

She nodded and they headed off, Donny and Margaret held hands all the way to their post in front of the wall. Suddenly she longed to be on the other side of that wall, protected from what was about to happen. As the sun sank behind the horizon, she took a deep breath, squeezed Donny's hand one more time, and let go. She grasped her weapon

just as several pairs of yellow eyes
appeared. The fight had now begun.

Chapter 17

The Droch slowly lumbered over the hillside. They were far larger than in the simulator, thought Margaret, and much uglier too. Suddenly, all at once, they began to gallop towards them, running on all fours like animals. Their weapons were strapped to their backs and the ground vibrated beneath their feet.

Craine looked toward Margaret seeing her white knuckled grip on the hilt of her sword, "Easy Margaret. Just do as you have trained to do."

She took another breath and relaxed her grip.

The first wave of Droch hit the outpost and the sound was unreal. Weapons clashed and roars surrounded them. The size and strength of the Droch took them all by surprise. Margaret had to focus her entire being into every movement, every strike, every kill. It was challenging beyond anything she had experienced in all her simulation. She could hear Donny screaming orders at his group, arrows whizzing by her head, and the primal grunts of the Droch.

"Move center!" Yelled Donny to his group noticing the entrance to the outpost had been exposed. Liam quickly shifted and fired a knife into the head of a Droch who had broken free and was making its way to the gate.

"Hold steady!" Said Margaret to her group who was bombarded by Drochs twice their size. She spun quickly her sword tearing through their tough flesh. The sword was sharp sliced through clean, but force needed surprised Margaret. She spun again slicing through the side of a Droch giving Lyra the chance to decapitate her attacker. She nodded in gratitude before moving on to the next.

It was all noise until it wasn't; suddenly everything fell into focus.

Margaret spun with expert grace towards a massive Droch. She miss judged the height of the beast and instead of slicing cleanly through his throat she cleaved his head in two. The broadsword sliced through his skull like butter exposing the monsters brain. The body slumped to the ground in a massive heap. Margaret spun as a yell came across

the battlefield. A Droch had Liam pinned
down but Donny was too far to reach him in
time. "Bri!" she shouted up to the tower and
pointed. Bria looked down and immediately
took aim and fired straight through the
Droch's eye. Margaret briefly smiled up at
her friend, but it was a moment too long. A
Droch rose up behind her and she didn't have
enough time to react. He raised his weapon
high above his head but just as he went to
strike her down he began to shake his head
vigorously. Grabbing his head, he wailed as
if in pain and stopped his attack. Not
wasting any time Margaret grabbed her weapon
and decapitated the Droch. The head slid
from the body and a fountain of green goo
erupted from an artery on the Droch's neck,
covering Margaret.

"What just happened", she thought. Gathering
her composure, she commanded her people to
spread out as the next wave approached. This
pack was more determined to take the gate,
so she shifted her people again, this time
to the middle, just as Craine, Dorien and
Donny had done. These Droch appeared to be
more skilled with weapons. They weren't just
utilizing a static chopping motion, but were
more adept and used a larger range of motion
with each strike. The sudden change in skill
level threw several Locrian off. The kill
strikes became more challenging and given
the added level of difficulty some of the

269

Locrian were separated from the group; including Donny. Donny was fighting two Droch at once, the level of skill he possessed was astonishing, surprising even himself, but he struggled to make the kill. Every time he exposed the neck of one the other would intercept his blade. He was beginning to worry, he couldn't keep this up forever. The weight of each blow wearing him down.

Margaret spun around to scan the battlefield after her most recent kill and she noticed that the Locrian were scattered, the cohesiveness gone. The Droch has crept in separating their group. Margaret saw that Donny was isolated completely battling two Droch, her immediate reaction was that she had to get to him. She tore through the battlefield slicing down one Droch after another. She had tunnel vision, her only concern was reaching Donny. Suddenly she was upon them. Donny was holding his own but not making any progress. He had a large gash through his forearm and she could see exhaustion on his face. Margaret ran up behind one of the Droch slicing horizontally through his spine. The broadsword was made so well that it never lagged in slicing through bones and muscle tissue. She heard a crunch as the sword came out the other side. The beast howled in pain and turned to face her. Adrenaline fueled her attack, dodging several swipes from the sword. She sliced across his side, a leg and torso but nothing slowed him down. A howl erupted from beside her and the Droch turned. She jumped up, swung her broadsword and connected. The flesh tore easily as the sword slid through, a jerk was felt in her arms as the creature reared back in pain and she connected with the spinal cord. The beast fell and the green blood that once pumped through his veins now covered her face.

Donny spun around, "Thanks".

"Don't mention it." The pair ran back towards the outpost to regroup.

As they crossed back through the chaos, there were fewer Droch, the group of students came back together, regrouped and the fluidity of the fight was back. They were not individuals fighting, they were a unit and it was beautiful. Bodies were beginning to pile up and the Droch ran in retreat.

They crouched in place, waiting for the next wave to attack, but after several minutes, nothing. Margaret looked at Craine who looked just as confused as her.

"Is it over?" asked Margaret.

Craine kept his eyes on the horizon, "I'm not sure, this has never happened before." He shifted his feet. "Stay on alert."

They could see them in the distance now, a much larger group than before. They approached cautiously, as if hesitant to attack. After several minutes they began to move quickly and Margaret ordered her people to spread back out in an effort to cover more ground. The Droch outnumbered them two to one, but she was relieved to see that the Locrian's skill level was higher. Margaret spun around quickly, just as she heard the guttural grunt of a Droch behind her, slicing her sword across its throat. Green blood spurted in every direction, spraying her face and chest, dripping down her arm where her weapon had made contact, but he continued to growl and writhe - his head was still intact. As the Droch hit the ground, she raised her weapon high, and finished the job in one fell swoop. His head rolled to her feet, yellow, empty eyes rolled upward. In them she saw nothing human, just animal. She dragged her eyes from the lifeless corpse and saw Donny across the field, deftly decapitating monster after monster, his battle axe and body covered in the same green slime as hers. Another Droch rose up, suddenly right in front of her, but before she could attack, an arrow whizzed past her and directly into its temple. He went down with a loud thud, landing next to the decapitated head at Margaret's feet. She let out a breath she did not know she had been holding.

What she presumed were Bria's archery skills had bought her a few moments to scan the area, and she spotted Lyra nearly overtaken by two Droch. She was holding her own but wouldn't be able to for much longer. Margaret sprinted to her and slung her sword across the back of one's neck, dropping it to the ground and giving Lyra enough leverage to kill the other.

"Thanks," said Lyra, breathlessly.

Margaret gave her a quick smile and sprinted back to her post. The attack was slowing. The sun began to edge above the horizon and the remaining Droch took off back to their hole, but they were left with no trophies or souvenirs to drag back with them.

Margaret's emotions filled as she watched the Droch retreat. They'd made it through the night. Craine, looking exhausted, made his way over to her, "That was really something. Once we make sure we get all out people squared away I would like to speak with you."

She nodded. With the rising sun the Droch bodies that littered the field began to disintegrate. The only convenient thing about Droch was that they were easy to clean up. Margaret remained outside the gate, anxiously waiting to see if any of her people were hidden beneath disintegrating Droch bodies. She was relieved to see that no bodies appeared to be theirs and as she looked more closely, none appeared to be Craine or Dorien's men either.

She headed back into the outpost to check on the archers and to see if anyone was injured. As she walked in, she began to feel a strange discomfort. All the Locrian were staring at her. Had she done something wrong? Donny ran over to her, wrapping her in his arms - an act that would have been gross had they not both been covered in the same green gore. "You were amazing, Margaret!"

"Then why is everyone staring at me?" she said, still aware of everyone's eyes on her.

Donny followed her gaze. "Because you were incredible. I don't think you realize how many Droch you killed, your speed was unreal. It was like you were doing some sort of beautiful deadly dance."

Margaret looked from Locrian to Locrian as they crowded around her more closely, shaking her hand and patting her enthusiastically on the back. She didn't know what the big deal was. She had just done her job. But it was a good day, no one died and the anxiety was gone. She would accept the celebration, but it needed to be shared by all. They were all born to do this and that was evident in the success of the night. She took a step back, "I appreciate all the praise and congratulations, but I was not out on that field alone. You all had a part in our victory today. Thank you for being on that field beside me, as long as we work together we can anticipate more days like this."

"You know you didn't have to say anything, people were proud to congratulate you," said Donny.

"I know but this was not a victory won by one person." She smiled at Donny and noticed the red blood mixed with the green. "Donny you are hurt."

He looked down at his arm, "It's just a scratch, I will be sure to get it wrapped after a much needed shower."

Eventually everyone dispersed and Margaret was no longer the center of attention. She made a beeline for the showers. She lingered in the hot water, letting it wash away the caked-on blood along with the tension and anxiety she'd been holding onto for the past eight hours. The minor scrapes and abrasions she received stung her skin as she let her mind wander, the reality of their survival began to set in. The confidence she had in her peers and in herself was growing. They had trained well. They had done what they were born to do. She exited the shower and put on the clothes she wore every day at the abbey.

Once she had put herself back together she went looking for Craine. She found him in the hall. Sitting there alone he looked very small. He turned when he heard her approaching and stood, gesturing to a seat next to him.

"How are you feeling?" he asked.

She sat down next to him, "Honestly, I feel great. It went far better than I expected it would."

Craine nodded, staring at her, hesitating.

Leaning forward on the table he spoke to her in a near whisper. "Are you aware of how well you did?"

Her brows furrowed. "We didn't lose any people, and there were very minimal injuries so I would say pretty well."

He shook his head, "Let me rephrase. Are you aware of what YOU did?"

Margaret was visibly confused.

He leaned back in his seat, "Ok, that's a no."

"What did I do?"

He leaned forward and in a reassuring voice said, "You didn't do anything wrong, it just wasn't expected. You focused in such an intense way on your fighting. I've seen this before but never from new warriors or unnamed Locrian. I also noticed that when your people were in trouble, and needed aid, you could sense it." He paused. "You would begin to move in the direction of a Locrian who needed you before you ever looked in their direction."

Margaret shook her head, "No, I just saw it from the corner of my eye, and I was hyper alert. If I didn't have a Droch right in front of me I made sure I looked around. Like you said, I was in charge of my people."

Craine paused to emphasize this point. "You looked around, yes, but you knew precisely where to look. When you honed in on the Locrian in need, you never wavered slicing through Droch to get to your classmate without pause. You also moved incredibly quick, with a speed I have only seen in elves and Fae. I have seen fast Locrian before, once they have been named and received their power, but not to the speed that you exhibited, and not within a Locrian who is without powers. The ability to sense when your classmates were in trouble is called 'battle sense'. I have seen this as well in named Locrian but never to the degree that you displayed."

Margaret rubbed her face, "I don't know what you're talking about."

He shifted uncomfortably in his chair, "I know. It wasn't a conscious decision you had to make. It was instinctual. It just clicked on when you began to fight. If you had done this before I'm sure Myriad would have said something but as it is you have a gift. I can't wait to see what extra abilities you're gifted with once you're named.

What Craine was saying finally sank in and she sat up straight, "Wait, so I already have abilities without being named? How is that possible?"

"I can't tell you that for sure, but I'm grateful if that is truly the case. Those Droch did not know what to make of you. The third wave paused, I believe, because they weren't sure about attacking. You had their bodies piling up in front of you. It was beautiful to watch."

She stared at him, "I do have a question. One of the Droch snuck up behind me when I was distracted. He looked like he was going to strike me but just before he did he grabbed his head as if he was in pain and slumped over allowing me to kill him. Have you ever seen a Droch do that before?"

Craine shook his head "No, but I've never seen a Locrian like you either. Today is a day for surprises. Just be grateful that whatever happened bought you the time you needed to make the kill."

They stood and headed out of the hall. "It's time to get some rest. The larger group will be out tonight since it's the new moon."

They parted ways and for the first time in months Craine had hope for their cause. He walked away with a smile, something he hadn't been able to do in quite some time.

Dragas paced the cavern, "I feel her, she is here! She was on the battlefield. It is still early yet. She has not been named, but she is very strong." Dragas walked amongst the Droch who had returned to the cave following the battle. "One of you almost killed her! If I hadn't stopped you she would be dead! No one hurts her, is that understood?!" A collective grunt echoed through the cavern.

"I need to find a way to get her here. I need to speak with her directly." He continued to walk about the cavern, his mind spinning. How could he get her away from the group? What is her weakness? He paused with a sinister grin "Tonight we will make our move. Rest now my minions, for the change is coming."

Chapter 18

"He said he had never seen it before?" asked Donny

"No, he said he had but never in an unnamed Locrian. And my speed apparently rivals that of Fae and Elves."

Bria looked at her friend, concerned "Did you even know you were doing it?"

"No, I had no idea. All I felt was intensely focused. Was it really that crazy?"

Donny shook his head, "Honestly, I was concentrating on not dying so I didn't notice too much. There were a few moments in there where you popped up on me instantaneously, but nothing that I thought twice about. Although, I was grateful you did. You just seemed to know right where to be."

"What about you Bri?"

"All I noticed was how intuitive you were, like Donny said, you instinctively knew where to be, but I was so focused in on the targets I only saw you when I was shooting near you."

Donny touched her face, lifting her gaze to his, "Hey, at least this is a good thing, it means you're special. Which I always knew." He leaned over and kissed her on the forehead.

"Yea, and now that we know, when we return to the abbey you can practice and hone your skills so you'll get even better. Think about it, it's like you got your abilities early. Nothing wrong with that."

Margaret nodded.

"We've all had a long night, let's just try to relax before the sun goes back down." Donny kissed her again and went to go lie down.

Bria looked at Margaret. "Are you ok?"

Margaret shook her head. "I think so, it's just been so much these last few weeks, and even good news feels overwhelming right now."

"I understand, but now that you know you can really kick some ass tonight!"

Margaret smiled, "You always know what to say."

"I detect some sarcasm, but I'll take it. Get some sleep."

Margaret climbed into bed knowing her friends were right, it was time to stop worrying and start thinking like a Locrian.

Margaret woke up a few hours before sundown. The barracks were already empty. She went out to the courtyard to find the others, surprised that she had slept so long. All of her friends were prepping weaponry, socializing, and laughing. Despite what was going to happen once the sun went down.

Margaret spotted Donny and Bria beneath the tree where they had met Damien the day before. She began to walk toward them when she was startled by a loud ringing sound.

"What is that?" Asked Bria.

"The dinner bell," said Damien, coming up behind them.

"Oh crap, no wonder I'm so hungry. I haven't eaten since breakfast yesterday. Was there dinner yesterday? I didn't hear the bell."

"Yes, but it was when you three were headed to the hall. No sound gets in or out of there in order to maintain privacy."

"Great I'm starving," said Donny, already headed toward the dining hall.

"When are you not?" Asked Margaret as she jogged to catch up with him.

Margaret looked behind her to see if Bria was following and found her stunned into silence, yet again.

"Well, see you in there. Oh, and Bria is it? Nice shooting yesterday," Damien smiled and walked away.

Bria seemed frozen in place, her mouth hanging slightly open. Margaret made her way back to the tree and gave her a quick poke in the ribs. She jumped out of her daze.

"Stop doing that!" Protested Bria.

"I will when you can act human around him. That was really nice of him to say that to you. What's wrong with you Bri?" Margaret asked with a knowing grin.

They both ran to catch up with Donny who was too intent on food to notice their exchange. "Mags, my brain melts when he's around. He's my kryptonite."

"I think you really like him and you don't know what to say or how to act." said Margaret.

Bria shook her head, "I always know what to say."

"Clearly not with him. Just talk to him like you'd talk to Donny." said Margaret.

"Need I remind you how you acted after Donny kissed you?"

Margaret blushed. She still felt foolish over how she reacted.

"And you helped me see the error of my ways. Trust me, Bri. Just relax and be your sarcastic smart-ass self. He'll either like you or he won't but you'll drive yourself crazy in the meantime."

At the dining hall, the menu wasn't as diverse as the abbey, but they were starving and happily loaded up their plates with spaghetti and meatballs with garlic bread and chocolate pudding for dessert. After piling up their plates they looked for a place to sit down. Damien sat alone at a table and Margaret and Donny walked straight for it. Bria's legs turned to jello and her heart quickened. Maybe she couldn't do this.

"Do you mind if we sit here?" Asked Margaret.

"Go for it. Thanks for the company," said Damien.

Bria froze next to the table like a lost child. Margaret grabbed her and pulled her down on the bench beside her.

Damien looked over at Bria for a few seconds then addressed the group. "Last night you guys all kicked ass, I was really impressed."

"Thanks, Damien," said Margaret. "Bria is the best archer we have. I was glad to have her up there looking out for us."

He shook his head in agreement, "Yea, you nailed those Droch. Almost every shot you made was through the eye socket. Fifty points easy."

"What?" Said Bria, coming out of her daze.

Damien feigned shock, "Oh, you do talk."
Bria's cheeks flushed red. "It's kind of a
game we do as archers, twenty points each
for forehead shots, fifty for eye sockets,
ten for chest areas, thirty for throats.
After a while you just have a running tally
in your head. It's on the honor system, but
you get really good at adding quickly. Wanna
give it a go tonight?" asked Damien.

Bria looked around, "Who, me?"

"I don't see any other archers at this
table. Yes, you. You would definitely be the
one to beat," he smirked.

Bria puffed up - a bit ruffled - exactly what
Damien was after. "What makes you think you
will beat me?"

He extended his hand across the table to
Bria, "Okay, game on then."

Damien smiled at Bria and her cheeks flushed
again as she reached for his hand to shake.
The touch of his skin made her heart race
and she quickly drew her hand away.

"So you guys will leave after tomorrow night
to return to the abbey for continued
training?" asked Damien.

Margaret shook her head, "Yea, that was part of the deal that Asher made with Craine. Three days at a time for now to keep us from getting overwhelmed."

"I have to say I'll be sad to see you go. You guys have already made a huge impact on the fighting ratio here. I haven't seen the outpost this excited in a long time."

"Honestly I don't want to leave either. We're finally doing what we're supposed to be doing. But I also recognize that we'll be more helpful once we train more and get our names," said Margaret.

"Hey, at least you guys are here now, during the worst of it," said Damien.

As they left the dining hall, the sun was just touching the tops of the trees. "It's time to find our way to our posts." said Donny.

"See you guys after," said Bria.

The pre-battle anxiety was gone now that they had done it before, but now Bria had a whole new battle to contend with. As they moved to their post Damien let Bria climb the stairs ahead of him like a gentlemen. Once they reached the top Bria went to the right and set up her quiver full of arrows.

"Hey," said Damien sidling up beside her. "Do you mind if I stand here tonight? I just figured since you wanted to compete I would help you with the scoring."

"Smooth move." Bria blushed, not quite believing she'd said that.

Damien looked a bit embarrassed.

"It will keep you honest with the scoring, I suppose." Said Bria.

Damien smiled, "I can tell I'll have to keep my eye on you as well." That didn't help her nerves at all. Her heart was going a mile a minute. Not good for an archer. But before long the yellow eyes began to peek over the horizon and she forgot all about Damien.

Dragas stood with his minions on the hill above the battlefield, just outside the cave entrance. He could see the entire landscape and easily coordinate attacks while communicating with his entire battalion of Droch using his psychic abilities. Grunts and snarls were fine for them but he didn't know how to make heads or tails of it. His telepathic ability gave Dragas an advantage over the Locrian, all his minions could hear him at once, if necessary, or he could communicate one-on-one with individual Droch. He had watched with bemusement when their suddenly fluid strategy had caught the Locrian off guard. But tonight he wasn't concerned about the other Locrian. Tonight the goal was her.

Damien re-strung his bow after the first wave had been taken down. "Nice job, rookie, it's only the first wave and you've hit 270 points."

Bria tested the tension on her bow, "I'm well aware of where my points are, Damien," said Bria, gaining confidence. "What about you?"

"320, but there's no shame in losing. You're new to the game." He pulled back and launched an arrow to test it out on an unsuspecting Droch, lumbering across the hillside. "Oh wait 370, eye socket."

Bria growled under her breath. She hated to lose.

Damien grinned. This was the side of her he wanted to see. He found this side of her hot as all hell.

Down below on the field, Margaret was once again cutting down Droch after Droch. Donny paid a bit more attention to her this time, and couldn't help but think it was beautiful; her speed and ability to find those in need was amazing. Despite the green goo and sweat that covered her face, his love for her grew with each decapitated beast.

She caught him staring at her from a few yards away. "What?" she yelled, checking behind her quickly.

"Nothing. You look beautiful covered in Droch guts," he said.

"Right back at ya," she winked.

This new group of Locrian posed even more of a challenge to Dragas the second night of fighting, and he knew the root of it was her. He had to find a way to separate her from the group. He watched her for hours as they battled. Her speed and ability were astonishing. She was able to immediately

hone in on those in trouble on the
battlefield and provide assistance quickly,
which suggested strong telepathic abilities.
She never let someone go outnumbered for
long and raced to them to lend support. That
was it. He needed to endanger a Locrian away
from the group in order to draw her out. All
he had to do was wait for the opportunity.

It was nearly dawn when he saw it - two
Droch were fighting a blonde Locrian woman
on the far right side of the outpost. He
instructed his minions to lead her closer to
the woods and draw her further away from the
group. The blonde didn't realize how far she
had moved from the larger group. As soon as
Margaret was aware of her distance, she
raced to her rescue. Just as he had hoped.

Margaret saw Cassie being drawn into the
woods. It was nearly dawn and she didn't
want her friend to be vulnerable. She took
off in her direction. She burst through the
field severing the head of a Droch quickly
advancing on Cassie. With the pressure
momentarily off, Cassie struck down the
second Droch with all she had left.

She put her hands on the tops of her thighs, trying to catch her breath. "Thanks , Margaret," She panted.

"It was no problem. Now let's get back to the outpost, we're too far out."

As they took off back toward the main outpost, four Droch quietly emerged from the trees. Cassie saw them first and took off at a run. Margaret turned and had just enough time to cut the first Drochs head in two. This maneuver was successful, however, her sword was stuck in its skull. Cassie spun around realizing that her friend had fallen behind. She ran up to defend Margaret slicing through the neck of another beast. This bought Margaret enough time to free her sword from the fallen Droch. The other two Droch approached swinging wildly.

"Run!" Screamed Margaret as she jumped in front of Cassie.

Cassie blocked a blow from one of the Droch, "Not a chance."

The two were fighting with everything they had when the Droch suddenly froze. They began to shake their heads, rubbing their ears as if they heard something unpleasant. Cassie and Margaret swung their blades but they were deflected. The Droch looked at one

293

another and nodded. Margaret couldn't
believe her eyes, the Droch were
communicating. The blows were strong and
wearing them down. Cassie, weak from the
earlier fight, fell to the ground. She
attempted to roll out of the way but the
Droch caught her arm and searing pain shot
through her as she screamed. Margaret jumped
in front of the relentless Droch.

"Cassie run, I mean it this time!" Cassie
stood up and began to run towards the
outpost to get help.

The Droch continued to dodge every attack
that Margaret gave. She couldn't understand
what was happening. They had her pinned
down, blow after blow came and her arms
began to tire. One caught her off balance
and her sword flew. Fear filled her soul,
she was going to die. Then the Droch
stopped, one of them grabbed her by the arms
and attempted fling her over his back. She
bit him, the taste of his blood was awful
but he let her go. The second one blocked
her using his sword. Using the techniques
from professor Xavier's class she lasted
longer than she anticipated but not long
enough. The Droch she had bit had had enough
and used the hilt of his sword to knock her
unconscious. Grunting, he picked her up and
slung her over his shoulder beginning the
march back towards the caves.

From the other side of the field Donny saw Cassie running toward him, her movements were ragged, clearly injured. Cassie pointed behind her, Donny switched his focus in time to see two Droch heading back towards the caves with what looked like an unconscious Margaret.

"No!" He began to run in her direction, but Craine grabbed his arm with brute force.

"She's too far out, and you won't survive the caves. You'll be vastly outnumbered."

Donny struggled against Craine's strength, "I'm not going to just stand here and let her die!"

From her outlook, Bria had seen Cassie and Margaret's struggle and was already sprinting down the tower steps, Damien close on her heels.

"I cannot let you go," said Craine, just as Bria reached them.

"You're not our commander," she said. "She is and we're going to save her."

"I admire your spirit" Craine said impatiently, keeping his eye out on the battlefield, relaxing when he saw the sun peeking over the horizon "but you're also in charge of your people. What will happen to them if none of you return?"

In that moment Donny didn't care about "his people" - he only cared about one person. But he knew Craine was right. He quickly scanned the crowd of Locrian until his eyes landed on who he needed. "Liam and Lyra, you're in charge until we return," Donny shouted, "And we will not come back without Margaret." He said directly to Craine.

"If I cannot stop you, at least load up with weapons before you go."

Hating the wasted time, Donny and Bria quickly grabbed back up axes, an additional bow for Bria and another full quiver of arrows from the battlefield arsenal.

As they headed toward the gate with every weapon they could carry, they heard a voice behind them, "I'm coming too." They turned to see Damien loaded down with a full quiver and his longbow.

Donny shook his head, "Damien, no, they need you here."

Damien gestured around the outpost. "I hate to disagree with you, but they need HER here. Her capture will kill this outpost. I want to help. Let me."

With no time for more arguments Donny
conceded. "It's good to have you. Now, let's
go, we've wasted enough time."

The three of them ran toward the woods,
hoping they weren't already too late.

Chapter 19

Bria, Donny and Damien sprinted across the field towards the caves, moving to the tree line in order to get a safer view of the entrance. As they approached Donny froze looking at the ground, Margaret's sword lay in the grass abandoned. He had never seen Margaret lose her sword and his heart caught in his throat. Damien walked over and picked up the sword handing it to Donny. "Carry it for her, she will need it once we rescue her." The vote of confidence was all Donny needed as they approached the entrance to the caves.

Crouching behind some bushes the cave entrance was visible. From the cave opening, they could see a pair of yellow eyes looking out towards the forest.

"Do you think they can see us?" Asked Bria.

"No chance. Their eyesight is shit in the daylight," replied Damien.

"How in the hell would you know that? Have you ever seen one during the day?" Said Donny.

Damien's shoulders shot up in defense.

"Sorry," said Donny, "I'm just tense."

"It's ok, I know what you mean to each other, just looking at you I can see that."

Donny nodded. "So, how did you know that?"

"Myriad told me when I was at the abbey training."

Bria looked at him, "She hasn't told us that."

Damien looked toward the cave, "You have to know the right questions to ask. She's a wealth of information but not always the most forthcoming."

"Yea, we know," grunted Donny.

"So what's the plan?" Asked Damien.

Donny scanned the area, "Maybe there's a less prominent entrance with fewer Droch where we could sneak in."

"Not a good idea. We don't even know where Margaret is, we're going in blind." Said Damien.

Donny stood and turned toward Damien. "Look, if you have a better idea then -"

"Shush!" Bria cut him off. "I hear something."

Damien cocked his head, "Yea, I do too. It sounds like growling."

Donny began to hear it as well. "It sounds like Droch, I think it's coming from over here."

They followed Donny's direction through the wood, listening as the sound began to get stronger.

"Here!" Bria exclaimed. "Look, there's a hole in the ground."

"It must be a vent for air into the caverns," suggested Damien.

Donny nodded, "Of course! They have to get air down there somehow. Maybe there's a way to use these to figure out where they've taken Margaret."

Damien nodded, "Or at least when the opportune moment to strike. I mean, they have to sleep at some point, right? Maybe we can sneak in."

Bria held up her hand to quiet them, "Listen. Someone is talking. Is that a human? It sounds male."

"Yes, and I think I heard Margaret too," said Donny.

Damien clapped him on the shoulder, "I think you want to hear her, man, I don't think that is her."

Bria leaned toward the hole, "Wait I hear her too! She sounds mad. Let's see if we can widen the hole. Maybe we can hear where they're taking her or what their plans are."

"Droch don't speak English, so how will we know?" Said Damien.

Donny started to dig at the hole, "I hear English being spoken down there, it's hard to hear but it's not Margaret, that's for damn sure. It's someone else."

Damien began to think they were so desperate to find Margaret that they had both begun to hear things, but before he could point this out a female voice erupted from below. "Ok, now even I heard that. And you're right - she *is* mad."

Bria began to help Donny widen the hole, "Quickly, Damien, help!"

The stench as Margaret was carried into the cave burst into her nostrils waking her from her unconscious state. Her head throbbed as she hung upside down against the sweaty Droch back. Finally he stopped walking and he threw her to the ground. Her eyes adjusting to the darkness, she could see a cavern that would rival the Hall at the outpost. Hundreds of Droch surrounded her. There were so many, how could there be so many? What kind of evil were they dealing with to produce so many? Her eyes finally focusing rested upon a figure in the back of the cavern. Standing before her, in front of what appeared to be a throne, was the Droch who had haunted her dreams.

Forced to kneel in front of him she scraped the tops of her knees as she was shoved to the ground, she refused to show any sign of pain or weakness. "What the hell do you want from me you son of a bitch?"

Dragas shook his head, "Oh come now, is that any way to greet a long-lost friend Margaret?"

His voice was gravelly and deep. There was a Droch-like growl behind it, but the language was undeniably his own. He was human.

Margaret practically growled back, "We are not friends. And how do you know my name?"

Dragas stood up from his throne, tall and imposing, but noticeably smaller than the Droch who guarded the cave all around her. "I knew you in another lifetime, under a different name. Today you may call me Dragas." He crossed in front of her, his head tilted in an almost insect-like manner. "But, you do not remember me?"

Her face was flushed red with anger, "I remember you as the bastard who invaded my dreams and nearly had me killed."

He circled her like a vulture, "Now, now, such harsh words Margaret. Having you fall into the fissure was an unfortunate incident, but no harm."

"You're an ass. You disgust me!" She spat at his feet.
Dragas ignored her outburst and continued his diatribe.

"Let me tell you a story Margaret. Every 10 years at the base of the tree that lies in Kilkenny, a class of Locrian is born. Always in even numbers, always one at a time until one fateful day when, miraculously, two Locrian were born at the same time from the same root. This was as close as any Locrian had come to being siblings. In fact, they were considered twins, a boy and a girl.

The Locrian world believed this miracle would bring about a new era for the Locrian race that would allow them to finally shift the balance of good and evil back into their favor. As the children grew up they exhibited signs of their abilities and powers well before their naming ceremony. They held psychic abilities which allowed them to communicate with each other without speaking. They adapted skills much more quickly than their counterparts and excelled in their studies of weaponry. Their psychic abilities allowed them to sense when a friend was in danger during training.

All of these abilities are manifested in a few other Locrian throughout history but not to the strength and power that these two exhibited, and never this early on in life. One day, as the boy researched Locrian history, he realized that the Droch held special powers and abilities that the Locrian did not, and if the Locrian could tap into those abilities then they would be unstoppable. His discovery was not welcomed by the instructors at the abbey. His way of thinking was considered dangerous and unacceptable. He quickly became aware of a plot by the professors to cast him out into the darkness, leaving him for the Droch to do with what they pleased, so he hatched a plan of his own. Rather than being forced to leave the abbey, he decided to leave on his own terms. Under the cover of darkness one night he attempted to escape with his sister, but they were intercepted by the professors before they could escape. The same people who had sworn to protect him carelessly threw him out to the mercy of the Droch without a second thought, simply because they feared his way of thinking.

But the Droch did not kill the boy. He was able to use his telepathy to communicate with the beasts and he convinced them to spare his life by promising them invincibility. He learned through time that the Droch were the innocents and it was, in fact, the Locrian who were evil. The poor beasts had suffered for decades at the hands of the Locrian and they deserve to walk the earth free."

Margaret stared blankly at Dragas. "That is one hell of a story. You should write it down and publish that load of fiction."

Dragas bent down and moved in closely to Margaret, sending his hot breath down her neck.

"How is it that I can speak and they listen? Why do I look like a Droch but speak as you do? How do I know of your special abilities? It is simple, dear sister. We were born of the same root. I am your brother, Michael, and I have discovered the core of invincibility."

Margaret shook her head. *This is impossible, what was he talking about?* "No. Locrian don't have siblings." Gaining a bit more confidence, she nearly dared him to prove her wrong, "You can't possibly know where the tree is. There's no way."

"Let me tell you a secret, my darling twin. Invincibility, gaining knowledge, it is all so simple when you possess the abilities we do." He crossed the room to an unsuspecting Droch. Extending his claws he reached into the Droch's chest and ripped out its still-beating heart. The Droch fell to the ground in a heap. Not a single other Droch even seemed to notice the disturbance. Margaret wanted to turn away but refused to give him the satisfaction. He returned her stare, unblinking. "When I ingest this heart I gain all of my victim's memories and abilities," he said, grinning, then biting into it without a second thought. Blood ran down his wrist and forearm and dappled the ground beneath him. "I'll admit, I pay a price. I can no longer walk freely in the light, and my blood-red skin isn't the most flattering, but there are worse things I suppose."

He held out the heart, offering it to Margaret, daring her to refuse, daring her to accept. "Suit yourself." He tossed the remaining bit of heart into his fanged mouth, savoring it, as blood ran down his chin, splattering in the dirt in front of Margaret. Still she refused to avert her eyes. "The surge of strength is unbelievable. Consuming another creature's heart, doesn't just give you their knowledge, it also gives you their abilities, for a brief period of time. It was two Fae that gave their lives so that I could learn of the tree's location and garner the ability to pull you into my dreamscape when our psychic link wasn't enough to hold you."

Margaret's stomach boiled, bile worked its way up into her throat. "You disgust me. You're absolutely insane. If anything you are telling me is true…" she trailed off, almost not eating to finish the thought.

He brought his face within an inch of hers, the stench of breath so foul it brought tears to her eyes.

"Oh, but it's all true," he said, sneering through gritted teeth. "I have found that when Droch eat Locrian hearts, they become stronger; the ore has much less effect on them. If they consume enough hearts, they can become invincible. "Haven't you wondered what has been happening to all the Locrian bodies left on the battlefield?"

Margaret shook her head trying to distance herself from the foul beast. "You're a liar! I don't remember you, and I have had no abilities until recently so what you are saying doesn't add up."

He smirked, "Oh but you did. I'm guessing a Fae bound your powers after my escape and wiped your memory, as well as everyone in our class's memory, so that I would be forgotten."

She spoke as if to herself, "Who would do something like that?"

Then Margaret froze. A sinking feeling started in her gut, then traveled up her spine - her body trying to tell her brain something she didn't want to know, didn't want to accept. The fact that their class was only 79 instead of 80, the horrible, painful dreams and the dreams that often felt like long-lost memories, the secret that Myriad wanted to tell her. Was this what she had been hiding?

His yellow eyes bore into hers and his blood-slicked lips peeled back from his yellowed fangs into a gruesome, satisfied smile. "I see reality is starting to sink in. I have been working for years to try to communicate with you in order to bring you here, to show you what we could be capable of."

Margaret's eyes traced his body from the blood-spattered floor at his feet to his hideous eyes. This beast, not a man, was the most vile thing she had ever seen. How could they be connected in any way, let alone siblings?

She stood to face him, "What WE could be capable of? I will never be a part of this."

"Oh but you will, dear sister. You see, the world that I showed you in dreams is the reality that will come to pass. It is the future that awaits the world that you know. The time of the Locrian is ending. Your breed is dying. If you join me now, our combined powers could be limitless. We could rule this world - not just the Droch, not just the Locrian - everyone. Besides, once they find out that you and I are in essence the same, they will turn on you too. Their fear will take over, you'll see."

Margaret's head was spinning. The dreamscape was constructed by Dragas to show his plan for the future, not the actual future. And as for the other Locrian, she knew them better than he ever could. They would never turn their backs on her. He was bluffing.

He spun on his heels, "Oh, I can hear your thoughts sister. The dream was my doing, but the landscape was not. This is the future. We will burn the tree to the ground and there will be no Locrian left to relieve you. One by one you'll die and the world that held balance before will be consumed by the Droch, by darkness. You can spare yourself that agony if you reign at my side."

The bile in the back of Margaret's throat began to come up again. The stench of death lingering in the cave, combined with the odor of Dragas, was overpowering. She breathed through her mouth, willing her stomach to stop churning.

"There is no way in hell I will join you, I would rather die fighting against you than live an eternity beside you."

He turned his back to her, tired of the debate for now. "Given time for quiet contemplation, I am sure you will see my side of things," he said, sneering.

Her disgust was too much, and she spat on the floor at his feet again. This time his anger came to the foreground, and he wheeled around to face her, grabbing her throat. "You know, since you're my sister I was going to take it easier on you and lock you in the caves. It's a much more pleasant experience than the daylight caverns. But seeing how stubborn you are, maybe that's just what you need." He turned to the nearest Droch. "Throw her in the east side cavern." He snarled. "Maybe this will teach you some manners."

Fifty feet above, Damien, Bria and Donny had been listening. Most of the dialogue was too quiet and garbled to understand until whatever was down there began yelling. Donny was sure Margaret was giving him reasons to be pissed - she was a fighter, after all.

Bria started to lose patience, "How long do we stay here?"

Donny grabbed her shoulder and looked her in the eyes reassuringly, "We stay as long as is needed. This is our only hope for a lead, Bri. I know she's down there, I just don't know what is being said. I don't like waiting around any more than you do, but we need to stay here and hope that something will come through to give us an idea of where she'll end up."

Damien practically had his head down the hole, "Wait it's getting louder. I heard daylight cavern. What does that mean?"

"I'm hoping it means that daylight can reach it, which means we can reach it. But how do we find it?" Donny asked anxiously, hope creeping back into his voice.

Bria was thinking out loud, "The sun rises in the east and sets in the west so wouldn't something called the "daylight cavern" be exposed to as much sun as possible?"

"That's a place to start, Bri." Donny agreed. "Let's search the east side of the hillside first and keep your ears open in case there are more of those vents."

The trio took off at a jog, searching the hillside for clues that would lead them to their friend.

Meanwhile, in the caverns below, Margaret could tell she was being moved nearer to the surface.

She was relieved to be moving up rather than down, and began to actually hope that she could figure a way out of here. She turned towards the Droch that was dragging her along, if what Dragas said was true shouldn't she be able to communicate with these things too? She didn't have anything to lose at this point and she was growing weary of the silence. "You do know that the sunlight doesn't kill me, right? I wonder if you understand me. I guess you won't talk back, even if you did I doubt I would understand you. Why do you let Dragas push you around? He kills your kind to eat the hearts and that doesn't bother you?" Margaret shook her head, this was ridiculous. "I'm going crazy. I'm talking to a Droch. Margaret, get your shit together."

Her nerves were shot and she was exhausted. She needed to stop yelling at a Droch that couldn't even understand her and start finding a way out of this hole.

The Droch stopped and pointed at a door. Margaret opened it and the Droch shoved her

314

inside the small room, slamming the door
shut to avoid being exposed to the sunlight
already coming into the cavern.

She surveyed the room and was met with floor
to ceiling bars on the east side, carved
into the rocky hillside of the mountain
allowing a full stream of sunlight into the
confined space. The other three walls were
also carved into the hillside but the door
she had just been thrown through was steel
and had a small window at the top. Turning,
she saw the withered remains of a human-type
figure with a hole in their chest. This time
the vomit that had ben welling up in the
back of her throat couldn't be contained.
She retched long and hard, falling on her
knees and grasping at what she now realized
was a very empty stomach. She felt better
and worse at the same time. Slowly she sat
upright, and wiped her face with the back of
her hand. As she did, her eyes drew
magnetically back to the corpse and she
realized immediately that it was Fae. She
was suddenly overcome with sadness - not for
her own situation or fate, but for the
innocent Fae who met their end in this hell
hole. She knelt down next to the Fae and
said a prayer that Myriad had taught her
when she was a little girl and had come
across a bird in the abbey's courtyard that
had broken its neck when it flew into the
stone wall. She had cried as soon as she saw

315

it, and Myriad had taken the bird in her hands and recited the prayer that would set its soul free. But the memory quickly disintegrated into rage as she recalled everything Dragas had said about Myriad, and that she now understood to be true.

She ran to the door and began to bang against the steel, yelling, "You ass-hole! When I get out of here, and I will, I will have your head. I will rip the heart from your chest and watch as the light leaves your eyes."

"Would you shut up! You have no idea who you are dealing with. And just a tip, you may want to save your energy. That cavern heats up to over one hundred degrees over the course of the day. After a few days without water and food I'm sure Dragas will get you to do whatever he wants. The room won't kill you but it will break you just as it did the Fae. Now shut up!"

Margaret was taken aback. The voice had been undeniably inside her own head. She peeked through the window in the door and saw the Droch who had dragged her to this cell sitting just past the rays of sun. He stared up at her and the edges of his scaly mouth seemed to turn up just a bit. Had that been his voice? Was that possible?

She backed away from the door slowly and squatted in the shade. "I'm losing my mind." It was already getting fairly warm in the cavern and she hadn't had any water since the night before. This was not going to go well.

Beneath the cliff Donny stopped running, coming to a sudden halt.

Bria came up short behind him nearly barreling him over. "What?"

He looked towards the cliff face, "She's up there. I just heard something."

The three paused to listen. It was faint but there was definitely banging and some muffled yelling.

Damien's archer eyes scoured the cliff - it was flat, dead flat. "Ok, so at least we know she's somewhere up there. The real question is, how in the hell do we get up to her?"

"Good question," said Donny.

They split up and began to search every inch of the cliff-side for a way up the steep embankment. It appeared to be sheer all the way to the top.

There has to be a way to get up there, thought Donny. He would not let her down, not when they were this close.

The temperature in the cavern was rising quicker than Margaret had anticipated. She sat in the corner where the sun hadn't fully reached yet, attempting to keep herself as cool as possible. As she looked around she noticed dark scorch marks in the corner. This is where the previous inhabitants of the cavern had died in an attempt to seek refuge from the sun. This is where they would hide, praying it wouldn't reach them, inevitably finding out that it did. This realization proved one thing to her, the Droch were not animals, as she once thought. They had emotions and feelings, a need to survive. This made what Dragas was doing even more psychotic than she had originally thought.

As the sun's rays began to invade her corner the temperature became just short of unbearable. Having lived in Ireland her entire life, she could not remember a day where she felt this uncomfortable from heat.

Why is the temperature rising so rapidly, especially this far up the mountain? She stood, pacing the room, and noticed a sheen on the wall. It looked like a metal. She touched it in an attempt to figure out what material it was, and quickly pulled her hand back. Once the sun reached the walls they acted like a conductor. She was basically sitting in an oven.

Now she was desperate. She walked over to the bars, they didn't shine like the walls did. *It must have been discovered while digging out the cavern. Who would have thought a bunch of Droch would know how to do something like this?*

Down on the ground there appeared to be no visible way to get up the cliff side. Donny squatted down and began throwing his knives at the ground while he processed everything. They stuck in the ground, he pulled them out, and threw them again, over and over. He was getting frustrated. She was right there and yet they had no way to get to her. Enraged, he threw the knife at the rock face and instead of clanging to the ground, it stuck.

It took him a moment to realize what had happened. He walked over to the rock face and pulled out the knife. "What on earth?"

Damien looked up, confused, "I've never seen a knife go through a rock before."

"I'm not sure this is rock. This is something else, almost like solid clay." He scanned the cliff again. "Let me try something." Donny picked up two knives and threw them a bit higher up on the rock and they stuck as well. He climbed up onto the knives and hung limp with his body weight. "Yes, it holds." He jumped down.

Donny turned toward the others, "Do you guys remember when we were younger and the training exercises were more like an obstacle course to build our endurance?" They both nodded. "Do you remember the peg board we had to climb?"

Bria began to understand, "Oh! The one where we had two pegs and we had to move them up using only our arms and then back down placing them in holes along the way?"

Donny exclaimed, "Yes!"

"Yea, I hated that," Said Bria.

He smiled, "Well get ready to hate it again. We're each going to use two knives to climb the cliff face like we did on that peg board."

Damien's gaze went all the way up the wall. It was far. Extremely far. He rubbed the back of his neck, "Well shit, Donny." He looked him in the eye and saw desperation. He needed to do this. THEY needed to do this. "Ok I'm in if this is the only way to get to her."

"Yes! Thank you, man! Bri?" Donny pleaded.

She sighed, "Me too."

Donny stuck four more knives into the cliff side. "Come on, we have to get moving. It may take a while and we have to get back before sundown."

Studying the cavern Margaret realized something; the bars were spaced in such a way so as to allow the maximum amount of sunlight into the space, which also meant they were far enough apart that she could fit through them. However, it was a straight drop of at least 200 feet to the ground. She considered climbing upward, but realized the

cliff side was completely flat in both
directions. She walked back to the door
where her captor had been sitting and saw
that no one was there. They must be
confident in their jail cell.

———————————

"Donny, this sucks," grunted Bria.

He climbed a bit more, straining to pull
himself up "Yeah it does but I think being
trapped by the Droch is worse, don't you?."

Bria looked up at him, "Ok, I'll shut up."

———————————

Margaret kept looking down; she couldn't see
the bottom of the cliff. She reached through
the bars to feel the edge, it was smooth but
oddly soft, almost like clay. She leaned
closer, pressed her face into the bars,
reached her arm out and punched into the
side of the rock face. It gave way beneath
her fist leaving a divot in the side of the
cliff face. "Maybe I could hang over the
side and use my feet to create handholds all
the way down," she thought out loud.

"Or you could use these."

For a moment she thought the Droch's voice was back in her head, then she looked over the edge and saw Donny, Damien and Bria all hanging on the side of the cliff. Donny, hanging by one arm, removed two knives from his belt and tossed them in her direction.

She snagged them while still holding onto the bars, "I have never been so damn happy to see anyone as I am to see you three right now."

"We're glad to see you as well," said Bria breathlessly. "Now let's get the hell out of here."

Donny inched over to the cave bars and hovered just beneath her, "Use your feet to create the initial grooves for support while you dig your knives in. It doesn't take too much to break the surface. As you move downward keep digging your toes in to give your arms a break."

She eased through the bars and over the side, making herself parallel to Donny.

He winked at her, "You ready?"

She nodded vigorously, "Never been more ready for anything in my life."

It took about 20 minutes to scale back down the cliff. As soon as their feet were on the ground she ran to Donny and leapt into his arms. "I never want to know that feeling again."

"What feeling?" Asked Donny.

Tears began to well up in Margaret's eyes, "The feeling that I may never see you again. I love you Donny."

The grin on Donny's face was unmeasurable. "I love you too Margaret."

He leaned down and kissed her for a long time, never wanting to let her go again.

Damien cleared his throat, "Um, guys. That's awesome and all but we should probably get moving. The sun is starting to hang a little low in the sky and I for one want to put some distance between us and the Droch.

Bria pushed forward, "Besides, I haven't gotten my hug yet."

Margaret ran to her best friend and hugged her hard, then turned to Damien. He held out his hand but she batted it away and hugged him too. "Formalities are gone. You risked your life to save mine."

"Damien is right, we need to get going," said Donny.

"Sure, when she's hugging me you're suddenly in a hurry," Damien said as Donny punched him in the arm.

"Come on." They were sprinting back towards the forest line near the entrance to the cave when they heard a deafening roar.

Margaret stopped in her tracks, knowing the sound was too loud to have been from within the cave, "Where the hell did that come from?"

Bria turned as she kept running, "Vents in the ground for air, you can hear through them when it's loud enough. That was how we found you. My guess is they have realized you're gone."

Margaret nodded and took off again. She wanted to fill them in on everything that had happened but there would be time for that later. They had to get back to the outpost before sundown.

Donny turned suddenly and stopped, "Oh, I almost forgot, here." Donny handed Margaret her broadsword. "Figured you'd want it, just in case."

She kissed him on the cheek, strapped it to her back, and kept going.

————————————————

Craine was in the tower overlooking the field. Dorien climbed the stairs and stood next to him. "Still holding out hope?"

Craine kept his gaze on the horizon, "Yes, aren't you?"

Dorien was hopeful but he knew if they were not back by sundown they wouldn't be coming back. "We need them," he said.

Craine looked at Dorien, his eyes deliberate, "The world needs them, the group of them, there is something special there. Even Damien, who has always been a top marksmen, has grown in his specialty since their arrival. If the four of them do not return it could be the downfall of this outpost."

They stood in silence. Dorien's eyes twitched toward something in his peripheral vision, but it disappeared. A bird, perhaps. He sighed and shifted his attention back to the battlefield. Another flicker of movement drew his eyes to the far corner of the field. "Craine, over there!"

Craine leaned over the edge of the outpost, "Raise the gate, they have returned!"

The entire outpost came alive, someone had returned from the caves! The gates were lifted and Margaret, Donny, Bria and Damien were all greeted by thunderous applause. Craine and Dorien came down to greet them and made their way to the front of the crowd. "We are so glad you made it back. You'll have to tell us all about your adventure, after you rest. Sundown approaches."

"Rather blunt isn't he?" Said Bria as they walked towards the barracks.

"Eh, go easy on him, the past few years have been difficult on all of us. You're new, but given time you'll understand," Damien said.

Damien left the trio at the bunkhouse and continued on his own. Margaret looked at her friends, "I need a shower."

"I think we all do," Said Bria. She leaned over to sniff Donny, "Some of us more than others." Donny started to make a comment but then smelled himself and realized she was right. They all grabbed fresh clothes and headed to the showers.

Margaret stood under the hot water feeling truly relaxed for the first time in more than 24 hours. She didn't want to eat or fight, she just wanted to sleep but she knew she had to fuel up and get back out there. Another battle waited. She placed her goo-covered clothing in her bag she brought to return to the abbey and made her way to the dining hall.

Craine headed her off on the way, "I'll be brief because I know you need to eat." There was that winning personality again. "You were clearly the target last night. Now I know I can't afford to keep you out of the fight, you have brought more confidence to this group in 48 hours than I have in 100 years. But I will not let you on the field."

Margaret opened her mouth to protest.

Craine continued, "You will be in the tower with Bria and Damien to protect you. You can show us your archery skills from there. I understand you are better with a broadsword but this is my decision. You leave tomorrow and when you return we will be better prepared. I will be able to focus on the fight knowing you are protected and off the main battlefield. Under no circumstances are you to leave the tower, understood?"

Margaret nodded.

"Go and eat, the attack begins soon."

She walked into the dining hall feeling a bit defeated. She wanted to be with her people, the ones she had helped safely make it through two nights of fighting. She wouldn't be stupid enough to fall for the same trick again. They would not be able to ambush her like that. But what if they used someone else to get to her and they were injured or suffered. No, Craine was right; she would do the right thing and stay in the tower. Once they were all safely back at the abbey they could develop a plan to protect not just her but all of the Locrian and the Kilkenny outpost more effectively.

Donny and Bria were already at a table with Damien. The good thing about all of this was that Bria could apparently talk to Damien now, and they sat comfortably close to each other at the long, wooden table - laughing at some retelling of their journey that day.

"Everything alright?" Asked Donny with that knowing look on his face.

Margaret plopped down next to him. "Yes and no, Craine just ordered me to stay in the tower tonight with Damien and Bria."

The three of them looked at her as if waiting for a bomb to go off.

Bria dropped her fork and touched her friend's hand. "And you're ok with that?"

Margaret nodded, "I wasn't when he was ordering me, I don't take orders well."

They all looked at the table.

"Yea, I know it's not a secret. But he's right I'm a target and I don't want to endanger anyone else," said Margaret.

Donny looked into her eyes, "You were the target last night, but it could be anyone today."

She shook her head, "No Donny, it's not random. I can't explain right now but it's better for me to be off the field right now. I'll still have your back from up there."

They gave each other a knowing glance, and dropped the subject in favor of their dinners.

After dinner, Margaret walked with Donny for a few minutes on her way to trade in her broadsword for a long bow. "Are you going to fill me in on what happened?"

"I will. I promise, but not tonight. It's too exhausting to recount and we'll have plenty of time later. Besides, I haven't even had time to process it all myself yet."

Donny accepted her decision with a hug. "Don't take this the wrong way but I'm glad you'll be in the tower."

Margaret's eyebrows arched and her lips tightened.

Recovering quickly Donny said, "Not because I don't want you fighting with me, but because I know you'll be safer and I can fight better for it." He grasped both of her hands and struggled to get out the next few words. "Mags I couldn't think, not until I found you. I was lost without you. The thought that I wouldn't see you ever again was the most terrifying thing I've ever experienced."

Margaret nodded and choked out, "I know the feeling."

Donny kissed her lightly, "I love you Margaret and tonight will be fine, and you will be fine. Tomorrow we'll all go home and try to keep doing this."

Margaret hugged him one last time before reporting to the armory. Donny watched her trade out her favorite weapon for her least favorite. He knew how hard it was for her.

He walked her to the base of the tower, "I'll see you when it's done."

She nodded, "Just don't blame me if I accidentally shoot you in the butt."

Donny turned with a smirk, "I will 100 percent blame you."

He smiled and exited the gate as she climbed the tower. Bria and Damien were already up there. "Hey, you ok?" asked Bria.

Margaret followed Donny's movement to his station, not taking her eyes off of him, "Yea, just try not to show me up too much ok?"

Damien nudged her to try to lighten the mood, "Not a chance."

Once the fighting started she fell back into her element. Her vision kicked into high gear once again but still didn't come close to Bria or Damien's talents. Still, she managed to avoid hitting any of her own people, and that was something. The Droch had definitely dwindled, she could tell they had made a dent in their numbers over the past few days. Either that, or they were being exceptionally cautious. As she fell into the groove she began to relax and enjoy herself until… *"Oh sister, you should not have escaped. Next time I get my hands on you you will not be treated so carefully. You WILL rule beside me and help me conquer the world, but as my slave not my equal."*

The voice froze her with an arrow pulled taut against her bow. Slowly she released the tension of the weapon and stared at the horizon where she knew he was, *"What makes you think you'll capture me again?"*

"I know your weaknesses." Visions of Bria, Donny and now Damien flashed through her head. *"You will give anything to keep them from harm, foolish girl. You will lose because your heart is weak. I have nothing to lose."*

The sun began to peek over the horizon. *"Until next time, dear sister."*

His voice brought her back to the cave, to his foul stench and blood oozing between his sharpened teeth and the familiar feeling of nausea overcame her.

The fighting had ceased and Bria noticed her friend's greenish pallor and blank stare, "Hey." Margaret jumped, startled. "Sorry, you faded out there for a bit, are you alright?"

"Yes," she said, color slowing coming back to her face. "Sorry, I'm worn out from everything. My mind is full and tired."

"Yea… that must be it." Bria decided to drop it for now but she knew when her friend was hiding something. "Well let's get showered and changed before the transport comes. I don't know about you but I could sleep for a few days."

Margaret yawned as if on cue, "Yea."

After cleaning up the group reported to breakfast and waited for the transport. "I really wish you all didn't have to go, it's been so helpful having you fight alongside us these past few nights," Damien said. "Not having anyone disappear or die has been an added bonus. Well permanently disappear anyway," he said, smiling at Margaret.

Margaret smiled back, she was glad they had found such a good friend in Damien and she couldn't help but feel a little guilty for leaving. "We'll be back before you know it."

Just then Liam appeared in the doorway of the dining hall, "Transport is here."

They stood and gave hugs and said their goodbyes to their new friend.

Damien hugged Bria last, and as she turned to go he stopped her, "Bria. I wanted to give you something."

Margaret and Donny were waiting in the doorway for her, "Go ahead guys I'll be there in a minute."

They nodded and headed toward the transport and Bria turned to Damien who had pulled something out of his pocket.

"What's that?" She asked.

He looked down, rubbing it, as Bria could tell that he did often. "This is the first arrow-head I ever broke off in the head of a Droch. I ran out to get it after the sun had come up; I mark my arrows on the tips so that I can track my kills." She cocked her brow at him, "What can I say, I'm competitive. Anyway I've kept it in my pocket ever since. It's kind of my good luck charm."

Bria was confused, "Why do you want me to have it?"

Damien took a deep breath, "I'm hoping it will bring me luck again." He leaned in and softly kissed her on the lips. "Something to remember me by and bring you back to me."

Bria flushed in the cheeks as she took the token, grasping it tightly.

"Thank you. I will keep it safe." She turned to leave and then ran back to hug him. "Please be safe until I return." She looked him in the eye and returned his kiss.

"Until you return," he nodded.

Bria ran to catch the transport and Damien smiled after her. He now had a new reason to live for all eternity.

Chapter 20

The mood in the transport returning to the abbey was in stark contrast to the trip to the outpost just a few days earlier. All 79 members of the class were returning home, victorious. Margaret was proud of her classmates and their defeat of the Droch. As their leader she had watched them grow their skill sets in recent weeks and face a daunting challenge, passing their "final exam" with flying colors. Now they had to get back to work fine tuning their skills, honing their abilities, and creating battle strategies to continue to defeat the Droch.

Margaret tried to enjoy the excitement and the camaraderie that surrounded her. On the outside she smiled but on the inside she was torn apart with worry. Dragas was in her head, literally, and she had to find a way to keep him out for good, for everyone's sake. The more Margaret thought about Dragas and the loss of her early memories, the more confused and upset she became. Seeing how dangerous he was, how disgusting, made her grateful for having her memory wiped. But

337

they were her memories and she deserved to know the entire truth. The secrets stopped today.

When the transport pulled up to the abbey she let the group exit first with Donny, Bria and herself bringing up the rear. The professors were all waiting to see how they fared and the smiles on their faces said it all. They had completed their task. They had done what was asked of them with no casualties or serious injuries. All the students and professors joyfully applauded as the three of them exited the transport. Margaret made her way through the crowd getting high fives from the younger Locrian and pats on the back from her peers. She nodded and smiled all the while scanning the crowd for her Myriad. Finally the celebration died down and she was able to approach the professor, "We need to talk when you can." Myriad's face changed instantly.

Nodding, she replied, "Alright, meet in my classroom in 30 minutes?"

Margaret agreed and turned toward Bria and Donny, "I would like it if the two of you were there too, I don't want to have to repeat myself." She turned and headed towards her room to unpack and gather her thoughts from the past three days.

Margaret arrived at Myriad's room before anyone else. She walked to the balcony just outside of the classroom and stared out over the hills like she had done hundreds of times. She was confused and wanted answers, but she also knew that Myriad's actions were only meant to protect her.

Myriad approached the classroom and saw her standing there as she always had, but this time she did not approach her, she knew Margaret would come in on her own.

Margaret heard her professor open the door and waited a few moments before heading inside. Myriad was waiting for her and for the first time it was awkward being in the room with the professor. The air was tense but Donny and Bria arrived right on time, laughing and talking, breaking the awkward silence in the room.

Bria looked from Myriad to Margaret, "Wow, you could cut the tension with a knife."

Donny elbowed her in the ribs.

Myriad's expression was serious, "Now that we are all here, how would you like to begin Margaret?"

Margaret took a deep breath, "I'll begin with what happened to me on the battlefield, but I will need you, professor, to fill in the gaps with needed information."

Myriad's face fell into deep concern, "What happened to you?"

Margaret's gaze softened at her worry. "I was taken captive by the Droch during the second night of battle."

"Wait, what!?"

Myriad looked to Donny and Bria who nodded in confirmation.

"How could this have happened?" Inquired Myriad.

"The Droch had a plan to isolate me, and take me to the caves. I was their intended target."

Myriad had to sit down, she couldn't believe what she was hearing. "How on earth did you escape? How are they organized?"

Margaret shook her head, "I will get to all that. I want to start with the first night of fighting. We discovered that I developed abilities, that I was able to move at incredible speeds and sense when others were in danger, to the degree that Craine said he rarely saw this type of ability in named Locrian, let alone an unnamed student."

Myriad looked down at the floor. The Fae's response confirmed that she had known about Margaret's abilities, and her anger flared briefly, but she continued. "Regardless I took this news in stride. Because of my new found talents we were able to make a sizable dent in the Droch population and we all made it through the night. The second night started out the same as the first but the Droch appeared more hesitant to attack because of the impact we had made the night before. Just before dawn I saw Cassie in trouble by the tree line. A pair of Droch were luring her out and away from the group. I went after her, just as they suspected I would, and we killed the two Droch attacking her. As we headed back to the outpost I was cut off from the group by four Droch. Cassie returned to help me and we were able to kill two more, but she was injured and we were overpowered. I ordered Cassie to run and they knocked me unconscious in order to capture me."

Donny cringed remembering how he felt seeing her carried away to the caves.

She looked directly at Myriad before continuing, "They took me into the caves to a cavern several hundred feet in diameter. It was filled with Droch and their leader who called himself Dragas.

Myriad was confused, "Wait the Droch spoke to you?"

Margaret's memories came flooding back to her, "Yes, the Droch spoke to me. Dragas was the one invading my dreams trying to get to me so that he could speak to me. He has an ability to sense my presence when I am near; his abilities appear to be telepathic in nature."

Myriad stood quickly and crossed to the other side of the room, gathering her thoughts as she stared out the window. Margaret continued, "He wanted to tell me a story about the Locrian tree and the unique situation that surrounded the birthing of one of the classes of Locrian. He told me in one of the classes that a pair of children was born at the same time from one root, that the Fae present during their birth called them siblings, twins."

"What? That's impossible, that doesn't happen. Does it?" Asked Donny suddenly chiming in.

Margaret's gaze never left Myriad, "I said the same thing. He continued to tell me that these children were the only set of siblings in Locrian history. These children exhibited early talents and abilities that other Locrian did not. It was as if they were born with their gifts instead of having them bestowed on them during the naming ceremony. According to Dragas, everything was going well until the boy decided to experiment with the concept of not only becoming immortal as a Locrian, but also invincible. He was convinced that he could find something to make the Locrian invincible, something having to do with the Droch, that would forever shift the balance in their favor. But the boy was criticized for this and seen as dangerous because the professors believed that no being should ever be truly invincible."

Margaret crossed over to the window where her professor stood. "The balance between good and evil can shift slightly but no one side can become truly invincible for the world, as we know it, to continue to exist," whispered Myriad.

She touched her professor on the shoulder getting her to look her in the eye. "The professors saw the boy as a threat and decided to cast him out at night to let the Droch take care of their problem. But the boy, given his special talents, found out about this plan and tried to escape earlier in the night with his sister in tow. The professors caught him and exiled him the darkness, assuming the Droch would finish him off. His sister remained at the abbey, her memory, and those of her classmates, altered to delete his very existence."

Bria's eyebrows furrowed, "I don't know Margaret, that seems kind of out there."

Margaret looked at her friend and nodded, "I thought so too. What he told me next was the most unbelievable part of the story. He told me that I was the girl and he was the boy, my brother. That we are the twins and that with our combined abilities we could overthrow the Locrian race and rule the world."

"What? That's absurd, you can't possibly believe that, can you? He is just trying to get to you, to mess with your head." Donny shook his head. "I just don't believe it."

Margaret shrugged, "It's honestly hard not to believe Donny. He can establish a psychic link with the Droch and communicate with them. She paused for a moment. "I have it too. I didn't do it intentionally but one of the Droch and I spoke telepathically. I suddenly have abilities that I never had. I thought it was my adrenaline but I did things on that battlefield that you yourself witnessed. The more I thought about it the more it added up. Why do you think we only have 79 in our class instead of 80? Why was I able to control myself in the dreamscape and communicate with the Droch? I hate to say it but it all adds up."

"Erase our memories? Who would do such a thing? Who COULD do such a thing?" Bria looked puzzled for a moment, "And why would you only have your powers now though if all of this was true, wouldn't you have had them all along?"

"Dragas had a theory on that as well. He assumes that not only was our memories altered, but that my powers were bound. I realized if this were true, the reason my abilities suddenly presented themselves might be because I am close to my 21st birthday or I needed them in the heat of battle. But I thought to myself, this is ridiculous, who could do that?"

Margaret looked back towards the window where her professor stood.

Realizing what Margaret was insinuating Donny and Bria leapt to their feet, "Margaret don't be ridiculous. Myriad would never do anything like that to you, or to any of us."

Margaret never wavered with her gaze, "It's true isn't it professor?"

Donny and Bria stood frozen in place.

"It's true," said Myriad. "But there is more to the story than what he told you."

Margaret felt relief at her words. She looked at Bria and Donny, who were clearly still trying to process all the information themselves, "I expect there is and I need to hear it."

Myriad turned at this, and looked shocked, "You aren't mad."

"I was at first, and then I just felt hurt and betrayed. I trust you as much as I trust them," gesturing to Donny and Bria. "But I had some time to think when I was captured and I realized as much as you care for us, there is no way you would do this unless you absolutely felt you had to."

"I am so glad you see it that way, and in all reality, it wasn't my decision to make, but I still followed orders so that is my burden to bear."

Margaret understood, grateful for the honesty. "What more do we not know?"

Myriad's small frame visibly relaxed, and she sat back down before beginning, "I will start with the night you were born. I never told you, but I was there, I was able to name you. Another Fae named him, I refused, even then something didn't feel right about him."

She nodded, "He said it had been Michael."

Myriad smiled a little at the memory, "Yes, I was not assigned to the tree at that time, I was teaching here at the abbey, but I was visiting a friend of mine who tended to the tree and happened to be there for the birthing. I was the only one to witness your birth. When we got back to the abbey we began to notice drastic differences between the two of you. You always attracted the other children, while he repelled them and enjoyed being alone, unless he was with you. He hated that you had friends and when you were younger, Donny, he scratched your face pretty badly because you were friends with Margaret. As you got older your powers grew.

I knew that you were the great hope for the Locrian and I still believe that. What you said was true, we did cast him out, but only because his actions towards you were beginning to truly scare us. We caught him trying to feed you the heart of a pig that he had gutted; he had camouflaged it to appear as if it was an apple. His abilities at the time were more advanced and pronounced than yours. Attempting to harm you was last straw for us - we had to save you from him. The night that he tried to escape with you, you were not even awake. He had put you in a trance of some sort; you were not leaving on your own accord. We did what we had to do to protect you."

Margaret nodded and shivered at the thought of him, "I understand that, he is a vile and a horrible creature. But why wipe our memories and bind my powers? If I was ten or eleven-years-old I could have been told and reasoned with I'm sure."

Myriad grasped her hands, but Margaret pulled them away gently, the sting of being lied to was still present. "We weren't concerned with you knowing the truth so much as we were worried that he could get inside your head and manipulate you because of the telepathic abilities you shared. So I bound your powers, the spell was to be released on your 21st birthday, but maybe being near

Michael again triggered them a bit earlier than intended. I wiped your memory because you were extremely close and we thought it would cause you less pain to never know he existed. Because I erased your memory of him I had to erase everyone else's too."

Margaret took a moment to process, "He is the Droch's advantage. The way he communicates with them is flawless. They are far more organized than we've ever seen. He's found a way to eventually make himself and the Droch invincible. They are eating the hearts of Droch, Locrian and Fae to make themselves stronger, and it's only a matter of time before they're successful. Dragas became a Droch through the consumption of Droch hearts and by doing so he has become some sort of Locrian-Droch hybrid."

"I always knew he was evil but I never expected anything like this," said Myriad. "We truly believed he died the night we sent him away."

"There's more. By eating the hearts of his victims he gains their memories and abilities. The abilities he acquires are temporary but I am not sure how long they last."

Margaret turned to Myriad, sadness was written on her face. "He knows where the tree is because of a Fae. He killed them and ate their heart. I saw the body where I was being held."

Myriad nodded grimly, "I assumed as much. Dorien informed me of two Fae who had gone missing, but I was holding out hope."

Bria looked shaken, "Is there any good news?" She asked with a nervous grin.

Margaret replied, "He has a weakness."

Donny looked at Margaret, "What is that?"

"Me."

Chapter 21

Over the next week everyone returned to
their classes and old routines, but it felt
different. They were all the more confident
and the fear of the unexpected was gone.
They were more unified than ever and the
competition between them were fun and light
hearted. Everyone was driven to help one
another succeed.

However, in the back of everyone's mind were
thoughts of returning to the outpost, to the
fight. They all thought they belonged there.
They had made such a difference in three
days time; they could be doing even more
now. Training began to feel like an absurd
formality when they knew the actual effect
their skills had in real life.

Bria was the most concerned about those at
the outpost. She kept Damien's token with
her at all times. Margaret had loved seeing
her friend with Damien but she never thought
about how it would affect her once they
left. The worry consumed Bria.

Bria was only with Damien a short time, but she felt she connected with him in a way that not even Donny and Margaret would understand. She prayed that he was alive and safe. Holding the arrow head tightly in her hand she sat next to Margaret, "Six more months of this is too much."

Margaret understood the way her friend felt. She was grateful that Donny was here with her and not in harm's way but she had a similar need and desire to be there with everyone else. "I agree, I want to be there too."

Bria stared at the arrowhead. "Do you think he's really ok?"

Margaret looked at her friend, "Damien? Absolutely, he's one of the toughest people I've met. But I understand why you're worried, it seems like we're at a serious disadvantage and they're facing that head-on every day. We need to stay positive Bri, we'll be out there soon."

"I just hope it's soon enough," she thought.

Bria paused "I want to believe you, but you aren't facing the challenge that I am, at least Donny is here and safe. I know I haven't known him long but I feel so connected to him. What if I met the perfect guy and I never see him again?" Her voice broke at the question and she looked upward to keep the tears in her eyes from breaking loose.

Margaret took her friends hands in hers, "It won't happen that way. I know."

"How do you know?" She asked staring at the sky.

Margaret couldn't explain it but when she thought of Bria and her future with Damien she saw happiness instead of sadness. There was no way that it would end in bloodshed. "I just do, trust me on this."

"I know you have super powers and all but you don't know everything," snapped Bria.

Margaret was taken aback.

"I'm sorry, I know you mean well, I'm just on edge."

"I understand."

Feeling a bit awkward, Bria changed the subject, "What about you?"

Margaret looked at her confused, "What about me?"

"You and Donny, all in love and everything, how is that going?"

Margaret smiled and shrugged, "It's good. We haven't really even had time to process it with everything going on. We've been so caught up in planning the next move and dealing with my satanic brother that we haven't even really talked about us."

"Mags, we're going to be dealing with all of this for quite some time, if you can't learn to live a little now you may miss the opportunity."

"Wow, so profound." She cooed with a sideways smile at her friend.

"Shove it, you know what I mean. He's hot so take advantage of it while you can."

Margaret laughed, "I know you're right, maybe I'll surprise him with an under-the-stars sort of date tonight, just us."

Bria smiled, "Ok, SO cheesy, but do it! How much alone time do you think you'll get once we're out there full time?"

Bria was right; in fact Margaret realized that she and Donny had never even had a real date. Heading back to her dorm that night to shower and change, she slipped a note under

Donny's door. She told him to meet in the spot where they used to play hide-and-seek as kids. Back then it frustrated Bria to no end because she could never find them. Eventually she would give up and play something else. Donny and Margaret were always so patient and waited her out that she never figured out where they were hiding. Margaret smiled just thinking about it, she hadn't been there in ages. It was one of the only areas along the wall of the abbey that you couldn't see into from the windows upstairs. Layers of ivy had overgrown the area giving it a tent-like feeling, but there was enough of a view overhead to let in moonlight and stargaze.

She gathered up some sandwiches from the dining hall and went to their spot. It was dark outside so it would be even more secluded. She spread out a blanket and waited for him, both nervous and excited as she spotted him in the distance. Her heart skipped a beat.

Donny approached with a huge grin on his face. He had wanted to be truly alone with her since they kissed in the hallway. "Well aren't you full of surprises." He said as he ducked down into their old familiar hideaway.

She shrugged, "I just realized today that we've never even had a real date, and I felt that more than enough time had passed to have one."

He sat down next to her, "We tend to do things a bit backwards don't we."

Margaret looked concerned, "What do you mean?"

"I mean, we kiss, we fall in love and then we date. Seems a bit backwards to me."

Margaret laughed. "Well it's not like we lead 'normal' lives."

"This is true, and it's not like you haven't had a lot on your mind. Speaking of which, how are you doing with all that? I haven't even talked with you about it since you spoke with Myriad that night."

"I'm dealing with it the best that I can. I don't have any feelings towards Dragas, whether he is my brother or not has no bearing. I will see him dead at the end of this. He is pure evil and must be stopped."

He wasn't expecting to hear the venom in her voice. "Still, it has to be hard on you."

Softening her tone, "It is, but mostly because I'm gravely concerned about how powerful he is and may become. I'm not sure we can stop him."

Donny touched her face; she was even more beautiful in the moonlight. "You can, I know you can. I saw you do some incredible things Margaret, and you don't even have your powers yet. You could be even stronger than he is. Maybe that's why you were born together. You are the greatest light I have ever known. Maybe you are destined to fight his darkness."

She began to blush at his words and his touch.

She looked at the ground, "I'm so bad at this."

"What?" asked Donny.

Margaret sighed, "Dating. Give me a sword and I can handle any man. Get me alone with one and I'm complete goo."

Donny smiled, "But you're my goo. And correct me if I'm wrong but isn't the 'goo' feeling a good one?"

She smiled back at him, "I guess so, but it's a feeling I'm not used to and it throws me off."

Donny made sure she could see the sincerity in his eyes before he spoke again. "Margaret, I have loved you since we were little but I didn't know how to say it, or how to ask you out or anything. So I remained your friend. A friend you beat up and beat in general because that was what was easy. But I realized that I can love you and be with you as you always were. The reason I fell in love with you is not because you were a gooey gushy girl, although that looks great on you as well, but because you're a total badass and it's hot. You're beautiful, confident and strong and you've inspired not only me and Bri but our entire class. I know that being a Locrian is your passion in life, as it is all of ours, but you have a gift unlike any that I've seen or probably will ever see. I'm fine coming second to that gift, all I ask is you come back to me every night and love me just the same."

Margaret was dumbfounded; how was it possible for her to love him even more? She stared into his eyes and kissed him, savoring the taste of his mouth, the smell of the air around them, the feeling of the grass - she wanted to be present. She wanted to remember this moment forever.

Their lips parted and they looked into each other's eyes, "Donny, I love you so much. And I hope you don't take this the wrong way, but I need you to know that I'm just not ready yet."

"Not ready for? Oh! That. Don't worry, I'm not either."

Margaret released the breath she was holding.

"It's not that I haven't thought about it, but we still haven't really had a chance to just be us, I don't want to rush into anything."

"Mags I get it, I feel the same way. I love you just the same. When the time is right we'll both know."

Margaret nodded, relieved but at a loss now that the moment was over. "Sandwich?"

Donny laughed, "I thought you'd never ask, I've been smelling them since I got here. My growling stomach almost ruined the mood."

After they ate they lay on the blanket to watch the moon rise overhead.

Margaret thought she might finally understand the meaning of the word bliss. "It's nearly a full moon, I can't believe it's been almost two weeks since we were there."

"It is really beautiful. Because the moon dictates our lives I often don't appreciate it for its simple beauty."

"You always seem to know just what to say." She looked at him under the moons soft glow, "Don't you think it's crazy how we're driven by the moon as they are? How we're drawn to it just the same?"

Donny shrugged, "Well, it's the Droch that drive us, and the moon that drives them. It's a vicious cycle."

They laid in silence for a few minutes watching the sky and holding one another. "Thank you for tonight, Donny."

He leaned down and kissed her forehead, "You as well. I don't think my heart could be more full. My stomach either."

She punched his shoulder.

"Hey, just being honest."

They stayed that way, watching the moon in silence, both savoring the rare moment of true relaxation. It was well past midnight when Donny walked Margaret back to her room and kissed her goodnight.

"How did I get so lucky?" She asked.

"Funny, I was just thinking the same thing. See you in the morning."

With one last kiss Donny left Margaret. She watched him walk down the hall. Opening her door she felt weak in the knees and slid to the ground, smiling all the way down.

Chapter 22

Margaret fell asleep instantly, the smell of grass still lingering on her skin. She had pleasant dreams of the moon and stars and cuddling with Donny.

Suddenly she became very aware that she was having a dream.

"Do not worry Margaret, I am not Dragas and I am not here to hurt you." Came a disembodied voice.

Margaret found herself lying on the grass almost like she was with Donny a few hours before, "Who are you?" She spoke out loud.

"I am your beginning and your end. I give you life and when that life has ended you return to me through the soil."

"Ok cryptic much?"

The sky faded away and Margaret stood in front of the largest tree she had ever seen.

It was magnificent. *Can it be that this is the tree that gave her life?* She thought.

"Yes, I gave life to you and to all who came before you. But my time here is nearing an end Margaret. I tried to provide you with a substantial group of Locrian this last cycle but I failed. It was then I realized that I am dying. Your class is not due to come to me for several months but I must hasten that. Tomorrow during the full moon I will present you with your powers and your names. Tomorrow you need to come to me, all of you."

The dream began to fade. "Wait, I have so many questions!" She awoke in her room, the dream catchers still secure. It must have taken a lot of energy to bypass those. She knew what she had to do.

Myriad was sound asleep and dreaming deeply when the sound of aggressive pounding woke her. She meandered to her door and opened it coming face to face with her student.

"Margaret, what is wrong?" She asked, with a look of shock and concern.

364

Margaret stood in the hallway with her arms wrapped around her midsection. "Do you mind if I come in? I know we haven't been on the best terms lately."

Opening the door wider, "It changes nothing, I have always been there for you and I will always be."

Margaret entered the room and began to pace, taking deep breaths.

Myriad let her process for a few moments before speaking, "Sit down Margaret and tell me what's going on."

She sat next to Myriad, rubbing her hands on her knees, trying to figure out what to say. Finally she blurted it out. "What happens when the tree calls us?"

Myriad was very confused, "What does that have to do with…"

Margaret cut her off, "Please, just answer the question."

Myriad adjusted her seat, "Well, I'm not completely sure having never experienced it myself but others have told me it's like a tug in the back of their brain to return to their home. Others say they have visions of the tree in a dream."

Margaret paused. "Does it ever talk to anyone?"

"Talk? No, not that I'm aware of. It is a living being but to my knowledge it only communicates when you are in its presence. I've never heard it communicating during the call. Why?"

Margaret paused, "I had another dream."

Myriad grasped her hands, "Was it Michael, er, Dragas?"

She shook her head, "No it wasn't malicious. I was looking at the stars and the moon and then a voice sounded in my head, one I have never heard before. And then a vision appeared in front of me, the most awe-inspiring and magnificent tree I've ever seen."

Myriad got up and began pacing herself - her concern was obvious. "It appeared to you, now? And it spoke? What did it say?"

"It said it was dying and that we needed to go to it tomorrow. It said it would bestow our powers and our names under the full moon."

Myriad shook her head, "But it's too early."

Margaret shrugged, "I don't think it has a choice. If we are to become full Locrian we need to go tomorrow."

"Are you sure it's dying?" asked Myriad.

"No, but what happens if we doubt it, and we're wrong? What will that mean for us in the long run? Is it worth the risk?"

Myriad crossed the room and looked out of the window. Her window overlooked the courtyard, where she would watch the young ones play. Was it truly ending? "I guess we don't have the luxury of meditating on this for long. We need to do what it asks."

"Should we leave now?"

Myriad turned to face her pupil again, "We will wait until dawn to tell them, they may as well all sleep soundly tonight because their worlds are about to change. Your time here is ending sooner than expected, but the journey you are about to embark on is lifelong."
They sat in silence for a moment. Margaret shifted uncomfortably in her seat " Myriad, if this is my last night here, I need to tell you I no longer hold anything against you for what you did. Like I said before, I understand why you did it, and it hurt to

find out the way I did, but I don't see a reason to hold on to that grudge any longer."

Myriad's eyes began to tear up. "I am glad to hear that. I would never do anything to hurt you."

Margaret nodded, "I know, and in your position I probably would have done the same. After a lot of thought I realized I'd do anything to protect those I was fighting beside, and if I had to lie to protect them, I'd do it. But it doesn't mean I enjoyed it coming from you."

"Believe me, it was not fun for me either."

They sat in silence for a moment. "Promise me you'll never lie to me again, as much as it might pain you to tell me the truth."

Myriad grasped her hands again and looked her pupil directly in the eye, "I swear it on 100 lifetimes. I will never do that again."

Margaret smiled and gave her professor a hug.

Myriad walked Margaret to her door, "I will be accompanying you to the tree tomorrow. I

have always gone with each class so it's
not goodbye just yet."

Margaret nodded.

"Go and get some sleep if you can Margaret,
tomorrow your life changes forever."

She gave her professor one last hug and
headed out the door.

Myriad was fully awake. There was no going
back to sleep after speaking with Margaret.
She was annoyed but she had an idea. "Asher,
wake up! I know you're in there!"

Rolling around in bed hoping it was a
nightmare Asher piled pillows on top of his
head to block out the sound until he
realized it wasn't a dream.

"What the hell!" he exclaimed from the other
side of the thick, wooden door.

He gave into the annoyance, and swung the
door open, half-dressed and too groggy to
care.

"Do you know what time it is?!" He yelled at
Myriad.

Myriad shoved the door open, "Yes, and do you think I would be banging on your door at 2:00am if it wasn't important?"

He conceded, "Fine."

She scanned the room taking note of the clothes strewn all over the floor. Locrian can age hundreds of years and still have the habits of teenage boys. "Margaret came to see me."

Asher sat down with a groan. "Oh geez, not her again, what's wrong now?"

Myriad turned on her heel, "Asher, stop your whining this is serious."

He growled, "Fine, continue."

Myriad paced the room, "She had a dream, which she shouldn't have had because of the dreamcatchers I gave her. It was the call, Asher. The tree came to her and told her it was dying and that all of them needed to go tomorrow during the full moon to receive their names."

"Well it IS the full moon. You know birthing cycles and naming ceremonies all occur during full moons," He said as he yawned and rubbed his eyes, clearly not yet awake.

Myriad had enough and she slapped the back of his head. "Asher, it's six months early."

He sat and thought for a moment. "Could Dragas be behind any of this?"

Myriad shook her head, "No, she said it didn't feel as before, that it was different and peaceful. Dragas couldn't be doing this but we will have to be cautious going to Kilkenny. That is where his horde is stationed and they've been trying to destroy the tree."

Asher, finally awake, pulled on a shirt, "Let's make sure they don't have the chance. I want everyone available to accompany this class to the tree for protection. We can leave Lyas and Lorian here to protect the newborns and the professors of the younger Locrian can protect them. I want everyone else to come with us, we need to make sure they get their names."

"Finally you get the hurry up attitude!" Myriad exclaimed.

Asher raised his brow at Myriad and began rummaging through his clothes.

He found some socks and shoes in one of the piles on the floor, threw them on haphazardly, and they left together to wake

the rest of the staff and begin
preparations. He hadn't felt this alive in
years. He hated to admit it in the midst of
this crisis, but he smiled a little to
himself at the thrill.

"You look a little too happy about all of
this Asher."

"Not happy, just alive. It's been years
since I've hunted Droch."

"It's a full moon; there may not be any to
hunt."

Asher looked at her, "There will be."

———————————

Rather than return to her room to lie awake,
Margaret made her way to Donny's room. She
knocked on his door quietly, knowing she
should let him sleep, but wanting to just be
with him. She nearly walked away when he
groggily answered the door. As soon as his
eyes focused on her, he was wide awake.

"Mags? What's wrong, are you ok?"

She nodded and walked into his arms, "Yes, I
just want to be held if that's ok with you."

He smiled. He had missed her touch as well. "Of course it's ok with me, come on in."

The two of them lay in silence, Donny quickly falling back to sleep and Margaret contemplating everything that had happened. She wanted him to get a good night's sleep. He would find out in the morning, along with everyone else, what needed to happen. The warmth of his body and the repetitive sound of his heartbeat and breathing soon lulled her to sleep where she dreamt of star gazing and love.

———————————

She woke up the next morning in his arms and they walked to breakfast together. She wished every day could be like this but she knew everything was about to change. She waited until Bria joined them and told them both about her dream.

"And you're sure that Dragas has nothing to do with this?" asked Donny.

She nodded, "Yes, it felt like returning home. I was at peace. There was nothing malicious. Even if Dragas could manifest something like that I think it would always 'feel' evil."

"So we're going back to Kilkenny tonight?" asked Bria.

Margaret looked at Bria, "As far as I know, yes. They're going to address everyone in a few minutes but I wanted you to know. I believe we'll leave in a few hours. It's time to say goodbye to this place."

Bria looked around the hall, the place they had met every morning since she could remember. And just outside was the glade where they played as children. She sighed, "It's bitter sweet isn't it? I mean we spend our entire lives training to get out of this place, and a few weeks ago going to Kilkenny was so liberating and I wanted to stay. But now, knowing there is no coming back home, it's a bit sad."

Donny nodded in agreement, "It is, but we're needed out there. It's our time to make a difference, and from what we witnessed the last time, our presence matters."

"We are literally the last true Locrian if the tree dies. We need to make this count," said Margaret.

The professors entered the room and the dining hall went silent. Everyone knew that something was going on. The students began to scan the room looking for Margaret, and when she realized what they were doing, she got up and walked to the front. She realized that over the past few weeks it was her, not her professors, who her fellow students had come to rely on for leadership and reassurance. As the professors spoke to them, she was proud of what she saw. The faces of her fellow classmates were filled with determination. They were not fearful of what was to come because they had already met it and they were ready to take it on again.

Once the situation had been explained, the group was dismissed in order to pack their rucksacks, the ones that would carry them throughout their lives. Back in her room, Margaret put her few worldly possessions into her own pack. As she moved her uniform from her drawer into her sack, she realized it was no longer needed. She packed one pair of sweatpants and sweatshirt as a reminder and folded the rest and laid it on the bed. The rest of her sack consisted of her street clothes - mostly jeans and some t-shirts inspired by professor Caleb, featuring whatever rock bands of which he was currently a fan.

She grabbed The Great Gatsby from her shelf. She had read it probably a hundred times, and the binding was disintegrating, but she had to pack it, it brought her comfort. She carefully packed her dream catchers as well as the few pictures of Donny and Bria and herself that she had accumulated over the years.

Knowing they would be moving at a moment's notice, she packed lightly, with a silent prayer that wherever they were going had good laundry facilities for all the Droch gore she was bound to incur. Lastly, she packed her favorite broadsword in hopes that they would allow her to keep it. It had a black hilt and a 4-foot blade. It was simple but perfect for her.

She left her room for the last time with everything she owned in a bag. It felt strange knowing the room was no longer hers, and that she would never set foot in it again.

She went down to the courtyard where a few of her peers were beginning to gather. Liam saw her and approached.
"How are you doing?" he asked.

She smiled, "I'm doing well, and you?"

He looked around the courtyard, "It feels weird doesn't it? Not like before when we knew we were coming back."

She shook her head, "It does, but we don't need this place anymore, it did its job and now we have to do ours."

He smiled, "How do you do that?"

She looked puzzled, "Do what?"

"Just inspire people like that. You always know what to say." He said.

She shrugged, "I appreciate that, but I don't always feel like I do. I just do the only thing I know how to do and I just speak from my heart and hope it is the right thing to say."

Liam smiled "Well you're good at it, I'm glad to have you at my side out there."

"Same to you Liam."

As he walked away she thought about how few interactions she and Liam had ever had outside of classes. Liam and the rest of her classmates where her troops, now her compatriots and she knew she needed to make an effort to get to know each and every one of them.

"There you are," said Donny. "I was going to walk with you but you had already left."

She smiled at his concern, "I'm sorry, I just wanted to get down here to see how everyone was doing."

"Always the leader," he said with a smile.

The transport pulled up shortly after all of her classmates were present. Myriad, Asher, Bryan, Caleb, Murphy and Xavier were all traveling with them. After everyone loaded into the transport Bria, Donny and Margaret climbed in followed by their professors. Margaret, along with all her classmates, looked out the window of the vehicle until the abbey was but a dot in the distance.

She leaned back and tried to relax. The further she got away from the abbey the better she felt. It closed a chapter in her life and she was ready for the next one. Myriad was sitting next to her - their familiar companionship had been restored.

"Myriad, where are we going? Are we allowed to know the location now that we're on the way?"

She looked at Margaret, "We're headed to the outpost in Kilkenny."

Margaret wanted to make a "duh" noise but thought better about it. "We know that, but then where do we go for the tree?"

Myriad sighed, "It's underneath the outpost."

Margaret was taken aback. All this time it had been right under their feet? "Wait what?! No wonder the Droch are attacking so fiercely, it's right there? Can't they reach it from the caverns underground?"

Myriad shook her head, "No, it is protected, but not from within the outpost itself. That is why the Locrian are always bestowed their gifts during a full moon - to keep the Droch in hiding."

Bria leaned in, "If the Droch won't attack, why are all the professors here? Or is this normal?"

"My presence here is normal, but the Droch can still fight in the full moon and with Dragas in command, the risk is even greater. That is why they're here."

Donny, over-hearing the discussion, leaned forward, "So you're saying there's a possibility that they'll attack tonight, even under the full moon, because we're accessing the tree? But it's dying, what would be the point?"

"They don't know that. They just want to prevent you from getting your powers. And my guess is Dragas doesn't want Margaret to receive her powers most of all."

At this thought, Margaret's eyes shot to Myriad's.

"Margaret, getting your abilities may make you even more powerful than Dragas, no matter how many hearts he eats."

Margaret had never even considered the possibility.

"They may attack just because I'm here. I believe he can sense when I'm around."

Donny and Bria exchanged a concerned look. The last thing they wanted was for Margaret to be captured again.

Myriad grabbed her hand to calm the nerves that she could sense rising in her pupil. "Do not worry about that now, we will do what we can to make sure your powers are given to you. The process will not begin until sundown. The tree draws from the moon's energy; it is at its most powerful during that time. We will deal with Dragas if and when that is needed."

They all nodded in silence as the transport approached the outpost.

Chapter 23

Dragas paced in the caves, looking at the sleeping Droch that lay at his feet. He rarely set foot outside on a full moon - the brightness significantly weakened him and burned his flesh.

All of a sudden his mind began to race and a sneer formed on his lips, *she is here,* he thought to himself.

He turned away from his throne and let out a growl, "We attack tonight!!!"

The nearest Droch approached cautiously *"But master Dragas, the moon weakens us, it burns us, what would be the point?"*

He backhanded the Droch, sending him flying across the room. "Because, you fool, she's back, and back early, which can only mean one thing on a full moon."

"What?" Asked a Droch from a safe distance.

"The tree has called them to receive their names," replied Dragas.

Another Droch approached questioning his master's logic, *"But it's early master, surely they can't...."*

Dragas kicked the minion in the stomach. "Do not dare question me, you brainless piece of filth, we attack tonight, the tree will be vulnerable, we cannot allow them to obtain their abilities."

"Yes, Master Dragas."

The Droch began to assemble their weapons to attack. *It ends tonight,* thought Dragas with a grin.

The outpost rose above Ireland like a beacon. It was worn and old but it was a sign that they hadn't given up. In the weeks that had passed it didn't appear any worse for wear. This day had been filled with emotions, but as Margaret looked out of the window she had no doubt or anxiety. This felt right, like coming home.

As they entered the gate, the Locrian could sense that their presence was a relief to

those inside the outpost. They passed
familiar faces, with whom they had just
spent time on the battlefield, each happy to
see the other again. There are few things in
the world that make faster friends than
fighting side by side in war. Each Locrian
had experienced that, and it was no small
part of why they were happy to be back.

For Bria the approach took a lifetime. Every
few minutes she glanced outside of the
transport to see if Damien was among the
crowd of onlookers. Once they stopped, Bria
pushed past everyone and jumped out of the
transport to search for him. She couldn't
wait to see him with her own eyes and know
that he was safe. She passed person after
person looking for his face. With a sinking
feeling she wandered over to the tree where
they first met. "Where is he?" She sat down
at the base of the tree, fighting back
tears. She heard a snap above her and with a
smile looked up.

High above in the branches sat a shadowy
figure, "I thought you'd never find me
here."

Bria's heart leapt at the sound of his
voice, "Why couldn't you just wait near the
transport like everyone else?"

Damien sat perched in the tree with a boyish grin on his face. "Oh, but I like it when you're a bit flustered." He hopped down in front of her and gave her a welcomed kiss. "It makes you even cuter."

She returned the kiss and then hugged him, interrupted only by Donny and Margaret's presence.

Donny coughed a little, uncomfortably, as they approached. "Don't mean to break up the party but it's good to see you again, Damien. I trust that you're doing well?

"Yes, and even better now," he said, shaking Donny's hand and looking down at Bria in his arms.

"We missed you," said Margaret embracing him in a hug.

He broke contact with Bria for a second while he greeted Margaret but his arm went around her shoulders as soon as he was done. "I missed you all as well, some more than others." He winked at Bria. "I'm a bit confused though, why are you here? Not that I'm not excited but isn't it a bit early to return for your next placement?"

Margaret grinned excitedly, "This is our final placement, we're getting our powers tonight. This is now home."

Damien's joy could not be contained. He hugged Bria, then Margaret and Donny. "I'm so glad, I've missed you all. As brief a time you spent here you left a void when you were gone and we could certainly use your help. But isn't it a bit early? I thought you weren't due for a few months."

"It's a long story." said Donny "Why don't we get a bite to eat and we can fill you in."

Over lunch Margaret filled Damien in on all the details regarding her dream and what the tree had told her. He stayed quiet until the end.

Damien shook his head, "Wow, no offense Margaret but you attract some crazy stuff."

She smiled. "I know, the scary thing is I think I'm starting to get used to it."

"I can't believe that the tree has been below our feet all this time, that's truly insane. But tonight we celebrate! You only get your name once and with the full moon we'll have the night off."

Margaret smiled and wanted to believe that they would be able to enjoy their initiation into Locrian society but in the back of her mind she felt that it wouldn't be so easy. There was a constant buzz in the back of her brain that told her Dragas knew she was here.

After lunch the four of them went out into the courtyard where Myriad sat by herself beneath Damien's favorite tree. Margaret wandered over to see her while the others went to their quarters to start setting up a more permanent residence.

When she approached, Myriad's eyes were closed, "Mind if I join you?"

The Fae looked lost in thought at first. "Oh Margaret, yes dear please do."

She sat down next to her, "You seemed to be meditating, I didn't know if I should interrupt."

Myriad smiled, "You are always welcome to interrupt me. I'm simply preparing myself for tonight. The tree is beneath the courtyard, a stairway leads down to it but it must be revealed through the use of Fae magic because it is the Fae who are chosen to protect it."

Margaret nodded, "Is it difficult?"

Myriad shook her head, "Not particularly, but it always makes me nervous to expose the tree, especially when Droch are so close."

Margaret crossed her legs, getting comfortable, "Isn't it a moot point now that the tree is dying?"

Myriad adjusted herself as well, "Possibly, however, if Dragas ever got his hands on the tree there could be dire consequences. The Droch are born with the immortality that the tree presents to Locrian. If they were to also receive that immortality, in addition to that which they're born with, they could become invincible, and no weapon would be able to destroy them."

Margaret's mind began to spin, "Do you think that's why he wants the tree so badly?"

Myriad shrugged, "It's hard to say what he wants it for. He is not a very rational creature. He may simply want the tree to prevent you and those in your class from getting your powers. Or he could want it for more sinister reasons. The point is, we must ensure that he never gets the chance."

The pair sat for a while like they used to do at the abbey, although instead of watching the sunrise they watched it set. "It is still beautiful," Myriad sighed.

Margaret turned to her and smiled, "I'm glad to know that it never gets old. I'm glad you're here with me doing this." She paused and grabbed the Fae's hand. "I know we've had our differences but I'm glad we've moved past them."

They embraced for a long moment and as they released, Myriad looked at her as serious as Margaret had ever seen her. "There is one more thing I wanted to tell you, just in case you are ever unsure of your path. The night that you and Michael were born and I held you in my arms, I knew immediately that you were different. His skin radiated a red hue of light, while yours was pure white. I believe you were both meant to follow the paths that you did. You may have been born from the same root, but it doesn't mean you are the same. Never let him convince you that you were meant to be like him. But if anyone can destroy him, it is you."

Margaret nodded and breathed a deep sigh of relief. She had worried that she had the capacity to become like him. But knowing she was born in the light calmed her soul. "Thank you; you don't know what it means to hear you say that."

Myriad smiled at her, "Oh I think the relief on your face says it all. Always remember your true path and nothing can get in your way."

Margaret looked out over the horizon as the last of the light drained from the sky. She stood and offered her hand to Myriad, pulling up her slight frame - she felt lighter than Margaret's own sword.

"The sun has almost set, it is time." Myriad said quietly. She led Margaret back to the center of the courtyard. All the Locrian, Elves and Fae gathered around to witness the opening of the entrance. A collective calm bloomed among them. For a moment their war took a backseat to this sacred ritual. Usually only those getting named were present, and upon exiting the chamber forgot its location. This was a rare sight for those present.

Myriad took a branch from a nearby tree, snapping it quickly and with a flinch - as though she felt the break in her own body. Slowly, she made a circle in the dirt in front of her. Around it, she drew several Fae symbols, some Margaret recognized from her studies in her younger years. One meant peace, another hope, the last one she could decipher was the symbol for safety. Standing back, Myriad began a chant in a Fae language

that Margaret had never heard. As soon as
the sun had completely set below the
horizon, the ground began to glow and a beam
of light shot into the night sky.

"If there are Droch around, they'll know
what just happened," Margaret said, looking
at Donny.

Donny nodded in agreement, "Good thing it's
a full moon."

Margaret knew better, this is what they were
waiting for; the moonlight would not stop
Dragas. Nothing would.

Chapter 24

Up on the hillside the Droch lay in wait as the sun dipped below the horizon. They exited the cave into the moonlight that was so bright it blinded them briefly. There wasn't a cloud in the sky. Blisters began to form on their skin as the moonlight scorched the beasts.

Despite the pain, they waited for Dragas to give them an order. They looked over the rolling hills to the outpost seeing no Locrian present, no one waiting for the attack, and there wouldn't be.

Dragas sneered, "This is too perfect."

All of a sudden a bright light shot towards the sky, causing the Droch to shield their faces. Screams erupted as their flesh burned; many retreated back into the safety of the caves.

Dragas roared, "Come back here you idiots. They have opened the portal." The knowledge he had gained from Padua's heart had shown him this light - given him a glance into the portal that he knew must be opened by a Fae only.

"Oh I hope that's you Myriad. How I would love to rip your heart from your chest." He fumed at the thought of the Fae who had cast him out from his home, away from his sister, in hopes of his death. He read her mind that night there was no sympathy for him. She had seen him as nothing more than an animal, claiming his sister almost as her own. The thought disgusted him. Dragas wanted nothing more than to rip out her heart, gain the surge of power and ability with the infinite wisdom that the Fae contained. Although the powers were temporary, the knowledge, the true power, lasted forever. But first the tree.

"Attack now while they're vulnerable! Bring me my sister alive." Margaret's escape and the way she had looked at him in the cave that day flashed before his eyes. He amended his command. "Brutal force may be used as long as she is breathing when she reaches me. Kill all others and burn the tree! Tonight their world ends and ours begins!" The roar was deafening, if the Locrian didn't know it before, they certainly knew now.

The light disappeared and, in its absence, a dark staircase appeared. Myriad lit a torch and led the way down. One by one all 79 Locrian descended down the spiral staircase. At its base was an ornate wooden door inlaid with a forest scene. Myriad touched the door, her eyes closed and it swung open, as if greeting an old friend.

Inside was what appeared to be an underground forest. The ceiling was speckled with lights, almost as if the stars were overhead.

Margaret was in awe. She gazed at the ceiling, thinking it did not look so different from the stars she and Donny had gazed at together just a few short hours ago. But these were different, they were moving. "How is that happening?"

"They're moths," Myriad whispered. "They exist only in the Fae realm, but as the tree's protectors we have brought elements from our land here. The moths provide a bit of light but they also provide the plants with nourishment through pollination. It is a truly beautiful place. Everything in here is self-sustaining, which is why the Fae that protect the tree can survive here as

well. The forest gives us everything we
need."

Large hibiscus flowers the size of dinner
plates bloomed along with flowers she
couldn't even begin to identify. It should
have been dark, but there was a natural glow
surrounding the forest that Margaret was
unable to locate. It was also quite warm,
almost tropical, which explained the
expansive plant growth and species. Margaret
was in awe. The Locrian walked down a path
that led them deeper into the forest,
winding around plants and trees. It seemed
to go on forever in a beautiful maze.

Eventually the path opened up into a glade
that exposed the largest tree Margaret had
ever seen. Even in her dream it hadn't
appeared as magnificent as it was standing
before her - nearly as wide as it is tall.
There was a glow emitting from the tree, and
she realized that was the light she had been
seeing. "Welcome back Margaret, welcome
home," said Myriad in a whisper.

No one spoke, as each Locrian absorbed the
experience of returning to where they had
been born. The prolonged silence was full of
awe, but also comfort. From this place of
peace, a sudden voice entered Margaret's
head, the voice she had heard in her dream.

As she looked around it was evident that everyone else heard it as well.

"Welcome children. The time has come for you to earn your place among the Locrian. One by one I will call you forward to touch the branch from which you were born. You will know it when you see it. At that time I will tell you your name. Afterwards, the Fae that look after me will give you liquid to drink. This will bestow on you your powers and your immortality. This liquid is made of my sap. As you are my children it is only fitting that your strength should come from me."

From around the back of the tree two female Fae appeared. One, with long blonde hair wearing a luminescent white gown, looked incredibly young, almost childlike. The other looked to be around Myriad's age with short black hair and a flowing blue gown.

Myriad leaned over to Margaret who was watching the Fae prepare the sap. "The younger one is the apprentice, the older is showing her how to prepare the ingredients for you."

Margaret nodded in awe of all the intricate details.

397

One by one the Locrian were called to the tree. Margaret waited, her nerves beginning to show, not knowing what to expect.

From the back of the chamber came a loud crash. She turned quickly, not knowing whether or not the sound came from within the room.

"I'll check on the noise, you all stay here and continue," said Myriad.

She quickly disappeared through the forest.

One by one the Locrian were called forward. Cassandra was first. She touched her root and smiled, after a few moments she turned toward the Fae and drank from the cup. She glowed briefly and turned to the group. "My last name is Murphy," she said with confidence. Margaret nodded, she had come a long way with a broadsword. Liam was next followed by Lyra.

Nearly a dozen Locrian had received their powers by the time Myriad returned. Distress lined her face. She glanced deferentially to the tree and its protectors before saying loudly and firmly enough for everyone in the cavern to hear, "The Droch are attacking, they know the doorway is open. Those of you who have received your powers please come with me, we must protect the tree at all costs. The rest of you must continue - you will need your powers, and once you have them please return to the surface to help."

Those who had their powers took off immediately - ready to use what they were just given. Margaret squirmed - she wanted to go with them. When would her name be called? What was taking so long?

Myriad erupted from the portal, the Locrian trailing behind her. She led them directly to the armory. "Grab your weapon and head to the gate!" Screamed Myriad.

Craine ran up beside them. "Myriad they have nearly broken through."

A crash came, as if on cue. "Shit! Defend the portal entrance! Protect the tree." Craine redirected his people.

Steadily the newly named Locrian emerged from the portal into the fray. Asher and Bryan joined the fight clearing a path for them to reach the armory. Their fighting was like nothing the students had ever seen. If the situation was not so tense, it would be a sight to behold. Their fluidity rivaled all others on the field.

Murphy O'Sullivan was running around the wall like a mad man, shooting arrow after arrow at a speed that rivaled Margaret's on the field. One by one the Droch fell, but they kept coming. Caleb Murphy was near the gate trying to hold off the horde that was coming through. His movements were smooth and quick, the blade was nearly a blur. The Droch continued to fall but they couldn't be held back. The tree was the end goal and they did not care how many they sacrificed to achieve that goal.

All three professors were moving in unison, performing a deadly dance.

More and more Locrian emerged from the portal, the Droch were held but there was no telling for how long. The Locrian were becoming tired and the injuries were becoming apparent; but they continued to fight, they knew what was at stake.

Come on, we need to close the portal, come on. Myriad thought as she wished for expediency. The situation was becoming dire.

———————————

One by one the remaining Locrian heard their names called, made their way, as if

400

magnetically, to the root of their birth and drank the powerful sap. Finally Bria, Donny and Margaret were the only Locrian remaining. Bria was called first. She walked up to the tree and one of the roots emitted a soft glow, she walked over to it and touched it.

"Sweet Bria, your eye for accuracy knows no bounds. You will be named after your ancestor O'Sullivan, whom I believe you could out shoot. Your powers will include grip strength and sharpened vision, you will be able to see for miles. With your added grip strength your longbow will be more accurate and deadly in your grasp. Go in peace Bria O'Sullivan."

Bria let go of the root and turned to drink from the cup. She smiled at Margaret and Donny. "O'Sullivan" she said with a half smile.

"As if there was any doubt," said Margaret.

"I will see you up there." Bria took off running down the path to the staircase without further hesitation. Like everyone else, she was excited to use what the tree had given her.

Donny was called next and bent down to the root that glowed for him.

"Donny. Your skills with battle axes and knives are unmatched. Even your name sake would have a hard time competing against you. You are pure of heart and strong as an ox. Your name will be Doyle and your powers will be grip and arm strength as well as speed. You will be able to fly around the battlefield, your strength and endurance will be rivaled only by one other. It is fitting you are together, you are stronger that way. Stay strong Donny, and trust her, there will be trials ahead for you both.

He drank from the cup and turned to Margaret. "Doyle," he stated.

"Again, not surprised. You should go up to help as well."

Donny shook his head, "I'll wait for you, just in case."

She smiled, "Always the protector."

"Go on, it's your turn."

She approached the tree looking for her root. Near the base of the ancient tree she found a large, knotted root entwined. One side was glowing while the other looked charred. She bent to touch it.

"My dear Margaret. You are the most powerful of all. As you know, you were born with abilities that were kept from you, but you also know how powerful you are. You need all your abilities to stop your brother. You have the gift of telepathy and I will enhance that with empathy. You also have the gift of strength and speed but I will enhance those as well. Given your unique talents, I will create for you a new name, as I did for your ancestors.r I gave the founders their names to unite them, to give them a family through a shared namesake. Your name, though unique, will forever bind you to your class, your family. Your name shall be O'Dwyer. I have given all I have to this class, together you are a powerful group, as you know. I only thought it fair to give you all the last of my powers so that you might stand a chance against Dragas. You will be able to communicate with your class just like Dragas communicates with his Droch. You will be able to sense when they are in danger or need assistance. This should even the playing field. Use your talents wisely and always for good. Margaret, as you know, I am dying and once you drink from the cup, my sap will dry up. When I am gone the tables will turn, the world as you know it will no longer exist. You must do what you can to save it. I will leave behind a seed, guard it with your life, and when you feel the time is right *plant that seed in a safe place so that I may return to the world. This new world, where Droch run free, will have new rules, you will have to learn what to do. Please realize old ways may not work any longer. The old world must die for balance to be restored. The new world created after Dragas' defeat will bring peace to us all. This was predestined, so do not feel sorrow. Good luck my child, we will meet again."*

"Wait, one question, why are you dying? Why now?"

"Dragas poisoned me with his birth. He comes from evil, and his essence is deadly. I have held on as long as I could but I can no longer. You can still save me, plant the seed when the world is renewed and I will be safe."

Margaret stood back in shock. She took the cup from the Fae with trembling hands. Drinking it she returned it to the Fae. Nothing seemed to happen for a moment or two and then the ground began to shake. Donny grabbed her trying to move towards the stairs to safety.

She fought him, "No, we have to stay!"

Her voice was fierce and he dropped her arm. Light began to shoot from the tree like an

explosion. Donny and Margaret were knocked
to the ground and the light leveled the
forest and shot up the stair-well.

Outside, the Locrian guarding the portal
were beginning to weaken. The Droch were
only steps from the entrance. Damien and
Bria were running with their longbows trying
to get better vantage points. Bria could see
like a hawk. She loved her new vision but it
would definitely take some getting used to.

Myriad was using her Fae powers to push back
the Droch as much as she could while
creating shields for the Locrian.

Suddenly a light shot up from below the
surface, knocking all the Locrian flat to
the ground and sending the Droch sailing
back over the wall. Groans from the beasts
emitted from behind the wall as their burns
rendered them immobile. The Locrian on the
ground looked at each other, stunned. Craine
and Dorien sprinted for the gate to secure
the door. Others followed in order to hold
any remaining Droch at bay, but none
followed.

They all stood in a daze, taking stock of
the wounded. It was a miracle no one had

died. Slowly they made their way to the portal, where were Margaret and Donny?

Donny and Margaret stood up after the burst of energy and looked around. The tree was gone, as was the forest. The light had disappeared and darkness had fallen. Margaret allowed her eyes to get used to the darkness and approached the spot where the tree had stood only moments before. Off in the distance she saw a faint glow; walking toward it she found the seed. As she picked it up it glowed for a moment and they faded, as if to let her know it recognized her.

The Fae and apprentice who had once protected the tree nodded to Margaret with respect and walked towards the stairwell. Their jobs were complete.

"Is that what I think it is?" Asked Donny, coming up behind her.

"Yes, and we have to protect it if we stand a chance to restore the balance."

He nodded gravely, staring down at their small salvation in the palm of Margaret's hand. They made their way back to the staircase in silence.

As the two emerged from the portal, they were surrounded by confused Locrian, Elves and Fae. The Droch didn't return to the outpost, whatever the tree had done had bought them some time. She placed her hand against her chest where the seed was and said a silent 'thank you' to the tree that had given them life and then saved it.

She quickly scanned the field and did not see any serious injuries - but could feel their confusion and fear. Her telepathy was definitely in full swing. Margaret clutched the seed to her chest, afraid to take her hands off of it.

Myriad looked at her, "It is done?"

Margaret nodded and looked around, it was dark. The moon and the stars were gone, covered in a sheet of black. It reminded her of her dream. Dragas was right, it had come true, but it wouldn't remain.

"The old world must die for balance to be restored," mumbled Margaret.

Myriad stared at her.

Donny approached her, as did Damien and Bria.

She turned and realized everyone was looking at her. Something came over her, a need, and she stood on a rock so she could speak to her friends, her family.

"The tree has died." A small gasp was followed by fearful silence. "I hold in my hand it's chance of rebirth. But this new world is not fitting for it to survive. The balance needs to be restored. And to do that we need to kill Dragas." She paused and looked out into the crowd, found Donny's face and continued, "Until then this world will be cast in a darkness like we have never seen but WE are the light. This is what we were destined to do. I stand before you willing to fight. We can restore the balance and conquer this new world." One by one fiery eyes met her own. "I am Margaret O'Dwyer, I come from the light, as do all of you. Who is willing to fight with me against the darkness?"

There was silence at first, and then a roar came from the depths of their beings. They believed in her, they saw her, and they would follow her.

As the adrenaline faded and the crowd retreated, Margaret made her way up to the wall surrounding the outpost. As she reached the top, her eyes stared off in the direction of the caves. Fury swelled inside her as she projected her thoughts toward Dragas. *"I am coming for you, brother."*

He felt her thoughts invade his mind and he sneered, *"As I am for you, dear sister."* Dragas stood in the cave nursing the wounds he received from the blast, but he was not disappointed. The tree was dead and the world was his to control. Let them have this night the others would belong to him.

Epilogue

Margaret stood in the right tower looking out over the world that Dragas had sought. It was dark and tinges of red glowed in the atmosphere. The world looked angry.

Donny approached her from behind, "What are you thinking?" She turned towards him and welcomed his embrace.

"I'm thinking, this is overwhelming, and I'm realizing that without a second thought I have made myself their leader."

Releasing him, she walked over to look down at the Locrian who trusted her to keep them safe. Fires glowed in the courtyard providing them all with much needed light. As she looked on she watched them carry on conversations, smile and prepare their weapons.

"They don't even look afraid."

"They believe in you, as I do. You are special; we will figure this out together."

She turned back to the darkness.

"This is a tall order Donny; I only hope I'm strong enough."

"You are," said Bria who had come up the stairs followed by Damien. "So O'Dwyer huh? That IS a surprise."

"I guess I don't fit in a category."

"You know Margaret, I don't know you well, but I would say that you don't. Maybe none of us do. Maybe we need to think beyond the ordinary from now on if we want to be successful."

"I think you're right, Damien, we can't keep doing the same things, they aren't working," said Margaret.

"This is a new world with new challenges, we can't assume that everything will be the same in the way we fight, in the way we strategize, even the weapons we use." Said Donny.

A large crack sounded. The four Locrian looked on as a fissure opened in the distance, a red glow emerged from the abyss. As the four of them looked on in silence, they interlocked hands. Together they stood

against the darkness. As the fissure
widened, their fear faded; their eyes now
filled with rage, determination and
strength. The new world had begun and they
were ready.

TO BE CONTINUED...

P.C Brown is a native of Virginia where she lives with her husband and son. She received a Bachelors of the Arts from The Catholic University of America in 2006 and a Masters in Education from Old Dominion University in 2009. She has always loved to read and explore worlds others created. As a child, P.C. Brown lived in imaginary worlds when she would play with her friends, creating stories and adventures that inspired her to this day. When she was in middle school she was published in an anthology of poetry for young poets and she never looked back. From there her love of writing grew and she loves bringing readers into the worlds she has created.

Made in the USA
Columbia, SC
07 July 2019